The Payoff

The Payoff

BY

ATTILIO VERALDI

Translated from the Italian by Isabel Quigly

HARPER & ROW, PUBLISHERS
New York, Hagerstown, San Francisco, London

THE PAYOFF. Copyright © Rizzoli Editore Milan 1976. Translation copyright© 1978 by Hamish Hamilton Ltd. and Harper & Row, Publishers, Inc. All rights reserved. Printed in the United States of America. No part of this book may be used or reproduced in any manner whatsoever without written permission except in the case of brief quotations embodied in critical articles and reviews. For information address Harper & Row, Publishers, Inc., 10 East 53rd Street, New York, N.Y. 10022. Published simultaneously in Canada by Fitzhenry & Whiteside Limited, Toronto.

FIRST U.S. EDITION

Library of Congress Cataloging in Publication Data

Veraldi, Attilio, 1925-
   The payoff.
   Translation of La mazzetta.
   I. Title.
PZ4.V477Pay   [PQ4882.E63]   853'.9'14   77-11775
ISBN 0-06-014493-9

78 79 80 81 82 10 9 8 7 6 5 4 3 2 1

'Keep a steady hand. Too much may turn into too little.' *A customer at the Rhumerie Martiniquaise*

1

Every time I set foot in those three dreary rooms, my heart sank; they looked even uglier than they had the time before and the furniture seemed, if possible, even shabbier and more decrepit.

And this was the office of a man who was possibly the richest in Naples, Michele Miletti. I did all kinds of jobs for him and every year cobbled together some sort of tax return—not that it ever covered everything he had a finger in—so I knew more or less what he was involved in: import-export, though it wasn't quite clear what went in or out, naval equipment, shipping agency, market gardening, building, and a number of other things. All in those three rooms in via Marina.

The first room wasn't just the entrance hall and waiting room, but the office of the secretary, Marullo. Marullo plain and simple, without a Christian name. Maybe because he wasn't considered a Christian; not by Miletti, at any rate. Certainly—being short and spare and withered, with a scaly skin, and bent almost double, under a small hump halfway up his rounded back—he looked more like an ant-eater than a man.

I went straight into his room, then, and said 'Don Michele?' to Marullo, who was squatting behind a desk of sorts.

He didn't answer, but looked at me with his everlastingly angry, irritated expression. Then he nodded at the other door, straight opposite me. The only thing that made him unlike an ant-eater was the fact that his head, far from being small, was bigger than his chest and hump put together.

So I went into the second room, which was, in a manner of

speaking, a parlour, with a small table, two shabby straw-seated chairs and a sofa that must once have been black. The indicator on the third door, which opened on to Miletti's office, was lit up red, so I sat down on the sofa. That was what it was there for, after all.

Apart from the telephone, that sort of traffic-light was the only concession Don Michele had felt he should make to modern progress. And it was always lit up red because the old man never wanted to be disturbed. Especially when he was alone.

But that afternoon he wasn't alone. After a good twenty minutes, the door opened and a small elderly man backed out, bowing and scraping. He wore a shabby dark suit and, although it was June, carried a heavy cloth cap. With a final bow he backed out of the second door as well almost bumping into it as he took his obsequious leave.

Miletti's voice, or rather his chesty grunt, called to me from the end room. At seventy-nine he still kept up a smoking rhythm of one every five minutes.

'Come along in, sir.'

To be addressed so politely, in Naples, might mean nothing in particular. But perhaps I should consider it as a kind of promotion, a sign of all the jobs and business he was putting my way. I laid the ten-week-old copy of *Oggi* down on the table and went in.

'The door, sir,' he said.

I went back to shut it, then sat down at the dark old table he used as a desk, which only the wildest optimist would have called an antique. The rest of the room was as bare as a monk's cell. Two straw-seated chairs, obviously taken from the room next door, by the table; a folding chair, ridiculously painted red like the damask wallpaper, in a corner; and a grey metal cupboard so modern it screamed at you.

On another folding chair sat Miletti, in an obviously uncomfortable position, since under the table his feet didn't touch the floor. And yet this failed to diminish the air of authority in, above all, the expression of his cold blue eyes.

He was remarkably lean and slender for his years. Not a trace of paunch, hardly a wrinkle, even round the eyes; in fact a miraculous failure, in that long face of his, to betray age. But below the face an eye-catching oddity, a quivering abnormality that luckily distracted anyone speaking to him from those cold blue, staring eyes: a dewlap. A treble chin that seemed to have a treble life of its own, shivering at every word he spoke yet quite independent, and as noticeable as the remarkable thinness of the little fellow, who stood about five foot six.

'I knew you were there,' he said. 'You're generally on time.'

I'd been wondering how he knew I was waiting in the next room.

'That was Catello, the caretaker of my villa up at Faito,' he went on. 'He was here for the same reason that I sent for you.'

He'd rung me up that morning. Not in my office, where he knew he wouldn't find me, but downstairs in the bar, where I generally spend the first part of my working day. Here I meet the fixers—those who fix up business matters—and small clients. One of the local authority offices is just opposite, which explains everything.

'And here's the reason for it,' he said.

Out of the jacket pocket of his grey suit—the same double-breasted one he also wore in winter, or else an identical one—he took a piece of paper and handed it to me.

It was a sheet of writing paper cut carefully in half, with the imprint of a nail along the edge of it; which was certainly in line with the dislike of waste that prevailed in Miletti's home and in his firm. Anyway, in a wobbly and almost childish hand was written: 'I feel sick with rage and disgust and I'm not staying in this house another minute. Don't try and find me. Let me get lost and get lost yourself. G.' The initial, G., was almost unreadable.

I handed it back and said nothing, waiting for an explanation. Actually I hadn't said a word since I came into the room.

Miletti seemed disappointed. What to him must have been a bolt from the blue provoked no reaction at all in me.

'Haven't you got anything to say?' he asked.

'What ought I to say, Don Michele?' I asked.

Whether or not it was a coincidence, the fact was that Miletti always managed to send my blood pressure up and set up in my left ear a buzzing that had been bothering me for the past year. Sinus, a high-powered specialist had called it to justify his fee, but he'd done nothing to remove it. 'I suppose your daughter wrote it,' I said. His present wife—he'd twice been widowed and once divorced—was called Tina, in other words T. 'When did you get it?'

'I didn't get it, I found it,' he said. The gurgling voice was becoming smoother. When this happened it meant he was extremely agitated, and when he was agitated Don Michele was impossible to deal with. Not that he wasn't usually a man of quite unusual nastiness, though he had his points—one of them, for instance, the fact that he was my one and only really important client.

'I found it yesterday evening when I went home,' he continued. 'On the desk in my study. And not even in an envelope, for Christ's sake. Just to tell everyone our business. That nosey Idillia, for a start.' Idillia was the maid and housekeeper—Venetian, with a name like that. She'd been with him forever and they still found it hard to understand each other's talk.

'That's the least of your worries,' I said. There must have been a bigger one, to explain his agitation.

'Yes, it is,' he admitted. 'Well, Giulia didn't turn up for supper.' Until then, he had never used her name in talking to me. She'd always been merely My Daughter. Like a title deed.

'Your daughter?' I said, just to get things back on to their normal footing.

'My daughter, yes.' He'd had her very late in life, by his second wife who died giving birth to her. And he must have made her life hell—first with his possessive character, then with his two subsequent marriages. 'And she didn't come back last night, either.'

'Have you told the police?' I asked.

He looked at me as if I'd been a cockroach. The flap under his chin was working like mad: quivering like a triple membrane. If he'd been taller he'd have squashed me underfoot.

'And you say I'm impatient,' he said at last, calming down. 'Why the hell should I tell them? Dirty linen shouldn't be washed in public.' I felt flattered. 'And this lot would fill a laundry. She's disappeared and with her the file of those papers you know about.'

'The ones about the double contract for the drainage?' I asked. Double because there wasn't just the local authority contract put out for tender, worth two billion and legally won, but a second contract for five billion, never won but handed out on payment of fifty million, all in advance and in cash. I'd done all the negotiations and felt as if the money had been snatched from my pocket as well as his, as I was expecting a fair price for my efforts and already had ideas about how to invest it.

'That's right,' he said.

'And when did they disappear?' I said, beginning to smell something nasty. They were—how shall I put it?—delicate papers, and their disappearance might mean trouble for me as well as him.

'With my daughter. At the same time. When I found her note on the desk I looked in the drawer right away. It was my own writing paper and she must have opened the drawer to get it. It was in a mess and the hinge of the false bottom of the drawer was broken; and the file with the documents had vanished from it. Yesterday morning it was still there, I checked.'

'So she took the papers?' I said. 'But whatever for? She can't possibly understand them.'

'She's understood them perfectly well,' he said. Then, as if suddenly struck by a new idea, he went on: 'See what that creep Marullo's up to, will you, Iovine?'

I opened the door of the room next door and went in. It was empty, but the other door—the one leading to the hall—was open. I looked in. Marullo was sitting where he had been, his great head sunk over the disorder of his paper-strewn desk. He couldn't have moved from there: he might have been born in that position. I shut both doors again and went back to Miletti's room.

He was now standing by the long window, the windowsill almost at chest-level, peering out as if someone might have climbed up to the fourth floor and was crouched under the sill, outside the open window, listening. The sound of traffic, of which there was little at that time of day, was like a kind of swoosh on the wet tarmac.

'He's sitting tight,' I said.

He turned but I couldn't make out what his face was like—he was standing against the light and the dazzling sun, which had at last come out from behind those deceptive clouds. From the tone of his voice, though, I realised that he was worried and thoughtful.

'He's been with me thirty years, Marullo has,' he said, 'and I still don't know him. He may hate my guts but he's never let me see it. Or maybe I'm getting old and these are just notions of mine.' He came back into the shadowy room and returned to the table to stub his cigarette out on the ashtray, so that I was able to see his old face properly: but it was as inexpressive as a block of granite.

I couldn't see what connection there was between Marullo and the disappearance of Miletti's daughter and the papers.

'Marullo doesn't know anything about this business,' I said. 'We did all the work outside this office because those contracts are only to do with COOFA; which isn't dealt with here.'

Miletti had stayed standing, with his hands on the table, and, short though he was, he managed to be impressive. Then he shook himself and lit another cigarette.

'Only one is to do with COOFA, don't forget. The two billion one. The partnership with Casali has nothing to do with the other contract.' Nicola Casali was his partner in the imaginative and imaginary 'Co-operative of Financial Associates' (COOFA), which acted as a screen for a whole series of deals, in only a few of which I was consulted; a proper crook whom no one but Don Michele would have taken on as a partner, even if it was only in difficult areas. 'Those fifty million came out of my own pocket,' Miletti went on. 'They're my lifeblood. And the whole business was to remain between the three of us—you, me and the councillor who's getting his rake-off.'

'Why, are there more than three of us now?' I said. I couldn't follow it all. 'How does a fourth man come into it? What's Marullo got to do with it? Do you mean him?'

'I'm thinking of a fourth—and it's not a man. Not Marullo—it's just that he's got long ears and I didn't want him listening to us now. Besides, I agree with you, he knows nothing. I was thinking of my daughter and her threats. Of what they involve. I told you she understood the whole thing.'

'What threats?' I asked. 'There weren't any threats in the note.'

'She rang me up this morning,' said Miletti.

'So she hasn't vanished, then,' I said.

'She rang me up this morning,' repeated Miletti, glaring furiously at me. 'To tell me I'm neither a good father nor a gentleman.'

Clearly he couldn't believe his ears. The girl certainly showed no lack of spirit, or even of understanding. On the whole I found myself agreeing with her, but I was beginning to be anxious myself: the fine castle we'd built and perfected for over a year with endless effort and fifty million in cash was now in danger of collapsing on account of a chit of eighteen. And farewell to my percentage.

'Where was she ringing from?' I asked. By now I was really interested. 'Did she tell you that, too?'

'Yes indeed, she told me that too. No respect, no modesty. A stranger, that's what she sounded like. That's the thanks I get for all I've done for her.' Considering what he must have done for her over the past eighteen years, he could hardly expect much thanks. 'It was Faito she was ringing from. That's where she'd run off to. But she said she wouldn't be there long, that she'd be leaving and I wouldn't see her again. She even sent Catello to the house to get her things for her. Clothes, for sure. That's why he was here a while ago. D'you see? As if it was the most natural thing in the world to run away from home, send someone to get the clothes she'd forgotten, and then ring up and make threats.'

'What threats?' I asked. We still hadn't got to the point. As always he was sparing with his words, using only the few that were needed. He must have been more upset than he appeared.

'To send me to gaol. She said she'd finished with me as a father, and . . .' he hesitated, 'that I disgusted her. In any case she put that in the note. Then she went on to say that I mustn't dare to make a move, that if I made any attempt to force her home she'd really get her own back. Meantime, she said, she's not sure whether to send me to gaol, or turn someone I know against me.'

'Casali, that is?'

'Who else?'

'So she's understood all too well how important the papers are,' I said. 'It stinks.'

'Iovine, there are names, facts and figures in them,' he said. 'Does it take much to realise that the second contract is a fraud and that, above all, Casali's left out of it? A child could understand it.'

'Maybe,' I said, but still unconvinced.

'So it stinks,' said Miletti. 'How? What d'you mean?'

'I don't know, but girls of her age don't get ideas of that sort.'

'Girls are mature at eighteen these days,' he said.

So he wasn't calling her a child any longer.

'Yes, but not so mature as to realise from letters and photocopies of documents and receipts that it's all to do with a contract that—as you put it—is a fraud, and, what's more, that your partner's left out of it. What does she know about your relations with Casali? And above all how can she have realised that the work's never going to be carried out completely and according to the specification, but is going to be paid for down to the very last lira?'

'You mean someone's been explaining it all to her?' he said. 'Someone's put her against me?'

'It's a possibility,' I said.

'All right, but who on earth can have put her up to all this?' said Miletti. 'The only person I can think of is Casali, but my daughter's never seen him in her life.'

'That means nothing,' I said. 'And if she had, it would mean that Casali knew the second contract existed, whereas we've always kept him out of it, until now.'

He was grinding all this up in his mind, and soon showed the results of it, his small eyes staring into space, his legs dangling under the table, his feet crossed.

'No, the more I think of it,' he said, 'the more absurd it seems. My daughter in cahoots with Nicola Casali.' After that note and those threats. He was the one who was absurd.

'But she said she was able to incite someone against you,' I said. 'And even to send you to gaol. In any case, if it's not tactless to ask, what happened between you and your daughter to start all this off?'

'It's not tactless, because you're involved,' he replied. 'Indirectly, but you're involved.'

I now felt the need to smoke. When I smoke, I smoke Galas, and now lit one up. 'How's that?' I asked.

'Because of that Pino Gargiulo, remember him?' said Miletti. 'I can't think of any other reason. Otherwise, why would she have burst out so suddenly like this? I don't know how she's done it, but she must have found out what we did.'

Pino Gargiulo was one of those long-haired, bearded layabouts the girl had been going round with recently. A creep, in short, who wore denim even in winter, and whom Don Michele hated ever since he'd discovered that his 'little girl', who was now also dressed in denim, was beginning to like him rather better than she liked the rest of her gang. The old man had plenty of helpers and informers, but they were what you might call heavy-handed; whereas he needed someone with a more delicate touch to do what he wanted done, and so, when he'd decided to intervene, he turned to me. As he was, as I've said, my one and only important client, I could hardly refuse. But it was going to be the first and last time I did that kind of job for him. I now had an office that was becoming increasingly less of a front for my business activities, and with Miletti my relations had so far been purely and simply quite modest and professional. So I certainly didn't want to go back to being his dogsbody, a stooge and tough operator working professionally for him. Life was taking me in a new direction, and I wanted to stick to that.

'I'm involved in that business almost by chance,' I said quickly.

'But you got the boy away from her,' said Miletti. 'That's the truth, and that's what matters.'

This was what happened. The boy, Pino Gargiulo, had hanging over him an old charge for using and possessing a couple of grams of grass, as they call it; a tiny charge, scarcely anything but quite enough to ruin his life. And Inspector Lentizzi, a friend of the family, agreed at once to revive the charge, pick up the lad, and threaten him with everything he could think of. I turned up the very next day, pretending I'd met him by chance and suggesting I should fix the whole thing up for him on condition he vanished and never showed up again, as far as Giulia was concerned. Of course I sugared the pill a bit, but, even so, the fact was that he agreed, though reluctantly. That was all, then, and I couldn't see how such an unimportant episode could have produced results that were now endangering the plan we'd thought up and laid so carefully.

'I'm involved only up to a point,' I said. 'And I think your daughter's laying it on a bit thick. Besides, it happened over a month ago and it wasn't even the first time you've got her favourite boy-friend out of the way.'

He was annoyed that I'd remembered this other aspect of the truth (as he'd called it), and above all that I'd reminded him of it. For my part, I was annoyed to find him blaming his daughter's bright idea, even indirectly, on something I'd been dragged into most reluctantly. And I was even more annoyed, since she wasn't my daughter, that the first really big deal of my life seemed to be going askew. As far as I was concerned Giulia could go to hell and Miletti could die of wounded fatherly pride.

Anyway, Miletti was now behaving in his usual way, prowling round the whole business, admitting nothing, denying nothing. First he fidgeted on his chair.

'Look here,' he grunted, 'are we going to spend the entire afternoon talking about the whys and wherefores of what that little tart's been up to?' In the normal way he'd never have called his daughter a little tart to an outsider. And that's what I was, an outsider, even though, with his talk of washing dirty linen inside the family, he'd momentarily drawn me into it. 'I don't know—she must have been fonder of him than we thought.'

'I never thought anything, Don Michele,' I said. 'Let's get this straight once and for all. I intervened that time just because you asked me to. I've never thought anything before or after it. I'm not your daughter's keeper.'

He didn't answer. At any other time he'd have lashed out at me.

'Besides,' I went on, notching up a few more points, 'it happened over a month ago. Rather a delayed explosion.'

'She must have been brooding over it,' he said. 'In any case, let me ask you again: are we going to spend the entire afternoon dotting our i's and crossing our t's? There's no time to lose. We've got to get that file away from her before she does anything silly. Then I'll see about getting her back.'

So that was it; that was why he'd got me to come along. It was always a struggle, with Miletti dragging me in to do his dirty jobs, and me digging my toes in, thinking of my office and all the rest of it—including a pinch of respectability.

'We haven't understood each other, Don Michele,' I said. 'I'm a businessman, that's my job. Not running around as your dogsbody or whatever you like to call it. What you're asking is for me to persuade your daughter, nicely or nastily . . .'

'Oh nicely, nicely,' he said.

'. . . nicely, then . . . to give me back that wretched file, isn't that it? Let me say it again: we haven't understood each other.'

He was annoyed at this. 'Let me say it again too,' he said. 'There's no time to lose.' And he glared at me with those eyes of his that were like blue laser beams.

Oh, he could be persuasive, the old rogue. Using an expression, a gesture, anything. My one and only important client, but with a large promissory note from me, signed and agreed to, periodically renewable whenever he gave me a job to do, whether I liked it or not.

'Apart from everything else, your daughter will hate the sight of me,' I went on, thus losing the few points I'd won. Was I beginning to give way? Or was it a clear defeat? It depended on how he interpreted it, and he could be generous, if he had to be.

'Why should she?' he said. 'She knows nothing about your involvement. All she knows is that you're my man of business. No sir, she'll consider you quite neutral. She's not going to think you're a crook, as she calls all the others who do me a favour now and then.'

The laser beam was extinguished, but it had burned right into me. He himself tried to make things better by referring to his own quite genuine generosity.

'After all,' he went on, 'I never ask favours without paying for them. It's true that your percentage on the drainage deal would be enough to cover this little business, but you know I'm not sticky about such things, in a matter like this. In other words, if you can save the situation, which just means looking after your own interests, I'll reward you with a sizable handout on top of the rest.'

I'd been disorientated by my sudden, in fact precipitous, tumble. But in a few words Miletti had brought me back to reason. As he said, it was just a matter of looking after my own interests, and I told him so.

'Of course,' he replied at once. 'Yours and mine. Quite apart from the fact that my daughter's involved.'

'You're right,' I said, and no longer felt ashamed.

'But you've got to get a move on. That means getting going right away,' said Miletti.

'You're right,' I said again.

As I went through the room next door I found Improta, one of Miletti's henchmen, sitting on the sofa, a dark fellow in dark clothes but with glittering, mad, light eyes. He looked at me without seeing me, and so without knowing me.

Further on, in the hall, limp Marullo was still bent over his desk, as always. Perhaps he'd actually died in that position.

2

The road to Faito ran straight between tall grey buildings, from the outskirts of Castellammare. It had started to rain again and the whole of Campania seemed flooded. Reflecting the gunmetal sky, the dark puddles formed two continuous, gleaming parallel strips along the crumbling edges of the tarmac; and the curve of those two ribbons between the untidy new yards and sheds which had replaced the rows of grim houses warned me, just in time, that the road was turning right, westwards.

The bend turned out to be unexpectedly sharp—not, as it had seemed to me, a gentle one. I dealt with it by braking quickly, as I hadn't realised I was tearing along on the wet surface at over sixty. I was thinking of the Milettis, father and daughter, and swerved even more when the rear right wheel, at that speed, raised an oblique wall of yellowish water; then, skidding and slithering, I got back into the middle of the road.

I'd taken the bend too sharply and had cut across the puddle on the edge of it. Look out, I told myself; you'll be in trouble if you don't watch out. And to hell with Miletti.

The straight road was now left behind me, after its initial effort on the first broad sweeps uphill. It seemed to have narrowed as well: in fact it now looked like a sick old woman, with all those holes full of water that looked like burst pustules, on to which the rain was falling more and more heavily. I had the windows closed because of the buzzing in my ear, and the windscreen now began to mist up. I opened the window on my side and, as if I'd touched a switch, the buzzing at once grew louder. But I had no choice: it was either the buzzing or a crash down the cliff which lay in wait at every bend in the road.

After two more bends I could see, through the right window, the whole of Castellammare spread below me: a wide, gentle arc that narrowed in the distance into other dark built-up areas that faded into the misty rain along the grey waters of the bay.

When at last I reached the summit it was already dark, and the Teleferic Bar in the square outside the cable-car station was closed and dark. I stopped the Alfetta, lowered the window completely and looked around: in the rain, Faito seemed deserted, a place that had been emptied hastily, in fear.

The idea of announcing my arrival by telephone from the bar there hadn't been a good one, anyway. If she'd been warned that I was on my way, Giulia might have barred the windows and doors, instead of welcoming me in to shelter from the rain. I didn't believe what the old man had told me, because even clever people can be wrong and I was quite sure she loathed my guts. Better to try my luck and turn up unannounced.

I started up the engine and drove along the only road ahead of me. There wasn't much choice, unless I'd turned back, which, if only I'd known what was waiting for me, would have been a better idea. Along the road were the shadows of all sorts of houses, large and small, in line with the current notion that every beauty spot must be turned into an overcrowded holiday resort; and not a light shone out into the darkness. The holiday season, which had only just begun, seemed over already.

The villa Elena was right at the end of this passageway, at a fairly isolated point that must have had the best view: a kind of ridiculous chalet, Swiss or Norwegian in style, made of fake wood and genuine concrete, beside which, like a puppy crouched by its mother, stood the caretaker's almost identical but smaller-scale chalet. As for its name, that came from Miletti's last-but-one wife, the one he'd divorced.

I had to leave the car a good thirty yards from the shelter of the villa's jutting eaves because the property was absurdly fenced by a low wooden rail in the form of a tyrolean balustrade, and before I'd gone ten yards in the direction of the house, I was soaked through. Yet I stopped suddenly, puzzled. The darkness ahead of me was pierced by three unexpected points of light. One after the other, going higher and higher in the houses, three rows of windows were brilliantly lit, as if someone was frantically switching on the chalet lights on the way up from floor to floor.

I ran on. The front door was up a flight of wooden steps that ended in a balcony running all round the raised ground floor of the house. As soon as I'd set foot decisively on the first step, urged on by a kind of presentiment, I was shaken by the thudding of footsteps on the balcony. At that same moment someone was turning the corner of the chalet on my left, and doing so at a run.

I dashed up the steps and ran in the same direction, turning the sharp corner of the balcony just in time to see ahead of me, on the open space behind the house, the dimmed lights of a car. From the sound of the engine, that had just been switched on, I realised it was a Mini. I dashed down towards the gangway that linked the balcony to the uneven open space behind the house, but was only just in time to see the two headlamps flash away. Whoever was in that Mini was certainly in a tremendous hurry.

I went back, round the first and second corners of the house, and reached the front door again. It was unlatched and, inside, the small hall was brightly lit. I pushed the door open and entered, calling loudly: 'Giulia!'

Suddenly I had a feeling that the house was empty, abandoned like the rest of Faito, that the swift shadow I'd glimpsed from the balcony was that of the last person who'd been there—someone in a hurry, distracted enough to leave all the lights on. I carried on indoors, still calling to Giulia, still getting no answer, and entered the room on the right of the hall, which was also brightly lit.

It was a large rectangular room, on a corner of the house and so with windows on two sides looking out onto the balcony; and filled with so many flowers that it looked like a greenhouse: flowers on the wallpaper, on the curtains hooked up to the sides of the windows, on the upholstery of the sofas placed at an angle to each other, of the armchairs opposite them and of the cushions strewn about the floor between them. There were even some artificial flowers in a vase on the table that stood against the wall beside the open door. But among all these flowers—including some more on the fake-Chinese carpet—lying quite still in the angle made by the two sofas and surrounded by cushions, was the body of the person who must have been last-but-one to use the chalet.

With his young, relaxed-looking face, his beard and hair left stiff and tidy when the life flowed out of him, with his eyelids shut and his arms carefully arranged along his sides, surrounded by that amazing display of flowers, Pino Gargiulo looked as if he were lying serenely sleeping in a first-class funeral parlour.

Without touching him I leant over him, and only then saw the deep red gash across his throat, from which the blood had flowed down the other side of his neck, forming a great pool under the body and along the sides of it, like a kind of folded red cloth.

The upper storey was just as empty, just as brightly lit.

In the rooms, everything was tidy. Only in the one that must have been Giulia's bedroom was the wardrobe flung open, and the inside of the wardrobe in a mess. Clothes on hangers all in a muddle, no longer vertical, rumpled up together. Frantic hands must have pulled them carelessly about. On one dress, a thin, off-white one, there were several red stains at hip level.

I took it off its hanger and held it up to the bedside lamp. The stains were dry and might have been blood. I put the dress back in its place, glanced round the room again and left.

At the end of the passage the bathroom door was ajar. I pushed it open, poked my head in and withdrew it at once, instinctively.

There was someone else in the house, but at that moment I couldn't have said quite when this person had come in. Maybe it was the third-to-last, because while the other two must have been there only temporarily, even if one of them had stayed on, the one I'd seen in the bathroom had had time to undress and get into the brimful bath. In other words, it was someone who'd had a bath, and that someone was a woman.

There'd been no reaction to my intrusion—no protests, no outraged cry. I pushed the door further open, until the bath tap stopped it.

It was a fairly modest bathroom, compared with the pretentious decoration of the rest of the house: white tiles, white fitments and accessories and a single lamp above the basin. It looked like a deep-freeze—as the blast of cold air that blew into my face seemed to suggest. The rectangular window opposite the door was wide open on to the darkness outside.

I avoided the draught by going into the bathroom and shutting the window. When I turned I saw a woman's face, which had stayed quite still, showing just above the waterline: it was red and swollen and the eyes, which were wide open and glassy, had obviously almost jumped out of their sockets. The rest of the body was hidden by the foamy water, but it must have been bunched up because at the other end of the bath a pair of swollen feet with long red-painted toe-nails poked up. Not a drop of blood. I put a finger in the water: it was cold.

It was Tina Miletti, fourth and last wife of Don Michele, who was thus left a widower for the third time, with a divorce in between. And I was the one who would have to give him the news.

3

I went downstairs, then further down to a floor below, a kind of semi-basement, also brightly lit and as empty and silent as the ground floor. The kitchen was down there, in perfect order, as if all those people had never set foot in it.

I looked for a glass, filled it at the sink and drank greedily, as if I'd been thirsty.

Now I had to make that wretched telephone call; I couldn't put it off.

A telephone stood on the heavy wooden table in the room beside the kitchen, obviously the dining-room, which looked like the inside of a Norwegian hut: wood everywhere, on the walls, the floor and the ceiling. By the table stood a heavy wooden rocking chair. I dialled the number, yielded to the temptation to sit down, and did so suddenly, giving way to my sudden weariness, and at once started rocking.

Miletti answered at once. He must have been waiting with his hand on the receiver.

'Don Michele, it's Iovine,' I said.

'What the hell have you been up to?' he said aggressively. 'I've been waiting here in the office for hours and I ought to be home for dinner by now. What's happened? Have you found my daughter?'

I told him what I'd found, in place of his daughter, trying not to talk too bluntly, to find indirect ways of putting it.

At first he interrupted me with a couple of questions, from which I realised that he hadn't understood exactly what I was telling him.

'Found her? What d'you mean, found her? Where?'
'In the bath,' I said. 'Drowned.'
'Tina?' he said. 'But she's in Rome.'

Then he took it in and was suddenly silent, leaving me rocking with the telephone line buzzing in tune with the buzzing in my ear. I was still soaking wet.

'Don Michele?' I said.

'I understand, I've got it. How did it happen?'

'I don't know, she must have fainted and . . .'

'The geyser?'

'There was no smell of gas. And the window was open, anyway.'

'It's electric, what a fool I am,' said Don Michele.

'Don Michele, we've got to tell the police, we can't waste any more time. They'll find out how it happened.'

He couldn't have heard me, he was completely taken up with his own thoughts. 'How could it have happened? She left for Rome a couple of days ago. It was her mother's birthday and she'd gone up to see her. At least, so she said,' he added. 'I even asked her to take Giulia with her. If only she had.' This I couldn't follow. Either he didn't believe his wife was dead, or he'd rather his daughter had been drowned as well. 'But her mother doesn't like my daughter much and she didn't want to spoil her birthday. The fact is that Tina and Giulia don't get on very well. Didn't get on,' he corrected himself.

If I hadn't interrupted him he'd have gone on brooding aloud. I told him about the other body I'd found, and this time I was more explicit and direct. But his reaction was the same; and this time too I heard the endless irritating buzzing on the line.

Suddenly the old man burst out, almost shouting. 'What was he doing there with Tina?' he cried, as if this were the most important point to clear up.

'I really don't know, Don Michele,' I said.

'In the sitting-room, you said? Throat cut?'

Like a lamb, I thought, but didn't say it.

'And no sign of Giulia?'

I asked him if his daughter had a Mini and if he knew whether she'd been wearing trousers just then. If she had, then the shadow I'd followed pointlessly round the balcony might have been hers.

'Yes, she's got a Mini,' he said. 'But how she was dressed I don't know. She's always dressed in trousers these days.'

'Don Michele, we've got to send for the police,' I said. And I got up. The chair went on rocking, out of inertia, and banged against my legs.

'As soon as I get there. I'll come straight away,' he said. He must have been very confused and agitated to say such a thing.

'D'you realise what you're saying?' I asked him. 'Am I supposed to wait for your arrival before telling the police?'

'I want to see her before they do. Before they touch her,' he said.

I feel almost sorry for him. 'It's not possible, Don Michele,' I said. 'There'll be trouble afterwards. And anyway, she's hardly recognisable. You'd better not see her, the state she's in.'

'But are you quite sure it's Tina, my wife?'

'I'm sure, Don Michele.'

He gave way. He was really confused. 'Do what you like,' he said. 'Ring the police, tell Catello, do what you like. I'll set off right away.'

I was just going to put down the receiver when he added: 'The other one, is it really Pino?' He was obviously beginning to doubt the whole thing, perhaps even my mental state. Or perhaps it was just a crazy hope, the result of incredulity. Anyway, he'd called the boy by his first name, like that.

I reassured him, if that's the word for it, and hung up.

I now had another call to make. Easier, I hoped. I couldn't remember the number and found it in the book that lay on a shelf under the table.

A rough, disagreeable voice answered. 'Fiorentini police station. Fifth district.'

'May I speak to Inspector Lentizzi, please,' I said.

'He's not here at this time of day. Who's speaking?'
'Has he gone away or is he expected back?'
'He's gone. Who's speaking?'
'Don't you know if he'll be back? He's generally there at this hour.'
'Who's speaking?'
'I'm a friend of the inspector's.' This time I couldn't get out of saying it but it was better not to give names.
'I'll put you through to the deputy inspector,' he said, and did so at once, without giving me a chance to react to his idea.
'Hullo, who's that speaking?' Another abrupt voice, sounding only slightly less disagreeable.
'I'm a friend of Inspector Lentizzi's. I wanted to talk to him,' I said.
'Then why have they put you through to me?'
'I don't know,' I said. 'The switchboard...'
'In any case he's not here. Who are you?'
'I've told you, a friend of his.'
'You must ring later. He's gone out for a minute but he'll be back. What did you say the name was?'
'Lentizzi. Inspector Lentizzi.'
'No, you! What's *your* name?'
'Ah. Alessandro Iovine,' I said. Having got to this point, I might as well tell him the rest. 'To tell you the truth, I wanted to lay a charge.'
'Ah, then you must come in yourself. Charges are made in person or in writing, don't you know that? There are forms to fill in. In any case, what's it about?'
After all, my other telephone call had perhaps been easier. I'd never charged anyone with murder, either in writing or on the telephone, and I was beginning to fear that it might be unexpectedly complicated.
'Two deaths. That is, two corpses.'
'Corpses? Homicide?'
'One of them.'
'One of them what?'

'Only one of them seems to have been killed.'

'Seems? How can it seem? Was he or wasn't he killed?'

'He's had his throat cut.'

'Then it's a matter for the Flying Squad. Where are they?' he said, beginning to sound interested.

'Here, at Faito. Where I'm calling from.'

'Faito? You mean above Castellammare di Stabia?' Interested and surprised.

'Exactly.'

'And you're ringing us here in Naples? You must get in touch with Castellammare.'

In writing? I thought this, but didn't say it.

In the end he agreed to take down particulars and said he'd tell the Flying Squad in Naples, who'd be directly involved. In the meantime I must tell Castellammare.

'Tell me the address again,' he said.

'It's on the road to San Michele. The villa Elena. The last house as you come from the cable car station.'

'And now tell me something,' the deputy inspector said. 'Do you lay charges of homicide and accidental death only to your friends? You still haven't told me why you telephoned us here in Naples when you might have guessed that you should get in touch with the nearest police station.'

I replied that I knew nothing about these things, that it was certainly not one of the happiest moments of my life, that I was bewildered and wanted to ask a friend who knew about such things for advice about what to do and how to do it. This was only part of the truth. What really worried me was the fact that one of the corpses was that of Pino Gargiulo, and I really had meant to ask Lentizzi for advice.

The third telephone call, to the police at Castellammare, was mercifully less complicated.

4

I had over half an hour before they turned up, that was certain. So I thought I'd drop in on the house next door, the one that looked like a small-scale copy of the main house but, unlike it, was completely dark and looked unlived in. It had its entrance on the first floor as well, reached by a small outside staircase, this time made of concrete, which led to a small balcony that ran right round the ridiculous building.

I went up the few steps and banged on the door; waited, then knocked again. The small man who finally opened up was the one I'd seen in Miletti's office. This time he was wearing the heavy cloth cap and also an overcoat. Then I realised that the overcoat served as a dressing-gown: underneath it he was dressed in pyjamas.

'Good evening, Catello, my name's Iovine. Do you remember me? We saw each other this afternoon in Miletti's office.'

In the darkness he hadn't recognised me, but after a moment's hesitation he asked me in. The front door opened straight onto a kind of sitting-room, at the end of which, on a table against the wall, stood an unshaded lamp that gave less light than a candle. The rest of the room was in darkness.

'Yes, yes, I remember,' he said. 'You must excuse us, we were already in bed.'

He then invited me to sit down on a hard, uncomfortable chair by the table, while he stood in front of me, ill at ease. The dim light of the lamp, which struck him sidelong, threw the wrinkles of his face into relief and made it look a muddy colour, giving him a half-alive appearance. Clearly he couldn't have seen or heard anything that had happened in the main house.

So I told him, with less hesitation than I'd used in talking to the other old man. I told him what I'd discovered and when and why I'd come to Faito and made the discovery; in other words I told him about everything except the shadow I'd glimpsed and followed along the balcony and the Mini that had dashed away. He listened to what I was saying, his expression occasionally altering, as a mummy's might change when it had just had its wrappings removed. In that light, the colour of his face remained unaltered. Only his hands began to tremble. At last his agitation burst through those outsize wrinkles and he started stammering.

'Oh lord, what a tragedy. Poor Don Michele. That's the fourth wife he's lost.' Clearly he felt that death and divorce were the same thing.

Then, with a loud yell of 'Sisina!' he went to wake his wife, and they came back together.

Sisina, when she appeared, was a sight indeed. If she'd worn a bowler, she'd have been a perfect Peruvian Indian. She too was wearing a dark overcoat over a white nightdress; her face was crisscrossed with innumerable fine wrinkles, her eyes, invisible between the bags underneath them and the thick eyelids above, were set at an oblique angle in that ruin of a face, and her hair, which was remarkably black and scraped back into a thick pigtail, was as heavy and neat as a horse's tail dressed for a cattle fair. Not a hair out of place: hardly as if she'd that moment got out of bed.

Catello was telling her the news I'd just given him, continually calling on heaven to have mercy on poor Tina Miletti (it was clear he cared nothing about the boy), while she listened with an impassibility that was as much a part of her exotic face as the unhealthy complexion. Then, suddenly catching sight of me, she said:

'May we offer you something? A glass of wine?' Just as if I was there calling on my Aunt Sisina.

I didn't even answer, but turned to Catello.

'How was it that Don Michele didn't know his wife was here? You didn't tell him.'

'No sir, we didn't know it either.'

'How on earth was that? Here she was, practically on top of you, and you never noticed: now remember, the police are on their way and you can't expect to tell them that.'

'She told us not to say anything,' said his wife. Catello gazed at her open-mouthed, clearly frailer than she was, and less impassible. 'Caté,' she went on, 'don't you realise you've got to tell the truth at this stage?'

'But it's got nothing to do with us,' he replied. 'We're just a pair of nobodies and do what we're told.'

'That's right, that's just why we can't go getting into trouble,' said his wife.

She was more open to reason than her husband, who had now begun moaning like a whipped dog. So I turned and spoke to her.

'How long had she been here?' I asked. 'Signora Tina, that is.'

'Two days. She came on Monday morning.'

'Alone?'

'She came alone. Later the young gentleman with the beard arrived.'

'How much later? That same day?'

'Monday afternoon. She went to fetch him at Castellammare in the car.'

The chair was too hard, I had to get up. I stayed standing beside the table, like them, and we looked like three figures in a Christmas crib. I hadn't eaten and my stomach was craving something, so I said to Catello, who had stopped moaning and was now listening:

'That glass of wine—I'd be glad to have it now.'

'Of course, sir, of course. Right away. It's a new, light strawberry wine, it's excellent.' He was delighted at this interruption and the chance to get away.

Once again I turned to his wife. 'And they never stirred from here?' I said.

'When they came here together on Monday afternoon, after the signora went to fetch him at Castellammare, they must have stopped a couple of hours in the house. Then in the evening they went out again and that night I heard the car coming back. And yesterday morning they were here again and went out again. After that I don't know a thing. The car kept coming and going.'

The husband came back with two glasses. The second one was for him. His wife looked at him: impossible to say how, of course. I sat down again on the hard chair and took a sip. Catello sat on the edge of the shadows on a stool behind me. He was now doing the talking. His wife stayed where she was.

'Right, but when did it stop coming and going?' I asked.

'Yesterday evening, I think,' Catello said.

I turned to him. 'Yesterday evening?'

'Yes, yesterday evening,' he replied, and then was silent.

'Early or late yesterday evening? What time, in other words?'

'Late,' said Catello.

'Early,' said his wife. 'I don't know what time, but we were already in bed.'

'So it was late?' I said. 'Is Catello right?'

'We go to bed early,' she answered, still motionless and impassible, with her hands folded across her lap. 'At this time of year, when it's still daylight.'

'And didn't you hear any other car, after that?' I said.

'Yes, Miss Giulia's, this morning.'

I put my empty glass down on the table and rose again. Then I went and stood in front of Catello.

'So I've got to drag it out of you, have I? Can you only talk in dribs and drabs? Why don't you tell me what you saw and heard, in detail? The police will soon be here, as I've told you, and then there'll be trouble.'

It was the wife who answered. 'Trouble, why trouble?' she cried. 'How do we come into it? They're the ones who make trouble, and we're the ones who get involved in it. We never set foot in the house. We saw the signora because she came here on Monday morning, soon after she arrived, to tell us we weren't to tell anyone she was here. Not anyone. Not even Don Michele. And she gave Catello five thousand lire. What should we have done? Telephoned Don Michele? It's their business. We're the caretakers, that's all. And we heard them coming and going in the car, that's all.'

'But you saw them. You saw the young fellow with the beard,' I said. 'And I'm pretty sure he didn't come and give you five thousand lire.'

'Haven't we got eyes in our heads?' said the wife. 'They did it on the balcony out there, the filthy pigs!'

'Sisina!' cried Catello hoarsely.

I turned to him again, sitting on the stool, twisting his hands nervously. He looked up at me.

'It's their business,' he said softly, as if apologising.

'It may be their business but this time you're both involved in it.'

'No no, sir!' he moaned. 'We don't come into it. It's their business, not ours.'

The wife said nothing. Perhaps I'd scared Catello enough.

'Then Miss Giulia arrived this morning, is that right?' I said.

'Yes sir, this morning. And what a state she was in. A real state. She came here and told me I'd got to go into Naples with her. She'd take me in and then bring me back. Then she rang up. From here. Rang her father. You should have heard what she said to him. Then she took me to Naples.'

'Did she come straight here or did she go there first, to the big house?' I asked.

'I don't know, she came straight to the front here, in the car,' he said. 'As a rule when they come they go round the back and leave the car in the yard there.'

'What did you do in Naples?'

'We went to their house, the other house,' he said. 'She made me get out before we got to the gate and told me to walk right up the road. I wasn't to say I'd come with her. So I went to see Idillia, that nasty dark creature, and got her to give me a bag that was already packed in Miss Giulia's room. The old bitch didn't want to give it me, but in the end she did and I went back to Miss Giulia. She took me down via Orazio and dropped me off at Mergellina. She told me to go back by train. Now put yourself in my shoes—what should I have done? I rang Don Michele and told him everything, except that I'd come in with her. I told him his daughter had come out to Faito and had sent me to get her things from the house.'

'You didn't tell him his wife was at Faito too, though, did you?' I said.

He looked at me in terror, as if I'd been Miletti himself. Perhaps his eyes were actually wet; they certainly seemed to glisten in the dim light.

'No, sir. But you can see what a mess it all is. No sir, I didn't tell him.'

'Because of the five thousand lire?'

'Because of that lousy tip? No fear. Because it was their business and the old man was quite capable of taking it out on me. How can you tell what he's going to do? Always flying off the handle, if you'll forgive my saying so.'

'And what did Don Michele say when you rang him?'

'He told me I was to go to his place in via Marina at once. So I went and he wanted to know everything, straight off.'

'Everything? But you didn't tell him everything. Or did you tell him about his wife this time? And that his daughter'd come into Naples with you?'

'You should have seen what he was like,' said Catello. 'I couldn't risk it. No sir, I just repeated what I'd already told him on the phone.'

'So you didn't get muddled?'

'No, why should I? All I had to tell him was about the time since his daughter turned up here. And that I'd gone into town by train.'

'Whereas in fact,' I said, 'you only came back by train.'

'Yes sir. After you'd seen me when I was leaving Don Michele's office, I went and got the train back.'

'And didn't you see Miss Giulia again? When you got back here she'd gone?'

'When I got back we had supper and went to bed,' said Catello. 'No, we didn't see or hear her again.'

'And didn't you see or hear anyone else?'

'No one else.'

'When Miss Giulia took you to Naples, didn't she say she'd be bringing you back here herself?'

'Yes she did,' said Catello. 'Obviously she changed her mind.'

'And when she left you at Mergellina,' I said, 'didn't she tell you why she wasn't coming with you? Or where she was going, at least.'

'Why should she, what business was it of mine? Did she have to explain things to me? Can you imagine it? She's her father's daughter all right, and just about as sweet as he is.'

'Her father,' I said. 'Well, now her father's going to find everything out,' I added, poking at the wound.

'He will, sir, that's the trouble,' said Catello. 'That's the mess we're in. All because we tried to mind our own business.'

This time, behind me, the Peruvian Indian grunted.

5

It was still raining when I went back to the main house. I didn't know much more than I had before, above all in connection with the girl, and soon I'd have to answer all sorts of questions. A really pleasant evening.

I went round the house again, avoiding the sitting-room on the ground floor and the bathroom upstairs. Something had escaped me, the last time I went round.

When I came down from the first floor I saw the file, lying

there, hidden from anyone coming in by the front door. When I reached the last steps of the staircase I saw it lying a few yards ahead of me on the floor. I'd been near it at least three times, when I came in, when I went out, and when I came back to the house, and I hadn't noticed. Now, though, the door was shut instead of wide open.

It was lying beside a small new leather suitcase, and a fabric travelling bag, obviously a woman's; they seemed abandoned, forgotten in a hasty departure. But it was empty. When I picked it up and opened it I saw it was empty, the documents had gone. I unzipped the travelling bag and searched in it, thinking they might have been transferred there. It was packed full, and there were even books in it, I could feel, apart from women's clothes, but no papers or documents.

For the first time, too, I now noticed damp footmarks all over the hall, large ones and small ones, all sizes. Most of them pointed towards the sitting-room. But I hadn't noticed anything, before.

At that moment the police announced themselves from a distance with the shrill whistle of their siren. I hurriedly zipped up the bag, rose and stood there for a moment undecidedly, clutching the empty red file. Then I looked round. From where I was standing in the hall I saw a desk in the corner of the sitting-room opposite me. The whistle was growing louder.

When I tried the first drawer of the desk it refused to open. It was locked. And so were all the others, set in rows on either side of the person sitting at the desk. I tried them all. It was a double-fronted desk, with drawers on both sides, as I discovered when the whistle stopped in a kind of sob just outside the house. I was only just in time to shut the bottom drawer when I heard their footsteps running up the wooden steps outside, and ran to open the door just as they arrived on the threshold.

There were two of them, in uniform, young and serious looking.

'Urgent call,' said the taller of the pair. 'Was it you who rang?'

I said it was. We were all of us panting. Then they came in.

'The chief will soon be here with the rest of the squad,' said the second man. 'You haven't touched anything?' He looked around and immediately noticed the footprints. 'Aren't you alone in the house?'

'Nothing, absolutely nothing. Yes, I'm alone. I arrived just over half an hour ago and when I discovered . . .' I indicated the sitting-room with my open hand, 'I rang up at once. I haven't touched anything and there's no one else in the house.'

They went into the sitting-room, one behind the other, and stopped suddenly as soon as they had passed the doorway.

'Where's the other one?' asked the taller of the two men.

'Upstairs, in the bathroom,' I said.

'Here's the inspector,' he told me, as if trying to be reassuring.

He was arriving at that very moment, whistled in as they had been. With louder whistles, in fact; there must have been several cars.

The two men exchanged glances, then went over to the staircase and upstairs.

I still had my hand on the handle of the open front door when the rest of the squad arrived. Six of them in plain clothes, with and without ties, followed by another two in uniform and preceded by an elderly, shortish, potbellied, whiskery man, the inspector, who said at once as he came in:

'You're Mr Iovine?'

When they carried her down on a stretcher, they'd covered Tina Miletti with a sheet.

She looked enormous under all that whiteness: her belly must have been hugely swollen. I remembered her as slim and well built. But above all as young, thirty-five years younger than Miletti, whose wife she had been for less than thirty-five months. She was blonde, much too blonde.

They put her down in the hall beside the staircase, in a wide space between the steps and the sitting-room door. Pino

Gargiulo was already lying there, without a sheet over him, in his jeans and faded jacket and, oddly, stained with everything down the front except blood. And he was even younger than she was, in spite of the grave, solemn air that, both living and dead, that beard and those whiskers had given him: half-way between her and her stepdaughter, the pair that must have shared him as long as it lasted.

Now they were close together, alone and isolated, and seemed to be sleeping together, as they must have done God knows how many times before.

I was in the sitting-room, sitting at the end of the sofa beside the exactly similar one on which the inspector was sitting, also at the end, and among all those flowers. Between us, in the corner between the two sofas, was the outline of Pino Gargiulo drawn in chalk on the beige background of the fake-Chinese carpet and on the big red patch of dry blood.

We were waiting for Miletti to arrive in order to make the official identification, after which another series of questions would begin, unlike those I'd been asked, I hoped, and those used in the interrogation of the caretakers, at which I'd been present.

The plain-clothes men were still busy, up and down stairs and back and forth between the rooms, following the deputy attorney, who'd turned up after the rest of them but was no less active; he seemed to be making an inventory of the house, as if in preparation for a move. The men in uniform, on the other hand, were calmer, standing about here and there in the sitting-room and the hall and on the stairs, upstairs and down.

I was thinking of the file I'd been in time to put away, in a place that looked plausible enough for an empty—yes, empty—file, wondering what could have happened to those documents and what might happen to the whole business. And I could feel the inspector's eyes boring into me like a pair of little tacks.

I was also thinking of the girl and of what Miletti would tell the police about the shadow on the balcony and the Mini, which I'd mentioned to him but not to the inspector.

'What I don't understand,' the inspector was now saying, and I wondered if it was really a coincidence, 'is why on earth the father asked you to get the girl to come home. Couldn't he have come himself? To persuade her or to force her back?' It wasn't a question but a reflection, out aloud.

On this point, to tell the truth, I'd been rather vague. I'd called myself a friend of the family, careful not to say anything about a business relationship. Now I went back to thinking of my own affairs.

'Eighteen, you said, didn't you?'

His voice was mellifluous, like his gentle manner. He was called Assenza, and wasn't so much short as round. Looking at him closely during the interrogation and watching him going round the house, sticking his nose into everything, I'd altered my first impression of him. His incipient baldness, his puffy face, his suit, which was loose and at the same time short, above all his paunch, made him at first sight seem shorter than he was. What was really noteworthy about him, though, was his eyes: a couple of black pins that fastened on you and stayed there.

'Yes, she's eighteen,' I said. 'So she's of age. Force wouldn't get him anywhere. He'd thought of it, in fact it was the first thing he did think about. From what the caretaker couple told you, you'll have got an idea of what he's like. A friend of the family could get more. That's why he came to me.'

'Because you're a friend of the family?' he said, not waiting for my reply, which he already knew. 'The caretakers, yes. It's not that I doubt what they said, it's that I'm thinking of what they didn't say.'

'I thought they said all there was to say,' I said.

'Going to bed with the hens. It looks to me as if they went with the chickens,' he said, and grinned with amusement. He was the only one who did. 'When was it you talked to the pair of them?'

'I told you, after I'd rung up, while I was waiting for you to arrive.'

'And you'd telephoned Miletti first of all?'

'I thought it the first thing to do,' I said. 'It was his wife I'd found in the bath.'

Around us, everywhere, on the furniture, on the door frames and handles and windows, around the light-switches on the walls, there were black stains: the powder for fingerprints that had been dusted all over the house. The stains on the table in front of the inspector looked like a row of black beetles on the march: soon they'd climb up on to him, crawl all over him and gobble him up.

'Did you know her well?' he asked. 'The wife?'

'A bit,' I said. 'Her husband didn't take her around much.' I avoided calling him Don Michele.

'So you're not so much a family friend, then,' he said, 'as a friend of the husband.' God knows what he meant by that.

'Michele Miletti's an old-fashioned man,' I said, and God knows what I meant by it, either. 'And that reminds me, I wanted to ask you something: could you separate the two bodies? You know, to find the pair of them like that, lying side by side, might seem . . .'

'A hint of what happened?'

'Well, maybe. In any case, it's a terrible blow to him already.'

'You're right, but you know how it is, we've got to go ahead with a certain routine. All the same, there's no rule to say we can't lay them out in another way. I must ask the deputy attorney, though.' He rose and with unexpected tact went to remedy the effects of the routine, as he had called it. The black beetles stayed where they were.

When he got back he looked ready to rub his hands with satisfaction. 'All over,' he said. 'They're separated now.'

But he didn't go back to his place on the sofa, he went over to the window behind me and stared out.

'He should have been here a while ago, by now,' he said. 'So should the Naples flying squad. It must be the rain that's held them up. It's still raining.' And he went on, without a pause and without any apparent logic, as if the rain were part of what he was saying: 'Because they'd been married only a short time, hadn't they?'

'Less than three years.'

'And he knew nothing about the boy?'

'Nothing, as far as I know.'

'Did you?'

'Even less.'

'Never seen him, never met him.' Lentizzi would support me in this. It was the second time I'd denied ever meeting Pino Gargiulo.

'And she, the wife, brought him here. It wasn't by any chance official, was it? Officially ignored, that is?'

'The very idea strikes me as an insult to Miletti,' I said.

'Yes, it's insulting,' said the inspector. 'And didn't the step-daughter know anything either? Women are more intuitive in these things, you know.'

'You must ask her,' I said. 'You think I know more about the Miletti family than I do.'

'Well, you said you were a friend. The girl—Giulia, I think you said: she's a daughter of Miletti's second wife, isn't she?'

'Yes, but she never knew her mother, who died soon after she was born. She was brought up by the third wife, until she was divorced by the father. Who then married again, when Giulia was about fifteen.'

'A bit unstable, you might say,' said the inspector, who had now left the window and was standing in front of me, the rain forgotten. 'Changing mothers twice—in fact three times—in fifteen years isn't likely to make strong family bonds. That's what I meant by unstable. But I see you're pretty well informed about the Miletti family. Did she get on with her first step-mother? What did you say her name was?'

Either he didn't remember, or if he did remember he wasn't sure if he remembered rightly and was asking for confirmation of it. An odd memory. He'd muddle me up and make me forget the answers I ought to remember.

'Elena,' I replied. 'I know she was very fond of her.'
'And what about her second stepmother?'
'I think she was fond of her too.'
'If she was very fond of the first she wouldn't have taken to the second very easily, would she? D'you think they were friends? I can't find another word for it.'
'You must ask her that yourself,' I said.
'We will. When we have the pleasure of meeting her.' But he still didn't give up. Above all he seemed unable to take things in properly. Quite unexpectedly he continued: 'But why all these marriages?'
'You must ask him that,' I said.
He took no notice of my reply. 'Because he's rich? Because he *is* rich, as you told me, didn't you? And he must be a womaniser, too. Rich men generally are, or become one, as they can afford it. But at his age . . . There were thirty-five years between him and his last wife, weren't there? That's a lot, it's obvious she'd find her fun elsewhere.'
A thinker, this Inspector Assenza, compelled to be an inquisitor. He got back to the job right away.
'You know nothing about his first wife?'
'I know they were married a long time, about fifteen years, and that she died of some illness. And there wasn't a great difference in their ages,' I added at once, to forestall him, as he'd taken to doing his sums.
'Well, of course. He was young then. What about the second?'
'Giulia's mother? All I know is that they were married a couple of years. Then she died and he married again to give the child a mother. Or a stepmother, if you prefer.'
'And this third marriage lasted a long time too, since they were divorced, as you say, when the girl was fifteen and there wasn't any divorce in Italy. How did they do it? Of course, there's always been divorce for the rich. But was he already rich?'
'Yes he was, by then.'

'You know that for certain, do you?'

'It's not just I that know it. Everyone knows.'

'And wife number three was called—in fact, is called, as she's the only survivor—Elena. And she lives in Milan.' He was still thinking aloud. 'An odd father.' I didn't understand this conclusion, but I could now no longer follow him. I was tired, hungry, wet and my stomach was upset on account of the wine I'd drunk without eating.

Apart from the policemen standing about here and there, the rest had all disappeared, including the deputy attorney, who'd have to carry on the interrogation, a coda to the formal one which had already taken place, disguised as chat. Perhaps he was playing cards in the dining-room.

Then more whistles and more cars. The Naples Flying Squad. It arrived, I think, reduced to a minimum and almost at the same time as Don Michele.

6

The ancient stone that made up his face had suddenly crumbled, and lines had appeared on it. Michele Miletti now looked his age—ten years more than his age. They almost had to prop him up.

After he'd nodded repeatedly and with an absent-minded air at the brief ritual of the official identification, his chauffeur Antonio and one of the plain-clothes men from the Flying Squad had to take him to the sofa in the sitting-room. Then, just when he was flopping down on to it, the deputy attorney approached and made as if to shake his hand, but seized his wrist instead and whispered something, as if making an obscene proposal: it was his condolences, possibly the official ones.

The rest of us were plunged into an embarrassing silence. Having left the two bodies out there in the hall, close together once more, most of us had gone into the sitting-room. I was in the place where Assenza had been sitting, at the furthest possible point from Don Michele.

He had recognised his wife but not Pino Gargiulo, so things were now official: neither of us had ever seen him before. The blue flash of his eyes, when they looked into mine for a moment, confirmed that he had grasped the situation. How he had grasped it, God only knows. I always undervalued him, that was clear, or else he valued or overvalued me. However, he was now wrapped in grief and therefore impregnable.

In any case, there was no attack. The ritual continued on the level of courteous understanding, with the deputy attorney and the inspector rivalling each other in showing it. As for the deputy inspector from the Flying Squad, he did very little, in fact barely opened his mouth, what with coming late, and feeling somewhat in awe of the others. But, as was bound to happen, at a certain point the matter emerged.

'You confirm, then, that you sent Mr Alessandro Iovine, here, as a friend of the family, to persuade your daughter to return home?' the deputy attorney asked Miletti.

He'd settled down, if you can call it that, on one of the armchairs which he'd put in the middle of this family reunion, with the squad that had come from Naples standing silently behind him. He must have been uncomfortable and uneasy, for he kept changing position; he had long restless legs which he kept crossing and uncrossing continually. He was bald, wore spectacles and, with those legs of his, was a good deal taller than anyone else there.

Assenza, on the other hand, was settled in the real sense of the word on the same sofa as me, with his legs stretched out as far as they would go so that his feet nearly touched the head of the outline drawn in chalk on the big splash of blood on the carpet. At the deputy attorney's question he nodded his head frantically and looked at me with the air of an accomplice.

'Yes, yes, I confirm it,' grunted Don Michele. He'd lit his first cigarette since he arrived.

'And do you also confirm what the two caretakers said'— and the deputy attorney consulted a sheet of paper which he kept waving in his hand—'the Bellellas, that your daughter arrived this morning and left again at once?'

'Yes, yes, I confirm it,' said Miletti.

'Forgive me, Mr. Miletti,' Assenza broke in. 'But how can you confirm it if you weren't here? Don't you think so, sir?' It was a respectful reproach to the silly question.

'She phoned me this morning. From here. And Catello confirmed it when he came into my office. But I didn't know then that my daughter had come to Naples with him. I know it now.' He was silent. Perhaps he was thinking of how to get his own back on old Catello. 'It's true, I can't confirm that she left here immediately after she arrived, but the fact is that she did leave.'

'In any case, after that telephone call you sent Mr Iovine up here?'

The deputy attorney was silent now, and was looking from Miletti to the inspector with an interested air. Obviously he didn't feel excluded, as in fact he had suddenly become.

'That's right,' said Miletti.

'Why didn't you come yourself? Had you quarrelled with your daughter?' asked the inspector.

'No, we haven't quarrelled. I thought it was a harmless prank and that as Iovine knows what to do in such cases, he'd easily persuade her to come home. If I'd come it would have been different. You see, I'm old-fashioned and there are some things I won't stand for. So we'd have had a row. Iovine was more suitable.'

'When did your daughter leave home?' asked the deputy attorney, in a tone that suggested total innocence. Everyone's interest had now turned into curiosity.

Don Michele hesitated only very briefly. 'This morning,' he replied.

'Not before?' said Assenza, not letting himself be ousted.

'I found a note from her this morning. We have a big house,

but if she hadn't been at home last night, I'd have known it just the same.'

'What note? Have you got it with you?'

'No, I left it at home, in fact in the office. I showed it to Iovine; gave it to him to read when I asked him to come and fetch Giulia.'

Assenza turned to me, changing position on the sofa and crossing his legs. Making rather less of it than the deputy attorney, since they were shorter than his.

'And what was written in this note?' he asked me.

I turned three quarters of the way towards him, to avoid looking at Don Michele.

'That she was fed up with her father's strictness,' I said, 'and was leaving to make a new life for herself. That sort of thing, more or less. You know, the usual.'

'Undated?'

'I don't remember that it was dated.'

The deputy attorney continued to follow us with interest, the deputy inspector was all ears, and Assenza continued to do the talking. He now turned to Miletti.

'As this house of yours is large, mightn't she have left yesterday evening without your knowing?'

'I always know everything,' said Miletti.

'You didn't know your wife was here, though,' said Assenza.

Miletti flashed a glare of hatred at him, then turned the blue beam of his eyes onto the deputy attorney. He seemed deeply wounded.

'Do I have to stay here and be insulted?' he said. 'Is that how you interpret the law, sir?'

No longer interested, but embarrassed, the deputy attorney reluctantly entered the conversation again, trying to improve matters.

'Dr Assenza was only trying to do his duty,' he said.

'And this duty means a total lack of respect, does it? Considering the time and situation, at least,' said Miletti. His feelings seemed outraged.

40

The deputy attorney couldn't help giving Assenza a brief, useless glance of reproach. 'You know, Mr Miletti,' he said, 'it's very important to be sure whether or not your daughter was here yesterday evening.' It may not have been dawn at this point but it was well past midnight and so, in his official capacity, the deputy attorney quickly corrected himself. 'On Tuesday evening, I mean. According to the police doctor, the death of the two victims can be set, for the moment, at about Tuesday evening. So you must see that if your daughter was here that evening, her situation would become very embarrassing.' This was the actual word he used. 'So it's very important.'

Miletti had grasped the importance of the matter at once. 'No, she wasn't here on Tuesday evening because she was at home,' he said. 'I repeat, she left only this morning. That is, yesterday morning.' Then he was seized by an idea. 'The two caretakers were here, though.'

'What d'you mean?' said the deputy attorney, crossing and uncrossing his legs.

'This: that they not only didn't hear or see my daughter but that they were here on Tuesday evening. They've been here all the time.'

Assenza had been silent too long, and lost no time. 'We'll talk about the Bellellas later. What we want to know about now is your daughter.'

'You want to know. But what?' the old man burst out, without even looking in his direction. 'And what might this embarrassing situation be? Might you conclude that she'd cut the throat of that fellow there?' And with a gesture of his head he indicated both his own contempt and the corpse's feet, poking in at the door, from the hall.

The inspector, on the other hand, never took his eyes off Miletti. 'Stains have been found on some of your daughter's clothes that from a preliminary, superficial examination look like blood. We'll have that confirmed as soon as possible.'

'Blood?' The old man had been caught off guard.

'And all the rest of the house was perfectly tidy. Nothing has been touched or moved. Mr Iovine, here, said he found the door open, and in fact there's no sign of a break-in. Whoever was here went in and came out by that door.' And he too indicated those still feet, making Don Michele turn round. 'As nothing was touched, we can rule out theft.'

'I still don't see how my daughter comes into it.'

'We're not accusing your daughter, Mr Miletti,' said the deputy attorney, intervening once again. Obviously, in the contest with the inspector, it was he who had the old man's feelings most at heart. 'We're only trying to reconstruct the facts.'

'The facts,' said Miletti. 'In the whole of this business there's only one certain fact, and that's that I still haven't been told how my wife died. Drowned, you said. But how can anyone drown while having a bath? Drowned,' repeated Miletti and looked at me, who'd been the first to use the word.

'For the moment we must stick to what the police doctor said,' said Assenza. 'The autopsy will tell us more.'

'Autopsy?' said Miletti. 'Why, are you going to cut her up?'

'We don't want to cut anyone up, Mr Miletti. In cases like this, the law demands an autopsy. That's all. And now, would you be so good as to tell us where you think your daughter can be found.' He wouldn't let himself be side-tracked, he wouldn't lose sight of the point on which we'd have liked him to be blind. 'That is, where can she have gone? From here.'

The old man looked at him at last, but as if he'd have liked to tear out his eyes, no less. 'I've no idea,' he said. 'Ask Catello rather than me. He was the one who saw her last and went to Naples with her. Even though he may lie to you as he lied to me.' Pitiless and vengeful.

'We've already done that. But you must admit that you know your daughter rather better than he does and know more than he does where she may have gone. To Milan, do you think? To her first stepmother?'

'I tell you I've no idea.'

'She did get on well with your third wife, didn't she?' said Assenza.

'She did. After all, it was she who brought the girl up.'

'So it's not impossible she may have gone to her?'

'Not impossible, no,' said Miletti; and it seemed to me that he was now giving way not just to his own weariness, but to something else. The look he gave me this time was almost apprehensive.

Assenza, on the other hand, must have felt triumphant. He looked at me too, but with an air that seemed to be implacable.

'And when you were told by Mr Iovine that your daughter was no longer here, didn't you think of telephoning your ex-wife?' he said.

'When Iovine told me my daughter was no longer here, he also told me that this other wife of mine was dead. So you can imagine the state I was in. No sir, I didn't telephone. And anyway, why should I do so? How could my daughter possibly be there? Could she fly? She was still in Naples this morning.'

'Mr Miletti, there are such things as aeroplanes today, so she could in fact have flown. She might have got a seat on an afternoon flight.'

'Let's hope she did,' said the old man wearily.

'Were relations with your fourth wife good?' asked Assenza.

'Whose? Mine?'

Perhaps at this point Miletti was no longer following him; perhaps at that time of night, with those two corpses still out there, with those present, including me, exhausted and impatient and the deputy attorney ever more restless in his armchair, this interrogation was becoming a bit much. I began to see Assenza in a new light.

'Your daughter's,' he said.

'Extremely good,' said Miletti.

'They never quarrelled, as far as you know? You know how it is, sometimes even people who are fond of each other can have differences.'

'What are you looking for?' said Miletti. 'A motive for my daughter to come here and be in at her stepmother's death?'

'As the deputy attorney told you, I'm only trying to do my duty,' said Assenza.

'Let's forget your duty. You must see that I'm tired out by now. You're full of curiosity which you want satisfied straight away, without wasting time, whereas there's just one thing that I want to know—something very painful and entirely justified that I've asked and haven't been told. How my wife died.' He was trying to get away and was wrapping himself up again in his mantle of pain.

'According to the police doctor, she may have been taken ill. The water may have been too hot, perhaps.'

'Yes, perhaps,' said Miletti.

The ambulance had arrived, without whistle or sirens, and they were now carrying out the corpses. The plain-clothes men, who until then had been inert and silent spectators, were suddenly seized with energy, and the meeting broke up. Nearly everyone had followed out the deputy attorney, who had been called into the hall, and, crowded round the doorway, they prevented us seeing the stretchers being carried past. We heard footsteps down the wooden staircase outside, heavy, cautious steps, and then the group in the doorway broke up and I saw Catello and his wife at the front door, standing quite still at the foot of the stairs. They must have been made to wait in the next room—he trembling uneasily, she quite impassible—and they must have heard everything. But the long vigil wasn't yet over for them, they were still to hear more.

Assenza must have been a tireless nightbird. In the sitting-room the three of us had remained sitting, together with a uniformed man, but clearly he hadn't resigned himself to the idea that the party was over and that the company was going to depart without any official farewells, at least from the deputy attorney. So he came out, quite casually and unexpectedly, with a typically delayed-action question.

'So you've never seen or met that young fellow?' he said. 'We don't even know who he was. He hadn't any papers on him.'

It wasn't clear which of us he was addressing, partly because he was gazing at the outline at his feet, with the great dark blood-stain that seemed to be flowing out of the throat sketched in chalk.

So neither of us answered, neither Miletti nor I. The old man continued to stare at a point on the floor a long way from the sofa, and I merely shook my head. The marks on the table—those greedy insects—seemed to be growing and moving, crawling about.

'I wonder how long they'd known each other.' So, he was carrying on with his tiresome habit of thinking aloud, but now in a provoking, irritating way.

'Ask those two,' Miletti growled. 'They know everything. They've seen everything.' He'd noticed the caretakers' presence, although he'd never looked in their direction. The Indian and her husband were standing perfectly still at the foot of the stairs.

'How long have the Bellellas worked for you?' asked Assenza.

The old man hesitated, and with reason: the wretched fellow seemed to be started off at the beginning again. Then, still gazing into space, he said:

'Four or five years.'

'Do you know them well?' asked Assenza.

'I've known them four or five years,' said Miletti.

'So you've had this villa for four or five years?' said Assenza.

'No, sixteen,' said Miletti. 'Before, I had another couple who were caretakers.' He said it with a sigh, as if resigning himself to the fatal inevitability of this hammering interrogation.

'Did you dismiss them?' asked Assenza.

'No, they decided to go,' said Miletti.

'Have you ever had reason to suspect the Bellellas?' asked Assenza. 'For any reason at all?' As if the two of them weren't listening.

'I don't often come here,' said Miletti. 'In any case nothing's ever been missing, if that's what you mean.' And he now looked him in the face.

'But would you swear to their honesty?'
'I don't swear to anyone's honesty,' said Miletti.
'In other words, you'd suspect them?'
'Those are your words, not mine,' said Miletti.
'I'd be grateful if you'd answer clearly.'
'Ask clear questions and you'll get straight answers,' said Miletti. 'You're speaking of honesty. What's honesty got to do with what's happened in this house? A person may be honest and yet kill, and dishonest but incapable of cutting anyone's throat. As was done to that . . . gentleman.'

'I asked you a straight question, and that is whether you had any reason to suspect the Bellellas. As for the rest, I must admit that I can't follow your idea of honesty. It can only help to give me an idea of how you consider it yourself.'

What the hell was Assenza trying to say?

'Yes, sir, I suspect the Bellellas,' said Miletti. 'I've no need for reasons. I haven't got any at the moment and I don't need any.' This we knew perfectly well. 'As for the way I consider honesty, let's forget it. It's got nothing to do with the drowning of my wife, which, among other things, you still haven't explained to me.'

7

When we left it was nearly dawn. The sky was beginning to turn pale and far away, at the edge of the world, behind the dead volcano, a silver glow was spreading. The rain had stopped and across the sky were scattered and strung a few tufts of pink, as if the approaching warmth of that glow had already melted the few remaining clouds, the most determined. The day promised to be unlike the one just over.

Miletti must have recovered all his energy. When he rose from the sofa on which he had been sitting for so long he refused Antonio's help, and sent him to wait in the car; then he stretched to his full height and, small as he was, seemed to dominate everyone, including the tall thin deputy attorney. As for Assenza, his role in what was happening seemed to have been reversed: he had suddenly crumpled, his full face had slackened and his eyes had lost their lustre.

Thank heaven it was over, even though, when he said goodbye, Assenza threatened us with a tired smile: 'See you soon,' he said. 'I think we'll be meeting again.' This was to both of us, Miletti and me. The deputy attorney, for his part, was anxious to 'deal with a few formalities', as he put it. A nice man, after all. The ambulance had been gone some time.

At last we were all out of doors, and some of the cars were still moving off, the doors slamming noisily in the silence and the wheels crunching over the gravel. Like a dying motor. After what must have been the longest night of their lives, the Bellellas were still on the balcony, silently watching us all depart.

Miletti's ancient black Flavia was waiting outside the ridiculous gate, with Antonio's hand already on the door handle, impatient and ready to open it for him. But Miletti was coming across to the Alfetta with me.

'Please tell him he can go, Iovine,' he said. 'I'll go back with you.' After keeping him waiting all those hours, stuck in a corner of the sitting-room.

When I got back I found him already sitting in the car, waiting.

'No one'll hear us, this way,' he said. 'And we've got to talk.'

After which he didn't open his mouth until the end of the long winding road that went steeply downhill. Only at one point, in the middle of a sharp bend, did he mutter: 'Don't go too fast down this hill', then lapsed once again into a staring, settled thoughtfulness.

At last he shook himself, when we were on the edge of Castellammare. Suddenly he burst out:

'The little tart!'

'You mean your daughter?' I asked, after a puzzled moment. Considering the circumstances in which she'd been found—not to say surprised—the words this time might equally well have applied to his wife.

'Who else?' said Miletti, looking at me, or glaring, as I could see out of the corner of my eye.

'I mean, are you wondering where she may have gone?' I asked.

'No, I'm thinking of the mess she's got me into,' he said, and lapsed into silence again. Nothing more came of the talk he had promised me.

We were at the beginning of the motorway by now, which at that time had few cars upon it. Above us the sky was lighter, but the calm, clear day was darkened by Miletti's gloom: I could feel it sitting beside me with him, another travelling companion.

'D'you think you'll ring up your wife in Milan?' I said. 'It's quite likely your daughter's gone to her.'

He didn't answer my question. 'I didn't tell you, yesterday, that there was four hundred thousand lire missing from the desk drawer, when I checked it,' he said. 'The money was there, the previous evening. It was in an envelope, the one I keep cash for household expenses in, and the envelope was empty. She took it.'

I looked round a moment: he was staring through the windscreen, as if fascinated by that big red, distant disc. Far away.

'So it's obvious she was planning to go far,' I said.

'Far? On four hundred thousand?'

'Young people today know how to deal with money, they can make it last. They're quite capable of going round the world on a thousand lire.' I'd said what I had to say, I'd made my point; but now we must talk about serious matters. The girl's four hundred thousand could take those documents even further away from us.

'Yesterday evening, before the police arrived, I found the file,' I told him.

'And you're telling me only now? What were you waiting for?'

'For us to be alone. It was empty. The papers weren't there.'

'Empty? How's that?'

'Someone must have taken them. Maybe the girl herself—your daughter, I mean. She may have put them somewhere else. It was on the floor behind the front door, beside a suitcase and a travelling bag.'

'Green?'

'Yes.'

'They're Giulia's. Did you search the suitcase?'

'I wasn't in time to. Only the bag. The papers weren't there. Then the police turned up.'

'They found the bag and the suitcase?'

'Yes, they found them, examined them, and took them over.'

'Where can she have taken the papers?'

'She may have hidden them on her in a hurry, so as not to be cluttered up.'

'In a hurry. But you're not sure it was she you saw on the balcony?'

'I'm not even sure it was a woman.'

'That reminds me, thanks for not telling the police.'

'It's in both our interests,' I said, and imagined, or rather felt, his eyes upon me.

'Listen,' said Miletti, 'we've got to find those papers. And my daughter. We've got to find them before the police do.'

'What can I say, Don Michele?' I said, and really didn't know what to say to him. 'We'll get going, but I haven't the faintest idea where to start. From Milan?'

He didn't answer at once. He was thinking, now fascinated by the movement of the motorway. I had a feeling he'd forgotten his dead wife. Perhaps he had by now become used to her death, or rather to the circumstances in which she had died—that shocking proof of her infidelity—and this stopped him talking about it: anyway, since we left he hadn't mentioned her once.

At last he decided to say something. 'I don't think she's gone to her stepmother,' he said, 'but in any case we can start from there.'

'Why don't you try telephoning in the meantime?' I asked him, yet again.

'Her stepmother?' He never used his ex-wife's name; but by now there was no chance of confusing the first stepmother with the second—Giulia had only one left, and that was Elena.

'She may have got in touch with her in some way,' I said. 'For a while she may have been feeling overwhelmed.'

'Overwhelmed?'

'Don Michele,' I said, 'your daughter saw those bodies.'

I couldn't see his face, but I could sense his incredulity.

'How can you say that?' he asked, after a pause.

I couldn't believe my ears: it was too ingenuous a remark for a man like him.

'You can't possibly think your daughter rushed up to Faito and went straight to the caretakers,' I said, 'without first going to the main house.'

'She must have gone to them to get the key,' he replied. 'She hadn't got one herself.'

'But she must have seen the other car parked at the back there,' I said. Without a pause I went on: 'Because in fact your wife arrived by car. Hers, I imagine.'

'Who else's?' Miletti allowed himself to sneer. 'That oaf's, with patches on his arse?'

'In fact,' I went on, ruthlessly, 'she'd been to meet him on the train at Castellammare, the caretakers told me. In any case, your daughter will have seen the car and gone into the house. Catello said she was upset when she turned up at their place. And if she was the person I saw on the balcony last night, then she must have seen the bodies twice.'

He didn't answer, but I felt he still wasn't persuaded.

'Besides,' I said, to clinch it all, 'the suitcase and the bag are hers, aren't they? That's proof she went into the house. And when she got there, the pair of them were already dead.'

'Yes, there's the suitcase and the bag,' Miletti admitted, and then burst out, unexpectedly once again: 'The bitch!'

'Don Michele,' I said, 'you're angry with her because she's left home, I realise that, but it certainly isn't her fault that she found . . . those two.'

'She's a bitch because apart from getting me into a lousy mess she's got herself into one too. The police'll be after her now.'

'Yes, but they've got no proof she was there before yesterday morning.'

'Proof, proof. You read too many thrillers, Iovine. You think everything's got to be certain and scientific, whereas the police fix everything up in their own way. In a year we shall hear how my wife died and what those marks on Giulia's dress are. In the meantime they'll incriminate her without any trouble at all. As she's already vanished, that fellow Assenza will be perfectly sure she did the killing, and he'll be perfectly sure his reasoning can't be wrong, because he's perfectly sure he's right to start off with.'

'Don Michele, I loathe books, thrillers or straight,' I said. 'All I mean is that the police suspect everyone at first, whether they've got proof or not. Including your daughter, that means. The caretakers are suspect too, because they're nobodies. Did you hear what the sergeant said as he was leaving? That there's always a social reason for these crimes.'

Miletti said nothing, but when I looked round I had a feeling he was smiling. With his eyes shut.

'Everyone talks rubbish like that,' I said. 'Even coppers read newspapers. In other words, that couple's poverty makes them suspect. Though why they should take it out on that other poor wretch I can't see,' I added.

Still he said nothing, merely grunting impatiently.

'I wouldn't take Assenza too lightly, Don Michele,' I said. 'He may talk about your daughter, but he's got Catello and his wife in mind, first of all.'

'Then I hope he finishes them off,' said Miletti.

I looked away from the road for a moment, and glanced at him again: he was dreaming, his eyelids shut like a screen over the sparks his eyes must still be shooting out, considering the time and his thoughts. His head was still; only the treble chin trembled with the car's vibration.

More cars were on the road now. Gradually, as we approached Naples, the traffic seemed to be awakening from its brief torpor during the night. It was now nearly six o'clock and things would soon be back to normal.

I was day-dreaming myself.

'I wish someone would finish off that fellow Assenza,' I said. 'I have a feeling he's sniffed something out.'

'Such as?' From his tone I realised Miletti's thoughts were elsewhere.

'He didn't swallow that story about my being the family friend.'

'Oh yes, that reminds me: why on earth didn't you mention your famous career as a businessman?' He was beginning to shake himself out of his torpor as well.

'I did. In fact I said I was a businessman, but somehow . . . Anyway, I thought it best not to mention my real reason for going there. So I said I was a friend.'

'It's one of those pointless lies it's hard to wriggle out of, later on,' said Miletti. 'D'you think they won't find out that the situation's quite different? Anyway, why can't you be my man of business? The fact is that you just like things shady—it's your daily bread, that sort of thing. In any case, Assenza may refuse to believe all sorts of things but that doesn't mean he's ever going to find out about the papers. The trouble's quite different now: they're after Giulia.'

'And if they catch up with her they'll get to the papers,' I said, feeling it best to press my point.

'Not necessarily. I know Giulia, and if she took them out of that file she must have had a very definite reason and she won't be caught off guard.'

'But, as I said before, she may have taken them because she was confused and scared,' I told him. 'Why should she put them in her pocket and then leave the suitcase and the bag behind? Let me say it again: I think she felt overwhelmed for a while and then, in that state of mind, may have decided, quite automatically, to turn to her stepmother, if only for advice. After all, she was very fond of her, wasn't she?'

'As if she'd been her mother,' he said bitterly. 'Fonder of her than of me.' He sounded like a father betrayed, breathless, anxious.

I was thinking, on the other hand, of the hell life must have been for the girl from the time he took her second mother away from her. Of course none of it was my business. What I had to do was find out where those papers had ended up, and if I was to find it out I had to start moving, do something. What ought to have been mainly his worry, I was beginning to fear, was becoming exclusively mine. A small percentage, he'd said. Of course, compared with what he was pocketing, my share was nothing; but for that very reason, how could he now have forgotten it? Forgotten it so completely that he wouldn't even answer my suggestion that he telephone his ex-wife? What sort of a relationship could he have with her, to stop him rushing to ring her up, if only to see whether Giulia and the papers were there, available to us, admittedly, but also to the police?

'For that very reason, because she's so fond of her, she may have gone to see her, even on her way somewhere else,' I said, pressing the point again. 'She may have hesitated a little after her discovery of the bodies. What does it cost you to make a phone call to Milan, and check? At least we'll know if she went through that way.'

Miletti didn't answer. I looked in his direction and saw his still face, and the quivering under his chin.

'I shan't ring her,' he said at last, stubbornly, after what seemed like a thousand miles of driving. 'She wouldn't tell me a thing. When I'm up against the pair of them, they always gang up on me.'

'Don Michele, you know her well, after all those years of marriage,' I said. To hell with tact and discretion. 'If she's lying, you'll know she is. Apart from the fact that if your daughter's only passed through on her way somewhere else, that'll give you something to go on.'

'You sound like a child,' said Miletti. 'Worried, unsophisticated. Do it yourself. In fact, go straight there and do whatever you like. Get on with it yourself. I've told you, you've got to bring back those papers.'

'And what about your daughter?'

'Get back the papers and forget about her. Besides, when she's got something into her head there's nothing you can do to shift it. She'll be back when she's decided to come back, if she does decide to.'

'And suppose she doesn't give them back, once I've found her? Suppose Casali's got into the act, some way or another?' I wasn't letting myself be deterred by the bitter tone of his outburst. 'Casali may be a tough nut to crack.'

'Casali's a shit,' said Miletti.

'It was you who chose him as a partner,' I said.

'Only for the tough jobs, him and his gang. But now he's got to get out. As far as I'm concerned he can get back into that sewer of his.'

'He may be quite ready to get out,' I said. 'But with the papers. Once he's got them.'

'My daughter can't have given them to him.'

'He may have made her. Or he may do so yet.'

'Are you on again about Casali being behind this business of my daughter? Well, look into it and then we'll know.'

'It won't be easy,' I said.

'Didn't you say it was in both our interests, a while ago?' said Miletti. 'Well, then, it's in your interest as well as mine. Get a move on. I've promised you a big handout. Look, now I'll double it. I'll hand over ten thousand francs in Switzerland if you find those papers. Apart from your little stake in the matter, that is.' Generous and tricky at the same time: as he mentioned it he'd lingered over that 'little stake'.

'You're very generous, Don Michele,' I said. 'Thank you. But do you realise the difficulties?'

'They're your business,' he said.

'I don't even know where to start . . .'

'That's up to you. Ten thousand Swiss francs should fire your imagination. Or are you expecting me to find the papers, and then pay you?'

We had reached Naples by now. The rest of the journey to his house in Via Orazio was made in silence, in that car full of smoke which, in the sunlight, glowed like a blue mist.

8

I was woken by the thin, blinding ray of sunlight that came straight on to my face from the open window, and the first thing I heard was the noise of traffic in piazza della Borsa.

The constant roar reminded me automatically of the journey along the motorway early that morning. How early? How much time had gone by? What time was it now? I felt my stomach heave and at once the first conscious thought pierced the torpor of that sudden awakening: the windows and shutters ought to have been closed. As soon as I got home I'd gone straight to bed, but before giving way to my weariness I'd closed them tightly. An old habit, since I can't get to sleep when there's any light about, even a candle. Then I noticed something else.

There were two of them and they were sitting at the foot of

the bed, on the edge of it, one on each side, like birds of prey. Or like a pair of candlesticks at the end of a bier—which was even more macabre, I thought at once, mechanically. The second noise I had heard came from the one on the left, nearest the window: he had cleared his throat.

'Well, Sasà, are you awake at last? We've been waiting here quite a while,' he remarked.

'Nearly ten minutes,' said the other.

I could see this second one rather better, in the half-light. The first one was sitting with his back to the light, but when he got up I saw him clearly. Stocky and strong, with a thin line of moustache drawn straight on to his fleshy upper lip, he looked like a boxer dressed for a party, in a light grey suit that showed off his rippling muscles, salmon-pink shirt and tie and parti-coloured shoes, black and white. I saw the shoes because, without standing on ceremony, he put first one and then the other on to the bed and gave them a conscientious little rub with a piece of the sheet. After which he moved across to the middle of the room, directly opposite me. He was taller than the average.

So there I was, with a single candlestick at the foot of the bed. But the candle fantasy was only just over when it was replaced by another: the colleague of this apparition rose to his feet as well, and went across to pull back the curtain, as if the light wasn't bright enough already. Dazzled, I rubbed my eyes again frantically, and after this realised that the pair were dressed alike, a harmony of grey, white, black and salmon-pink. Even their moustaches were identical, and their hooked noses. In other words, each was a replica of the other.

'Who are you?' I said. What else could I say? I felt ridiculous, lying there on the bed with the pair of them staring at me, but I still didn't feel up to sitting.

'Look here, Sasà,' said the first, suddenly talkative, 'why don't you get up instead of wasting time asking questions?'

'Tonino's right, Sasà,' said the other, turning to the bed again. 'Get up. Lying there with that face, you make me think

I've come to visit a sick uncle.' Their voices weren't identical, though.

'He's Pasquale,' said Tonino, leaning on the dressing-table. 'And now that we've introduced ourselves, will you get up? Or do we have to bring you breakfast in bed?'

'Who sent you? Casali?'

'All right, if you want to stay in bed.' Pasquale came back and sat on the edge of it, on my left. Then he turned three-quarters of the way round, grabbed my foot with his left hand and twisted it, pressing down on the heel with his right.

I woke up completely, with a half-cry that turned into a croak. 'What d'you want?' I muttered plaintively.

Pasquale repeated the twist in the opposite direction, turning my foot outwards. This time it was more painful.

'Sasà dear,' Tonino explained at once, sounding full of concern for me, 'we don't want to do anything to you, we just want to ask for some information and then invite you to lunch. But it's past two and you still won't get up. If we keep on waiting, what time will it be? Aren't you hungry? Look, get up, tell us what you've got to tell us and we'll go off and eat.'

'How did you get in?' I asked, thinking of Luisella. She couldn't have opened the door to them because I hadn't found her at home that morning: she'd walked out on me yet again. But Pasquale made a movement to twist my foot again and I added hastily: 'I'm getting up, I'm getting up.'

And I got up. The room was in a turmoil. A cyclone had swept over it without waking me. Nearly seven hours fast asleep, and God knows how long the pair of them had been rummaging through everything. I hadn't heard a squeak, and the few pieces of furniture in the room looked as if they'd been actually chopped to pieces.

In the sitting-room, the same thing. They'd gone through it like furies and now, walking down the passage behind me, they had the calm, satisfied air of someone who'd at last settled what he had to settle. Outside the bathroom door they stopped.

'Just a pee?' said Tonino. 'No tricks?'

'What tricks could I get up to? A fart, at most,' I said, and went in.

'Better leave the door ajar, then we won't just hear.'

They alternated in their talk, speaking first one, then the other: this last remark came from Pasquale. There was no denying they were an amazing pair, yet I still couldn't believe my eyes and ears.

When I came back into the passage they were waiting for me on either side of the door, as watchful and cautious as a pair of suspicious cops.

'Can I make some coffee?' I said, not terribly keen on the way they looked.

Pasquale was undoubtedly the more violent of the two: he grabbed my arm and hurled me against the opposite wall.

'Now, let's stop playacting, Sasà,' he said. 'You're making us waste time and lose patience. Get dressed, we've no more time. You can talk while you dress.'

'But what about?' I said. 'What d'you want me to tell you?'

I'd scarcely closed my mouth after that when Tonino gave me a blow, the sort of smack you might give a naughty child: only it almost whisked off my head and made the buzzing burst out in my left ear. Pasquale was only waiting for this example: he straightened me up with a slap on the cheek that burned like an electric current. I had to lean against Tonino, who held me up, whispering into my ear:

'Do what he says. Can't you see he's annoyed?'

'Annoyed!' snorted Pasquale. 'I'm furious,' and he shoved me into the bedroom with great thumps on the back. 'Give me a hand,' he told Tonino. 'We'll undress him and dress him ourselves.' And he took off my pyjama bottoms, while Tonino held me up off the floor under the armpits. I'm not light, but to him I must have weighed less than a baby.

Then Pasquale did something unexpected and very painful. As I was dangling in mid-air, he first gazed at my exposed prick, then, with a calm, sweeping movement put the first finger of his right hand under his thumb and flicked at it, like a steel spring. I gave a yell.

Tonino dropped me and I crumpled on to the floor, where I found myself sitting limply. Then I straightened up at once—with pain again. He'd kicked me on the sacrum.

Pasquale, in the meantime, was collecting my clothes from the ruins of the bedroom. When he'd got them together he came over and flung them on top of me. 'Now get up and dress,' he said. 'And we'll talk.'

I obeyed, and stood up at once.

'Right, let's talk,' I said. 'But what about?'

I still hadn't learnt my lesson. I'd scarcely said it when my head burst open: another blow, this time so hefty it must surely have broken Pasquale's wrist.

When they thought I was recovering one of the two, Tonino I think, said: 'Look at you—still playing games. D'you still want us to believe you don't know what you've got to tell us?'

'I swear I don't know,' I said. 'I swear to God I don't know who you are or who sent you!'

The little energy I had left must have given my reply enough bite and speed to make it convincing. It was Pasquale who replied.

'All right, you don't know,' he said. 'Then we'll tell you. We're Don Nicola's Twins and he's sent us. He sent us for those papers, but we haven't yet found them. As you see, we've looked around but God knows where you've hidden them. And this is what you've got to tell us now—where you've hidden them. You tell us, we'll take them, and all three of us'll go and see Don Nicola, who's waiting for us. With the file and the papers in it. He's asked you to lunch because he says he'll be honoured to have you and because you've got to talk. And what he says we do: we're taking you to talk to him. But before that we must find the file. See?'

'But where can I find this file? What file and what papers, anyway?' I said, and regretted it at once; I was given another kick. And when I turned, my heart heaved: the second Twin,

Tonino, had pulled out a flick-knife. The blade was out and shining in the sunshine that poured in through the window.

'Get dressed and tell us where you've put it. We wanted to make it a friendly chat, but Pasquale's right, you're just wasting our time. And Don Nicola's waiting.' Meantime, balancing the knife on one finger, he was swinging it about, dazzling me with the sun's reflections on the blade.

'I haven't put it anywhere.' It was pointless to carry on pretending I knew nothing about the damned file. 'I haven't got it. I've never had it.'

'Dress while you talk,' said the First Twin.

I didn't wait to be told again, but picked underpants and trousers from the floor and started pulling them on, never losing sight of the flashing blade.

It was now the Second Twin's turn, since the pair of them alternated in the conversation. He stopped playing with the blade, grabbed the knife threateningly by the handle and spoke.

'So you haven't got it,' he said. 'You expect us to come all this way and believe everything you say, is that it?'

'It's true, I swear it,' I said, putting a leg into the trousers and almost losing my balance. Instinctively I leant against the First Twin's back, which was as solid as a marble table. He looked at me with those close-set eyes of his and an ugly, irritable air, so I put my foot down on the floor at once, recovered my balance and said quickly: 'I mean, I haven't ever had it. Besides, you've turned my whole place upside down, flung everything around and still haven't found it. If it was here you'd have found it, the mess you've made.'

'It isn't here, that's true,' said the First Twin, still looking darkly at me. 'But you've got to tell us about it: if it isn't here, Sasà, then where is it? Is it in your office?'

I was putting my head into my T-shirt at that moment and couldn't answer at once; and in his impatience the First Twin hurried me up: with a dry blow in the middle of my stomach with the side of his hand. My yell half stifled by the T-shirt, I was bent double, and retched violently, though fortunately I had nothing to bring up. But that wasn't enough for them: another blow came from behind, at the level of my left kidney, with the side of the hand this time, too, I think. From the Second Twin, though, the sly Tonino. I straightened up at once, like a robot obeying orders, and groaned through the vomit that had filled my mouth.

'Don Nicola's waiting, let's not make him impatient,' hissed the serpent with the knife. 'If you've got those papers in your office we'll run over there and get them.'

'I haven't got them. Not there either,' I said. It was painful and difficult to open my mouth, but I made myself do it, and shouted the words, poking my head out of the T-shirt at last and turning to avoid showing my back to the sneaking Second Twin. But turning it, instead, to the First.

Who lost no time and seized his opportunity. But this time he contented himself with a simple punch that almost crushed my neck in half. To the buzzing in my ears was suddenly added a thunderous roar that seemed like an amplification of the hubbub in my guts.

I was in a pitiful condition, but those two hogs allowed themselves no pity. Where had they come from, absurd and identical, stinking and stubborn? Who had invented them? They went for me with the same enthusiasm they'd shown in destroying my home. Inexhaustible. They stopped short of using the knife blade, but apart from that they used everything, steel fingers, fists like hammers, open hands like iron bars, parti-coloured shoes that seemed to dart about everywhere. I tried to shelter from them: with my arms folded over my head, bent double, flat against the wall like a martyr to give them only my back to vent their rage upon. But to them I was like a twig, a silly creature they could do what they liked with, twirling me round and round, slinging me back and forth between them like a sack of grain. The outburst ended with a double kick on each buttock, after which I flopped on the floor in the corner, facing the wall like a punished child, and suddenly fainted. A rag flung aside.

They must have picked me up and thrown me onto the bed, because when I came to we were back where we started. I mean, the earlier scene was repeated: I was lying on the bed and the pair of them were sitting on either side, at the foot. The horror continued.

So did the playacting: because their behaviour really was theatrical, the way they alternated in their talk.

'Waking up, then?' said the First.

'See what a time you've made us waste?' said the Second, quite unabashed.

'We can't keep Don Nicola waiting any longer. It's half past two and he'll have the pasta cooking by now. He likes to be punctual and he'll be cross with us.'

'It means we'll have to go without the file and you can sort it out with him,' said Tonino, without a pause.

'Are you sure you haven't got it in that office of yours? Because if you've learnt your lesson you can tell us and we'll all three of us go along there and get it.'

I shook my head, being in no condition to speak. They had roughed me up, I had fainted, all that violence had been vented on me and thirty years hadn't gone by—only half an hour. And the two beasts were starting off again as if nothing had happened. I'd learnt my lesson, though, and although it cost me pain, weariness and anxiety because of the taste of blood in my mouth, I muttered:

'I'm sure. As God is my witness, I haven't got them, either here or there.' I was so worried about my teeth that I was trying to count them with my tongue and see how many were missing.

The First Twin had been the last to speak, but this time there was a variation: Tonino lost his place and it was Pasquale who now spoke.

'Right, we've spent too long on this. Tonino's right, you can sort it out with Don Nicola. So get up and we'll go. Give him his jacket, Tonino.'

They almost carried me down the seven flights of stairs of that three-storey building without a lift, one of them holding me under the arms, like some stunned old man. I hadn't lost any teeth but I'd lost the use of my legs and felt I'd done so forever.

All the way to Posillipo, sitting in the back of the car between Pasquale and Tonino and with another chap I saw only from behind at the driving wheel, I brooded on a single thing. I began by calculating how much I was owed for each broken bone, the promised ten thousand francs in the foreground of my thoughts, and that imprecise bonus of millions which was my part in the business as their background; and I ended by calculating how much Casali would be spending on ruining the whole enterprise.

At this point it was clear that Casali had nothing to do with the disappearance of the file. It was merely that he was now looking for it, as well as me.

9

Nicola Casali was waiting, already sitting at the table, out of doors, under a rickety pergola. All he needed was a napkin tied round his neck; apart from that he was prepared for a meal: a glass of white wine in his hand, a slice of bread torn in half on the plate in front of him, crumbs on the plate and off it.

'My dear sir,' he said when he saw me. And he got up to come over to me, as if I were someone he wanted to honour.

He was wholly composed of fat. To protect him from attack from anywhere at all, he had an armour of lard all over him; his body was shaped like a cone with one end cut off, a round belly sloping up to narrow shoulders, from which poked a neck that looked like some great broken pillar, an ill appointed pedestal for a round but tiny head; its smallness accentuated by stiff grey hair, cut short to look like a wire brush. As for his face, it was pock-marked all over, and looked as if it was carved out of pumice-stone, with small black eyes sunk into the fat of the eyelids above and the bags beneath, in the shelter of which they withdrew anxiously from any unfriendly glance. A joke of Mother Nature, in other words, but one he was clearly unaware of, since he hadn't covered up the disaster but, like some dashing youngster, wore nothing but a short-sleeved white cotton shirt and a pair of tight, crumpled brown linen trousers, which turned his great legs into a pair of chocolate-coloured tree-trunks.

Dolled up like this, he came across and held out his hand to me, after passing the glass he was carrying over to his left hand.

I shook hands, feeling I had no choice, after which he stood aside with a clumsy twirl and indicated the table with his glass.

'Sit down, sit down,' he said. 'This is really an honour and a pleasure. I've taken the liberty of ordering already: sea food. What d'you say to that? It's their speciality here. Delicious. And before that a nice plate of spaghetti, with the same sauce.'

His mouth was square, with a small nick in the centre of his upper lip, which was thinner than the lower one, and at the corner of that obscene hole in the pumice-stone bubbles of saliva seemed to multiply without a pause, as if he was already enjoying the taste of the meal to come.

My appetite had gone, of course, though I hadn't eaten for exactly twenty-four hours, but again I thought I had no choice. So I went over to the table, and sat down at the place he was indicating to me with his glass.

'Really, Don Nicola . . .'

'Now, now, Iovine, don't make a fuss. You're not going to deny me the honour of your company, are you? You know what they say—a joyful feast . . . Well, you know what I mean. Come along, your glass. Give me your glass.'

'Don Nicola, I don't . . .'

'You're not going to refuse, are you?' said Casali. 'This wine is really something. From Lettere.'

There was nothing to be done: I held out my glass while the Twins took their places at the table as well, in silence: one beside me, one opposite. Casali sat alone at the head of the table, on my left.

The four of us were alone; under the pergola that covered the end of a small pier, the other tables weren't even laid. It was as if Casali had taken over the whole place. A few yards from our table some steps led down to the water, which looked dead, judging from its stillness, its colour and the rubbish of all sorts floating on it. Along the rest of the empty pier, some abandoned-looking fishing boats were moored.

I then made the mistake of emptying half a glass of the metal-polish they called wine all at once, and immediately the violent burning on my palate was repeated by a similar burning all along my internal organs as the drink gradually went down. When it got to the bottom there'd be an explosion. I realised I was going to be put through it again. The absurd Twins, in the meantime, had touched neither glass nor bottle: they weren't just non-smokers; they didn't drink either.

'Well now,' said Casali, 'I haven't seen any sign of those papers. What am I to conclude from that—that our two little brothers here haven't persuaded you?'

'We interrogated him, Don Nicola, but he wouldn't tell us anything. And as it was getting late we brought him along to you.'

Pasquale, the one opposite me, had spoken very respectfully. He was sitting with his hands lying on the table beside the plate in front of him, and seemed all attention. Yet Casali was annoyed, and glared at him with those restless little eyes of his that flashed out of their hiding place. Then he turned to me once again.

'I still haven't had the pleasure of hearing our friend here, so I'd like him to tell me about it. Well, Sasà, what have you got to say?'

'Don Nicola, I haven't got those papers,' I answered.

'How can you have reached your age and still be so dumb as to think I'll believe that?' said Casali.

'But why would I have them?' I asked.

'For two reasons,' said Casali. 'No, three. First, you're Don Michele's trusted man. Second, you organised the whole business. Third, Don Michele hasn't got them, either at home or in his office. So what can I deduce from that? That you've got them. See?'

So there I was, faced with another mathematician, and I couldn't tell him the tale of that wretched girl Giulia without setting off a general treasure hunt. But how did he know Miletti no longer had the papers? Not at home nor in the office, he'd said. How did he know that?

'Don Nicola, you must believe me,' I said. 'I haven't got them.'

'Tonino, fill up our friend's glass. You can see it's half empty. Who knows, drinking may loosen his tongue. How do they put it? *In vino loquacitas*. Ha, ha!' And he laughed, showing a lacy strip of black teeth. The brothers exchanged doubtful, sulky looks and finally decided to let him laugh alone. The mere sight of Tonino filling up my glass made me feel sick.

He'd just finished filling it to the brim when the first waiter I'd seen since I set foot in the restaurant arrived with the plates. Clearly they must all have been watching respectfully from a room inside, and now that I noticed this it struck me as a menacing sign.

Not more menacing, though, than the bowl filled with an indescribable mass of pasta steeped in a thick black sauce which the bald, lame waiter put in front of me without a word. I would now have to disentangle it and swallow it down, because Casali kept giving me inviting and at the same time impatient glances, and he'd already begun to gather his own up on the fork. He had a more or less normal sized plate in front of him. At least I'd have time to think what to say to him, I concluded in a resigned sort of way. And farewell diet.

He left me no time, though, the swine. He was sucking up his food, and even while he was enjoying it, with a piece of pasta still stuck to his black-slimed lips, he managed to slobber indistinctly:

'So you hadn't got them. Right. That means I guessed wrong. But you must help me to understand and correct my guess. This dish is delicious, don't you think?'

I now had a piece of pasta sticking to my lip as well. I sucked it up and answered. 'It's foul,' I said. 'And the sauce is too thick and tastes of sawdust. Anyway, how can I help you? I haven't got them, nor has Don Michele. I've told you. So they aren't there. That reminds me, how d'you know Don Michele hasn't got them?'

'We've looked,' said Casali.

'At home and in the office?' I asked.

'In heaven and hell, we've looked. Look here, are you trying to pull a fast one? There's only one person here who answers questions, and that's you. I'm glad about one thing, though—that you've admitted the existence of those damned papers.'

'But aren't we talking about the tender for two billion's worth of work for COOFA?' I said. 'Why shouldn't I admit their existence? We organised the whole thing together.'

He didn't answer at once; first, having nearly finished, he had to suck up the last mouthful. Then he cleaned himself up with his napkin, leant back in his chair, looked squarely at me and took aim.

'I thought you were more intelligent, Iovine,' he said.

'What d'you mean, Don Nicola?'

'I mean that you'd better get on and eat without interruption, from now on. The food's getting cold and spoiled. I'll do the talking.'

Then he was lured by the black sauce that was left on his plate. He tore a chunk of bread off the big slice, poked his fork into it and rubbed it round his plate. When he had chewed hard at the mouthful he continued.

'More intelligent because you should have realised that sooner or later I'd find out about your little game. I can see why Don Michele hasn't realised, he's grown childish with age and the loss of all those wives of his. But you, who are young and bright, even if you're a cuckold . . .' He paused very briefly, to give me time to think of Luisella; then he went on: '. . . Anyway, with your go-ahead office, your experience of the world and your knowledge of people, you should have considered this, my boy: Nicola Casali may have been born in Casoria but he knows the world all right.'

He broke in on himself for another rub round his plate. It was becoming a ritual. I took advantage of it to leave half my helping, and put down my fork and napkin while the Twins stared at me, silent, avid, grubby-faced. But Casali failed to notice.

'Five billion isn't peanuts,' he went on. 'It's a sum people still respect in Naples and their mouths hang open when they think of it. Which means they talk. And as we've got ears, we hear. Is that clear, now? Finish up your helping, now, you can't leave delicious food like this.'

So he'd noticed. I picked up fork and napkin, poked the napkin into the polo neck of my shirt and started pushing the pasta around. The Twins had also finished, in the meantime; at almost the same moment they raised their two great heads from the plates, straightened up and stayed there staring at me, seated but still on the alert, both of them. They'd never let up.

'You were right, it wasn't good,' Casali remarked thoughtfully. 'The spaghetti will be coming along now. I ordered both dishes because, as you've shown me, variety's the salt of good cooking. Now eat up your spaghetti, which is more of a classic with this sauce, and tell us the difference. You'll be eating it on your own, because we want to keep a little appetite for the sea-food. Tonino, give him some wine.'

And Tonino poured some for me. In silence, he gripped my arm tightly, forcing me to put it out towards the glass he had filled and I hadn't touched. I could feel the acid going down, but no longer into emptiness; the thick sauce was now waiting for it and I imagined the upheaval produced by the interaction of the two. I drank half the glass, and had to put down my half paralysed arm. My jaws ached too, from the blows I'd had and all the rest of it: I'd arrived with my face stiff and, after all this munching, would leave with a dislocated jaw.

Tonino immediately refilled my glass and Casali returned to his talk.

'Logically, I thought, the only way to soften you up properly, after the Twins had dealt with you, was to force you to eat and drink whatever we said. I know you like being slim and this means you don't go in for the good things available. But tell me, are you English, by any chance? You were born here and spaghetti's your national dish. Why d'you behave in this foreign way? Dieting, whisky, and so on. Just to please me, Iovine, eat up your pasta and drink up your wine, it's your national sustenance, you know. And even if it doesn't suit you, well, you can swallow it just the same. And if you do and we still don't see eye to eye, then I'll hand you over to the boys again. But, for the present, we'll have a sip each time we take a mouthful, right? Then if you want to stop and go back to your diet, tell me about those papers and I'll have the table cleared. Tell me what the second contract's like and above all where it is. Understand?'

My stomach on fire, I'd gone back to working away with the fork, when, like a ghost summoned by Casali's words, the silent waiter limped across and put a second plate of pasta down beside the first. It was no business of his and his mud-coloured face expressed nothing. Then he vanished as he had appeared: impassible and silent. Nicola Casali's little tricks can't have held any surprises for him.

10

I looked at the second plate of pasta and black sauce in front of me and wondered: how much would I earn, if I kept quiet, for each strand of spaghetti I swallowed? It certainly wasn't out of loyalty to Miletti that I determined to hold out: if Casali also had a large share in the business, my percentage would be smaller. But perhaps there was hope of a compromise.

'May I speak now, Don Nicola?' I said. 'May I ask a question?'

'If it's reasonable,' said Casali. 'Take a drink first.'

I took a sip, obedient, burning. Then I asked the question. 'Why are those papers so important to you?' I said. 'What use are they, if you know it all already?'

'That's reasonable but naïve. How do you think I can persuade Don Michele to respect the firm and split everything down the middle, including the second phony contract? With those papers in my hands, I can ruin everything for him. There'll be nothing in it for me, but nothing for him either. I can even send him to gaol—him, the whole town council and you as well.' Another good citizen eager to get respect for the law. A citizen whose lips were smeared with black sauce once more: Casali had now set to on the sea-food, sucking away as before. Every mouthful an octopus, tentacles and all.

At this point there was no doubt about it: the business of the second contract seemed to be growing more and more unlikely. What had the swine said? People talk, rumours get around. And besides, Giulia was carrying those papers with her, showing them to God knows who. Soon we'd have a posse of honest citizens, headed by Assenza, all chasing that sly fox

Miletti. They'd tear him to pieces and part of the punishment would fall on me as well. So we must run to earth, stuff up some of the holes at least; better a few than none at all. I didn't feel remorseful or a turncoat as I put down my fork and looked at the pile of pasta on my plate, hope rising in me once again.

Under the light grey suits the Twins' muscles twitched simultaneously: they were poised to jump. Casali stopped them with a gesture of his hand, his fork, and the sea-food stuck on it. Being more intelligent than they were, he had grasped the situation.

I was ready to make a deal. I even pushed the plate away.

'Apart from the fact that no one goes to gaol these days,' I said, 'least of all Don Michele, I haven't appeared officially in any of this. My name isn't written anywhere on any of those documents.'

'No one's ever seen you as a problem,' said Casali. 'You're the smallest cog in the wheel. In gaol or out of it, you don't count.'

'The buyer always pretends to despise what he wants to buy, Don Nicola,' I said. 'But whether I'm big or small, I'm the cog that made the whole mechanism work. That's not the point and you know it. There's the question of the fifty million. Losing a profit's one thing, losing what you've already spent is another. Touch him where he's spent money, his life-blood as he calls it, and Miletti will turn on you like a viper.'

At this point the stupid, meticulous Tonino filled my glass again. But I took no notice, and looked at Casali again.

'If we come to an agreement,' he said, 'we'll divide expenses as well as profits.' He was really becoming quite reasonable: it was clear that now he was going to spare me the sea-food. He'd already eaten his own and was stretched out on his chair, pushing out his swollen belly, satisfied.

'What are you suggesting to me, Iovine?' he went on. 'Giving me the papers? I can get them from you in any case, from you or Miletti or whoever's got them.'

'I haven't got them, Don Nicola,' I replied. 'I've told you I haven't and I can't see why I should go on lying about it.'

'Would you bring Don Michele to see reason, then?' he said.
'I can always try,' I answered.
'Bring him, I said, not try.'
'Well, you know Miletti,' I said. 'Sometimes he refuses to see reason.'
'I don't think he's in exactly the happiest period of his life,' said Casali, 'considering what happened yesterday.' So he already knew.
'So you've heard?' I said.
'I told you, people talk, whether there's real news or it's just for the sake of talking. You have to keep your ears open, that's all.' God knows what he meant by people. 'But first of all, let's talk about the guarantees I'll have.'
'What guarantees?' I said.
I was really worried, trying to get a clear picture of the situation. Did he know about Giulia, too? Did he know that we'd got to find her in order to find the papers? No, otherwise he wouldn't have sent those two beasts to my home and tried to make me explode by pushing those plates of pasta and that filthy wine inside me. Once again I wondered how, not knowing Giulia had them, he knew that Don Michele hadn't got them.
'For everything to end—how shall I put it?—honestly,' he said, and gave his belly a light slap. Full and pleased.
'What guarantees are you asking?' I said.
'I want the papers as a pledge. But don't try and get away from me. I must have those papers in any case, whether we come to an agreement or not. Or must we get going on the spaghetti again?' And with a disgusting smile he indicated the plate still in front of me. The waiter hadn't reappeared; as far as he was concerned the orgy must have been over.
The Twins straightened up, feeling they were involved again. I saw the whole scene that had just taken place and the one before it and shivered. The place was sheltered from the sun by the side of the hill, and at that point the hill formed an amphitheatre round the slimy water, which must have made the whole place amazingly damp: in the very middle of the day

everything was wet—china, cutlery, tablecloth, plates and glasses. Seen from below, in fact, the rickety pergola looked as if it was ready to crash down on top of us. And it wasn't the only thing that looked likely to crash.

'You know I haven't got them. But I can look for them,' I said. It was an idea, a hope of turning things in my favour.

'Look where?' said Casali. 'D'you realise that just as I can make you say where they are—if you know it—so I can make you say where you're going to look for them?'

'Oh come, Don Nicola, you know very well I don't know,' I said. 'I don't know at the moment, but I may find out, by looking around and poking my nose in where these two bastards would never reach.' He was holding them on the leash, I could say what I liked. 'Where did you dig them out from, by the way?'

He looked suspiciously at me, then shook himself. 'The Twins? Don't get into their bad books, they're good lads and good workers. For instance, while you were asleep they rang up from your place: the papers weren't there and they weren't in your office either...'

'They've been there too?' I said.

'What d'you think?' said Casali. 'That everyone sleeps the way you do?' He opened his great sewer of a mouth, poked a pincer-like finger inside to get at a tooth, and went on talking, in driblets, openmouthed. 'So we arranged this little meal... They already knew they wouldn't get anything out of you... Giving you the works was just a precaution... If you'd known, you'd have talked sooner... They're conscientious, I told you.'

I thought of my office and the state it must be in. They'd even suggested we should go over there and fetch the papers. They weren't fools at all. Everyone was becoming brighter than me, as far as I could see, Miletti to start with, who'd given me this hot potato to hold.

By now Casali had finished poking about in the sewer and continued, gathering speed.

'Well now, let's get down to concrete suggestions. You look

for the papers: suppose you find them, what do you do then? Hand them over to me?'

'I don't give you the papers,' I said, 'but I give you the chance of participation in the second contract, as you're a partner in the first.'

'That is, you make Don Michele see reason?'

'Make him face reality,' I said. 'Your share, with the repayment of your part of the advance paid . . .'

'Advance? What are you talking about?'

'The man on the council works for a—what shall I call it?—a group. He hasn't pocketed the whole of the fifty million himself. If he had it would be enough, being in cash and securities. He's shared it with the others in the group, and so the amount he's pocketed himself is much less than it might have been. They want another ten per cent of the payments, over and above the money already paid to them.'

'That's half a billion and fifty. Too greedy.'

'Well, they've got yachts and seaside villas to keep up. And don't forget, it still leaves four billion four hundred and fifty. For a contract that, it's been worked out, needs at the most a couple of hundred million for work that's pure moonshine. In other words, about four billion. There for the taking.'

'And your rake-off?'

'The usual. One per cent.'

'Of four?'

'Of five,' I said.

He looked at me, as if he already had the money in his pocket and as if he'd worked for it honestly and hard. Greed had lit a flame behind his heavy eyelids and the look that came through them was scorching.

It was the most delicate moment: if he accepted that condition, never so far discussed with Miletti, who'd left everything vague—a little percentage, as he'd put it—and became a partner in the share-out, I finally had an exact idea of the payment I could expect at the end of it all. In other words, Casali's entry into the business was to my advantage. I ought to have realised it sooner: dealing with two partners, each suspicious of the other, was easier and more lucrative than dealing with one alone, especially one as stubborn as he was greedy and despotic.

Casali made me realise this at once.

'Carry on,' he said, revealing himself as a practical man.

'Well, as I was saying: his share, with the immediate return of half the advance payment, or nothing. According to me he's bound to accept, because, among other things, you can undermine the whole thing. On the other hand, you can also guarantee people's discretion—obviously—and the success of the venture.'

'Discretion I can see, success not,' said Casali. He had his elbows on the table and a sleepy air. He was digesting sea-food and words. 'How can I guarantee success?'

'As you yourself said, Don Michele isn't going through the happiest period of his life just now,' I said. 'In fact, I've got a feeling this business has gone into second place, among his immediate interests. Whereas where I'm concerned it's always the most important, and I'm always anxious about it. I'm afraid Don Michele may not take the necessary steps. In other words, I have a feeling he may need someone to give him a hand— perhaps quite a strong hand. And why not the partner he competed with for the first contract? You, Don Nicola, with your eyes and ears open and the Twins and maybe a few other beasts of yours around, are in a position to create a complete ring of silence around the whole business. In this way success becomes automatic, as everything's already settled and agreed and the formalities are all respected. Don't forget that this second contract is the result of careful planning, in which I've played my part. And which amply justifies my one per cent, among other things.' Better stress this notion.

Casali was thinking, one large cheek resting on a clenched fist, and every now and then, raising his shutter-like eyelids, he glanced at me.

'If I've understood the way you work,' I went on, glancing at the Twins, who were listening, quite still, 'your organisation is itself a guarantee. Don Michele knows it, or we'll tell him, and he can only feel safe, because—apart from everything else—he's got no choice. And the partners in the other group will feel guaranteed and won't be tempted to withdraw. As you see, it's a matter of having a guarantee that's also automatic. In other words, your entry into the affair will quieten everyone's fears, including mine.'

'And what about the papers?' Casali said.

'Don Nicola: I think you know everything there is to know about the whole situation. You must know it all—names, facts, addresses. What's the use of, say, the photocopy of a Swiss bank's cheque made out in favour of someone you already know, for a sum you already know?'

'It means I know more. For instance, the number of the Swiss bank account. Apart from that, it's a support—documentation, if you like—together with all the other photocopies.'

'Documentation that's important as a means of exerting pressure . . .'

Casali woke from his torpor. 'Call it blackmail, I don't mind the word,' he interrupted. 'You're ingenuous but tactful. And reasonable too. I like this new attitude of yours.'

'I've told you, I'm anxious about the whole thing. With your coming into it, it loses nothing. We stabilise it and gain peace of mind.'

'We haven't stabilised anything yet,' said Casali. 'First you wouldn't open the trapdoor a chink, now you're talking too much and too fast. Get back to the photocopies.'

'As I was saying: they were important as long as Don Michele hadn't agreed, but they'll be almost useless once he has agreed. In any case, I repeat that I can look for them. At this point, it's just a matter of patience and trust.'

He looked at me again. The two watchdogs beside and in front of me had crouched down, but when their master's eyes flashed they lifted their heads, on the alert.

'Trust you? On the strength of what?' Casali said.

'Everyone's own interest, but chiefly yours and mine. Also, because you've got no choice, Don Nicola, as we haven't got the papers, any of us.'

'And as long as we haven't got them we can't rest easy,' said Casali. 'I know, don't tell me again. You still haven't told me how you're thinking of finding them, though, and that isn't playing fair with me.'

'I don't know how I'll find them, but I'm damned if I won't. You want to keep them as a pledge to make Miletti stick to his agreement, and I'm looking for them because until we've got them safe and sound our money isn't safe. There's nothing hiding under that, Don Nicola, you needn't worry. Just leave it to me. Give me a bit of time.'

'You sound like a government minister. They also ask for time and trust. How much d'you ask of both?'

'As far as time's concerned, a week at most.'

He stretched out on his chair again, obviously preparing to break up the meeting.

'Right. A week, not a day more. Do what you like, but do it in seven days.' It was a benediction, in almost the words I'd heard from my other boss, in another mandate to achieve the same end. 'In the meantime, I want to give you a hand.'

'What's that? In what way?' I stopped my secret chuckling.

'It's not that I don't believe in your ability to persuade Don Michele. It's just what you might call a precaution. If not, I'll have just a pinch of doubt.'

'Which means?' I was alarmed, thinking of Giulia.

'Nothing, a trifle. I just want to meet Don Michele to remind him that old partners shouldn't be treated this way, it's just not done. He may be persuaded a bit quicker. Why so worried?'

'I'm not worried. I'm just afraid that if you press him too hard the old man may dig his heels in. Well anyway, you don't need my advice, Don Nicola.' Miletti wasn't my father, why did it horrify me so?

Casali poked his nose up, as if sniffing. There was a stench in the air, although we were out of doors. A stench of everything. From their shelter his little eyes flashed out at me like two distinct drops of suspicion.

'As I told you, you haven't played fair with me,' he said, 'so don't forget I'll be watching you this next week and the minute you step out of line I'll take it out on you too.' And he made a move to rise.

As if at a signal, the two watchdogs scraped their particoloured feet under the table.

'How can I step out of line, Don Michele?' I said. 'Within the limits of our respective percentages, we're all tied by the same interest.' And, to prevent him having time to reflect, I hurried on: 'There's something else, though.'

He sat down at once, turning his head to the Twins. 'I had a feeling there was something else. Go ahead.'

'I need an advance,' I said. 'On what you'll be paying me when it's all settled.'

He remained a long time without answering, stroking his belly. In the end he spoke.

'The cart before the horse,' he said. 'Tell me, then: what for?'

'As a guarantee. Of our agreement. A guarantee for you that you've got me on your side and for me that you'll stick to the bargain.'

He didn't laugh, but he nearly did; and that was a good sign, after all. 'As if we were gentlemen. I pay you to come over to my side and in exchange I've got your word that you've done it. I've got a feeling you're holding all the best cards. Apart from having no guarantee myself, I've got to give you one, paying you for looking after your own interests. And in exchange I'm not even going to get the papers.'

'I'll give you the papers,' I said. I'd thought it over in the meantime. 'I'll make a photocopy of the photocopy. Can't say fairer than that.'

'Once you've found them.' A nasty gleam of mistrust had joined the suspicion in his eyes.

'Once they're found, of course. Do you still not believe me?' Casali fended off my question with an abrupt gesture of his plump hand. 'In other words, I send for you, give you a going-over, organise this funny little meal and as dessert put money in your mouth.' He wasn't indignant, but his honour seemed offended.

I had to save the situation. He was a full-blooded fellow, less dry and more credulous than Miletti. I might even manage to bluff.

'Don Nicola, don't forget that I can even withdraw from the whole business,' I said. 'In the sense that I can hand the second contract over to others. All I need do is whistle and they'll come in packs, wagging their tails like dogs after a bone. Those involved in the group know and recognise me only and will be very pleased to get out of this situation. The advance can even be given back and all evidence cancelled, once the money collected has been wiped out and the payer's name has disappeared.'

This time Casali looked at the Twins as if he had a pair of useless mastiffs with him.

'Well, just for laughs, how much would it be?' he said. More credulous than Don Michele but also more practical: why run any risks? Basically, it was just a handout.

'Ten thousand francs,' I said. 'Swiss. To be deposited in a bank in Lugano.'

11

I opened the door and had a shock: the office was in an even worse state than my flat. In the hall they'd even ripped the carpet up off the floor, as if I might have hidden those wretched papers underneath it. As they'd gradually moved away from the four corners where they'd cut and lifted the pieces, they'd stopped only because of the tough adhesive. That wasn't just care, it showed hatred. The swine.

In the office they'd vented themselves even further, heaping everything up in the middle of the room, as if to make a great bonfire: papers and books, drawers and files and their contents, even the chairs on top of all the rest: all they'd forgotten was to put a lighted match under it. They'd remembered to overturn the bookshelves, though, after throwing the few never-read books on the pile. And in the euphoria of destruction they must have danced on the desk: the top of it was broken.

I went across to it and as soon as I leant on it, it heaved over to one side, as one of its feet was broken. My fountain pen, the single survivor on the raft, had lost its cap in the storm, but now rolled over and fell on the floor. I followed the way it had gone and my eye fell on the last lot of post that had arrived and was scattered over the floor, on the edges of the bonfire. Among the undamaged envelopes lay the folded yellow sheet of a telegram. I picked it up.

I knew it was hers. It didn't take much imagination to guess that, because it was something repeated every time she walked out on me: promptly next day, a telegram. This time it must have been sent between the morning and afternoon of the previous day, Wednesday, when everything had begun. That is, a few hours after Giulia had also run away. Coincidence.

Instinctively I looked at the telephone, lying on the floor with the receiver off: a phone call generally followed the telegram. She must have calculated the time to the minute, precise little bitch that she was, and known just when she'd find me in the office. It was now five o'clock. I'd left Casali not long before and now had another ten thousand Swiss francs practically in my pocket and that telegram in my hand.

I stopped the buzzing on the line, which was maddening now that I'd noticed it, put the telephone back on the tilted desk, and unfolded the yellow sheet.

The text of these telegrams was always a result of the mood of the moment: it was never the same. This one said: 'I'll explain everything. Forgive me and don't worry. Luisella.' An unbelievable promise and a pointless request; she was only too well able to look after herself.

I tried to tidy the room up a bit and in less than five minutes was exhausted. So I picked up a chair, put it up against the desk and sat down. Grazing one of my bruises while I was doing it was enough to set off, all at the same time, the pain in the others scattered over my body. Bending down just a little seemed to have broken the few healthy bones left to me. In other words, I couldn't stand up, and was a single aching mass, just as if I'd been pounded to pieces by the Twins that minute.

The telephone rang. Dead on time.

'Sasà?' Her voice had a new pitch.

'Where are you ringing from, Luisella?' I asked. 'Where have you gone?'

'You ought to be asking me *why* I've gone,' she said.

'We'll leave the whys till later. Besides, I think I know. Where are you ringing from? I can hear it's long distance.' The telegram had been dictated by telephone from home, obviously before she left. In fact, it bore my own telephone number.

'For the moment I'd sooner not tell you. You don't seem to me the least upset or sorry that I've left.'

'What ought I to be doing? Crying the minute I pick up the receiver? Haven't you got me used to these bolts of yours? Who with, this time?'

She hesitated. 'Sasà, it's not the way you think,' she said. 'This time it's not like the others. Yes, well, it's more serious and, I'm afraid, it's definite.'

Bless the girl, she never changed. 'Then why send a telegram and ring up?' I asked.

'I didn't want to chuck you suddenly'—as if she'd left the house gradually, the other times—'and I thought you'd be interested to hear the reason. Yes, I know, you think you know it. But you're wrong. You've always thought you knew all about me, but you don't know anything. I wanted to leave you a letter, but writing isn't my strong point . . .'

'So you sent the usual telegram,' I said. 'When did you leave?'

'Yesterday morning, soon after you'd left.'

I'd left her asleep. Obviously she must have made her decision while she slept. I told her this.

'You're a beast, as usual,' she said angrily. 'I wanted to explain to you . . .'

'You said that in the telegram,' I said.

'All right, I was wrong to send it, but now I realise I was right to leave.'

'And were you wrong to ring me?'

'Maybe,' she said. 'No, maybe not. You've confirmed that I made the right decision.'

'As always, we're talking only about you,' I said.

'Why, have you reacted in any way? From the way you're talking, from what you say, and from your voice, I wouldn't say so. Where are you? Who are you with! Let's put it off till later! Who d'you think you are? Irreplaceable?' She was becoming hysterical, and this wasn't like her. 'You can go to hell, for all I care.'

'Right, I will. To please you and to get me out of this whole ridiculous business of bolting, telegrams and phone calls.'

'Aren't you a dear. But the business that seems ridiculous to you isn't altogether so. As for the phone call, that at least has another reason. It doesn't matter, though, I'll manage on my own from now.'

She'd never quarrelled with me in these phone calls, even when I was in my very worst mood. The uneasiness I had felt since the phone rang increased.

'What d'you mean, Luisella?' I asked.

'Nothing. In particular, nothing that concerns you. Goodbye.'

'Wait a minute,' I yelled.

'The phone's expensive, remember.'

'To hell with that. No. Anyway, you make me frantic, unable to understand a thing.'

'But what d'you want to understand?' she said, suddenly cold and remote. I no longer knew her, I swear. 'We've decided you don't understand a thing.'

'All right, I don't understand a thing. But you must tell me what this second reason for ringing is.' Even I couldn't have said why I was so determined to know it, but the uneasiness I'd felt in my aching bones must have been a presentiment; this was clear to me now. 'I want to know.'

'Why on earth are you so keen to? Right then. But it's got nothing to do with us, mind—with you and me.' My anxiety was increasing.

'Who then? Who has it got to do with?'

'Giulia Miletti,' she said.

I leapt up with a jerk that was so painful I had to sit down again at once. But my worry was appeased. Instead I had a feeling almost of satisfaction. I grew calm again and, thinking I might have exaggerated and fearing she mightn't say more, became thoughtful.

'Do you know Giulia Miletti?' I asked.

'I know her now. Before, it was she who knew about me.'

'So you've seen her? When? Where? Where are you ringing from?'

'Why are you so interested in her? You don't give a damn about me and you can't wait to hear about Giulia.'

Christ, I thought, now she's jealous. That's all I need.

'Luisella, you've never been jealous,' I said. 'Are you going to pick this particular moment to become so? This call's expensive, as you said yourself, and besides, Giulia's run away from home.'

'I know.'

'And d'you also know that her stepmother's died? Tragically.'

'I know that too. I know everything.'

'Did she tell you?' I was now seething.

'Yes, and she told me not to tell you. But she's in trouble and I don't know how to help her. That's another reason why I'm ringing you. I wanted you to suggest something.'

'She's in trouble all right, the police are after her. They

haven't got anything against her, but she can't just vanish suddenly like this. So they're looking for her. And if she doesn't turn up, they may pin something on her. You know they can easily do that. What sort of suggestion d'you want?'

'When I said trouble I meant something more serious. Giulia's pregnant.'

'Pregnant?' I said. Then anxiety took over from surprise. 'Louisella, please don't make me drag it out of you. Pregnant by who? Since when? And where is she now?' Things, I felt, were becoming more complicated instead of simpler.

'I don't know where she is now, she told me she'd ring me or come round. She's nearly two months pregnant. Don't worry who by. I wanted you to . . .'

'Where are you, Luisella?' I asked her. 'Tell me and I'll come along at once.'

'I imagine all this anxiety is for the father rather than the daughter,' she said. 'You don't give a damn for her situation, you just want to get into that old swine's good books and get his daughter back home. You don't give a damn about anything.' Which, as a conclusion, seemed to be really brilliant at that particular moment.

'Luisella, let's not start again, please,' I said. 'For my sake, for Christ's sake, for anyone you like's sake, don't carry on like this.' Then I realised that above all I mustn't provoke her. 'Forgive me, I'm a bit upset. My office has been smashed to bits and I've been beaten up. And d'you know whose fault it is? Your blessed Giulia's. She's taken something with her that her father wants back, and so do some other people—and they aren't the sort to play about with. It was they who beat me up like this . . .'

'What are you talking about?' cried Luisella. 'What's your office got to do with it? Who beat you up? Are you trying to make me feel sorry for you?' She wasn't incredulous, she was joking.

'Didn't Giulia tell you she'd taken something? Something belonging to her father?'

'Something? She told me she'd taken four hundred thousand lire. She was desperate and needed it. After all, her father's money's hers.' Which made marvellous logic. I'd really infected her.

At this point, although I didn't want to, I had to tell Luisella about the file. It was the only hope I had of persuading her to let me help Giulia and so come to her; that is, to tell me where she'd seen her, and to get her to say, when she turned up again, where she was now.

'Nobody wants to take that money away from her,' I said. 'It's hers, as you say. But she's also carried off some papers. Important papers. And she's got to give them back. That's why I want to see her and talk to her. I don't want to take her back to her father, I'm not trying to get into his good books, I don't want to be unkind to her, I don't give a damn if she's pregnant . . .'

'I'm not surprised,' said Luisella. 'It means I was stupid to ring up. You have no respect for anything.'

'Luisella, for the love of God, try to understand. All I meant was that I wasn't shocked to hear she was pregnant, that I just wanted to help her. To have an abortion, if she wants it, or to have the child . . .'

She broke in again, annoyed. 'You really make me sick. How could I have thought that you'd really be able to help us?' That's just how she put it—in the plural.

I was letting myself be carried away by excitement. Like that, I'd never persuade her. 'But I want to help you both,' I said. At that moment I'd have promised to help the whole world.

'What's behind this? What's in it for you, in this whole business?' she exclaimed contemptuously.

'What can I possibly get out of it? Why d'you always see everything in a false light? I'm not going to gain a thing by getting Giulia out of the embarrassing situation she's in—because of the police and because of those people I mentioned. They're going to chase her so as to get hold of the papers, and it'll be a great deal worse for her then. Tell me something: don't you think it's a lot better for her and for everyone else if she hands the papers over to me rather than to the Twins? Because they'll make her hand them over. And how.'

'What are you talking about? Who are the Twins?' she asked.

'The blokes who turned my office upside down. But let's not worry about them. Listen, Luisella, just for once be a dear and believe me. Giulia's in very bad trouble because of what she's told you but in even worse trouble because of what she hasn't told you. If you tell me where she is we can help her out of it.'

'I don't know where she is now,' said Luisella.

'But she'll tell you. She's going to ring you, isn't she? Or come and see you, anyway? Well, when you see or hear from her, get her to tell you where she is. Maybe without saying anything about me, in case it scares her off. Meantime, where are you?'

'Sasà, why are you trying to be clever?'

'Because this phone call's costing millions, that's why. Luisella, let's not waste any more time. I swear I'll help her. I swear I'll join you right away.'

'But darling, that's exactly what I don't want.'

'Is that how you're going to help your friend Giulia? By letting her be beaten up by those people? Because it's what they'll do to her, that's for sure. And she'll never be able to deal with the police on her own. If you really want to help her . . .'

Luisella then made a remark that had all her feelings concentrated in it. 'So you're not coming for my sake?' she said.

'For who else's?' I said. 'For your sake, and for Giulia's as well.'

'You've never been as upset as you are now, so you must be coming just for Giulia's sake. Who, let me tell you, isn't a friend of mine but just a poor little thing who's turned to me for advice.'

'Exactly. And is this the way you're going to help her? You're not going to start being jealous again, are you?' I was losing patience. 'Just tell me where you are, and you can find out later why I'm coming. Right? Oughtn't we to talk? Weren't you going to explain everything? Do we have to carry on forever with this playacting?' The word reminded me of the Twins; were they really looking for Giulia? They didn't know she had the papers, but Casali always got to know everything.

'You call it playacting?' Luisella said.

'Just to avoid calling it farce,' I said. 'Because it certainly isn't drama—at least your part of it isn't. Where are you, in Milan?'

'What on earth would I be doing in Milan?' she said. 'No, I'm at my mother's.' At long last.

Then I remembered the classic old lie about going home to mother, and the fact that she wasn't my wife didn't alter a thing. 'At Formia?' I said.

'Yes, at Formia, seeing she's never moved house or left the place.' She was annoyed at having let it slip out. 'And what are you going to do, now that you know?'

'I'll come,' I said.

'What for? To save Giulia? To save me?'

'Save you from what? I swear I don't follow.'

'You never have, and you certainly aren't going to start following now. It was a big mistake, ringing you. The whole thing's been a big mistake.'

'Leaving me, as well?'

'No. Your irony confirms that that was the only wise thing I've done. Everything, all the rest, meeting you, loving you, coming to live with you, the whole thing, was a big mistake.'

'You know that's not true,' I said. 'You know that what you call my irony's the result of your instability, your unpredictable character, your intolerance.'

'Intolerance? Now you're really stirring things up. Well, that's typical of you.'

'Look, Luisella, let's give it a rest for the moment. We can talk when we meet.'

'For the past two years we ought to have been talking it over. What am I supposed to think now? That you've suddenly decided Formia's the ideal place to talk in? Is that why you're coming? Or because Giulia's here and you've got to help her?'

'Right, I'm the louse you've always said I was and you're the victim I've always forced into all sorts of things. I'm a louse and I'm coming to save Giulia so as to creep into her father's good books and earn myself a pile of money. And as I'll be there, we can talk about ourselves and our problem at the same time. Once and for all.' It was the only way to deal with her unpredictability. Because it was true: to me at least, she was quite unpredictable. 'So you've got to let me see you.'

'Don't worry, I won't run away again,' she said bitterly.

'And you must get Giulia to tell you where she is. Did she go to Formia with you?'

'She brought me here by car yesterday morning,' said Luisella. 'We talked throughout the journey and she told me everything. Poor thing.'

'Poor thing, indeed. And then? Did she stay on there?'

'She dropped me off at my mother's place, saying she'd ring up or turn up today. But she hasn't yet.'

'So she may not be in Formia any longer? Didn't she stay the night there?'

'She's not at Formia, that's for sure,' said Luisella. 'I asked her to stay at my mother's if she liked, but she refused. She said she had to get back to Naples.'

'Couldn't you have told me that before?'

'Why? Don't you want to come and see me now?'

'Of course I do. I've told you, I'm a louse and I must come in case she turns up herself instead of ringing.' There weren't many probabilities, but I couldn't run any risks. 'Whichever she does, you really must get her to tell you where she is. Try and gain time. I'll leave at once. And don't tell her you've spoken to me, mind. That's not tricky on your part, believe me. She won't agree to see me otherwise. And it's really in her own interest to see me, you know.'

'Right, I won't say anything. You know my mother's address,' said Luisella, and hung up unexpectedly, leaving me surprised and uncertain, with echoes of voices and distant crackles on the line. These seemed to cover the impression that the sudden weariness of her voice had left upon me, like a fingerprint.

12

I was still sitting at the desk, aching and worried, when the phone rang again. This time the ringing caught me unprepared, deep in thought, indecisive as well. I didn't feel like setting off on more than an hour's driving, yet I had to do it, although I doubted whether Giulia would go back to Formia. Why should she? To talk to Luisella again and get advice? To start with, I couldn't imagine any possible connection between them. She knew Luisella. How? They'd never set eyes on each other.

I started with a jerk that shook all my aching bones, and picked up the receiver I'd only just put down. It was Miletti.

'I've been trying to ring you for over half an hour and it's been engaged the whole time,' he said. He always had to have clear roads and open doors ahead of him.

'I was talking to Luisella,' I said. 'Has something else happened, Don Michele?'

He grunted, and at the same time spoke. 'They've been here, that's what's happened,' he said.

'Ah.' I thought at once of the Twins; they hadn't wasted any time. 'Where are you ringing from?' I asked. 'The office?'

'No, from home. I've been trying to get hold of you the entire afternoon and it was engaged then, as well.'

'That's because they were here as well. They turned the whole place upside down and took the phone off the hook. At times it looks as if they'd been trying to knock down the whole building. What about you?'

'They ransacked the place and made an appalling mess. It must have happened during the night, while I was out, though Idillia says she didn't hear a thing. They were looking for the papers, clearly. They didn't find them here and went on to you. Casali's men.'

It was now clear how Casali had known what he knew: he really had known that Miletti hadn't got the papers. But then, when the swine had promised to turn up at Miletti's, was he talking about something quite different?

'They turned my flat upside down too,' I said.

'Then they must have gone to my office, as well. I didn't go in today and that creep Marullo hasn't telephoned. I'll ring him now. Will you do something for me, Iovine? Are you busy? Could you come over to me?'

'Actually . . . I was just off to Formia. Possibly to see your daughter.'

'Giulia? Have you found her? Talked to her?' A note of anxiety had come into his gruff voice.

'Not talked to her directly. Luisella's seen her. She's . . . in trouble.'

'We knew that already. Or is there anything else?' He sounded suspicious, I thought.

'Let's talk about it when we meet.'

'No, right away, now. Were you off to Formia without telling me? To Formia, of all places. What's she doing there? How on earth did . . . that girl see her? Did they know each other?'

'Don Michele, your daughter's pregnant,' I said. Better make him swallow it right away, on the telephone, at least to spare me the sight of him.

He said nothing. For a long time he was silent, as he'd been when I told him about his wife's death. But I had a feeling that this news was a lot more painful to him.

He broke the embarrassing silence at last. 'Come over,' he said, 'I'll be waiting for you.' And hung up.

Down in the street the car-minder—or parking attendant as, with professional pride, he likes to be called—spoke to me.

'Sir, there were two odd blokes looking at your Alfetta,' he said. 'Studying it.'

'Studying it—what d'you mean?' I said. 'Did they pinch anything?'

'No sir! With me here? You must be joking. What d'you think I'm doing?'

'When did it happen?'

'Now, I must get this right,' he said. 'It must have been several hours back. Soon after you arrived. Then they vanished. They were pretty odd, though.'

'Odd in what way?' I asked.

'Well, how can I put it?' he said. 'They might have come out of a theatre. The only funny thing they weren't wearing was boaters. I've only seen blokes like that in musicals, but years and years ago. And believe me, sir, they were alike as two peas.'

The Villa Elena (but how many Elenas had there been in Miletti's life? And how many villas had he called after her?), white with green shutters, was built on top of a natural eminence that rose like a buttress from the steep tufa ramp along the top of which ran via Catullo. You got to it straight from the road through a small gate with an electric opening mechanism and intercom, along a stone pathway with steps on it; in a more roundabout way from below, from via Orazio, through a wide gate with tall columns on either side, and then down a long, winding, treeless drive that climbed up to the house.

To avoid this drive, I went beyond the bend in via Orazio to the crossing, there turned into via Catullo, crossed the uneven ground to the tradesmen's entrance and stopped outside the small gate.

It was open. I pushed it and went on to that sort of bridge made of marble steps. Further on, I saw, the outer door of the kitchen, which gave on to the long balcony at the end of the bridgelike path, was also ajar; between the door itself and the doorpost was a thin bright strip of white light. Then I heard the shot.

A dull, almost muffled sound that at once raised an echo from the tufa ramp. This was followed a few seconds later by another shot, the noise of which thudded again along the entire rock-face behind the villa. A double-barrelled shotgun. The second time, though, it must have been pointed in a different direction from the first.

I dashed into the kitchen and found Idillia flopped over a stool by the central table, which she was clutching. Dressed entirely in black, leaning on the marble and framed entirely in white, she looked like a fly perched on a vanilla pudding, still and frozen. When she saw me she started and gave a cry of fear. As if one intruder wasn't enough; it nearly finished her off. Finally she recognised me and started moaning.

'Mother of God, they're killing him!' she cried.

'Where's Don Michele?' I shouted back.

'He was in there, in the sitting-room. They're burglars and they're killing him!' With a trembling finger she indicated the door at the end of the kitchen, after which she went back to calling on the mother of God.

I ran through the house, which at that hour in summer was about as brightly lit as an undertaker's parlour at midnight, switching the lights on one after another and cursing Miletti's mania for spending his whole time closing windows and shutters. Only in the sitting-room, at the end of all those dark rooms which I'd left illumined behind me, were the windows and the french doors open on to the terrace outside. I went through the french doors and, in the space between the house and the garage, saw Miletti.

He was bending over the body of Antonio, the chauffeur. Seen from behind, kneeling on one knee, his hands clutching the barrel of the gun which was planted on the ground in front of him, he looked absorbed in prayer.

A reddish shaft of sunlight, pouring between the house and

the rock-face, lit up the pair of them, the living and the dead, throwing a long shadow that reached as far as the wide-open double door of the garage.

Inside the garage a naked light bulb was switched on, its harsh white light, mixed with the red glow of the sun, making restless reflections on the chromium nose of the Flavia that stood, black, ancient and imposing, at the end of the building. On the ground, beside the right-hand front wheel, lay a rectangular black package.

At the sound of my footsteps on the concrete floor the living man turned, saw me and rose with difficulty, leaning on the gun as if it were a stick. He wore only a cotton shirt and a pair of linen trousers, and that unexpectedly young, sporty outfit, which I'd never seen him wearing before, showed up the old age which had swooped down on him in the past twenty-four hours more than did his familiar double-breasted grey suit.

'I was in the sitting-room, waiting for you, when I heard shouts and ran onto the terrace,' he said. His tone and voice were unchanged, he betrayed not the least sign of feeling. Perhaps he really had been praying. 'I found Antonio struggling in the garage doorway with a fellow, someone taller than himself. There were two of them, though. Inside the garage another one was crouching on the floor near the car. I went back to the house to get the gun, with the idea of firing at the swine and frightening them, but I wasn't in time. When I got back Antonio was lying on the ground and the pair of them were off. Over there.' With the barrel of the gun he indicated the road, in two opposite directions. 'I fired both shots but didn't hit them. They fairly streaked away.' And he added, almost wistfully: 'If only I'd had Improta here. But he's never here when you want him.' Then he turned to the body behind him: 'They split his head open.'

I looked at Antonio too: he was lying on the ground, three-quarters over, one leg folded under the other and a hand, his right hand, lying motionless at the height of his temple, as if to protect the great wound from the first flies that had quickly gathered. The blood was still filtering through his fingers and pouring thickly down his bare arm.

'They clobbered him with that thing,' said Miletti, indicating with his gun a bloodstained brick on the ground beside the body. 'A single blow. Pretty strong. And it must have been just one of the pair who did it.'

'Did you see whether they were dressed alike, by any chance?' I asked.

He looked at me with interest and curiosity, as if he found the question odd. 'No, why?'

'Because if they were, then they were the Twins.'

'Casali, you mean? D'you mean Casali's Twins?' So he knew them.

'The ones who turned my flat and office inside out,' I said.

'How d'you know it was them?' And he looked at me with even more curiosity.

'I saw them. And heard them. They spent the morning going over my flat and the early part of the afternoon beating me up. They reduced me to a pulp, the bastards. I found them almost in bed with me when I woke up and we had lunch together as well. A pleasant day. Casali was there too.'

'Where?' He had almost pinned me against the wall.

'Having lunch with us. I'll tell you everything later, Don Michele. At the moment think about those two blokes. I've got the car outside and I can . . .'

'Do what? Forget it, they're too far ahead of us by now. At least we know who they are.' Those blue eyes of his flashed again. 'So you've seen Casali. Tell me everything.' He'd forgotten his daughter, not to mention the body behind him.

'I'll tell you everything, Don Michele, but it doesn't seem to me quite the time for it. First of all, we must ring the police, and we must do it straight away.'

'So we'll have all those questions over again,' he said.

'D'you mean you're not going to tell them? I know, it never stops: but you've got to call them and put up with it.'

Suddenly he was no longer listening to me. His attention

moved to the package beside the wheel of the Flavia, inside the garage. He went over to it, leaving me there beside Antonio's body.

When he reached it, he said: 'What's this?'

It looked like a shoe-box wrapped in the sort of shiny black sack that's used for rubbish. He moved it a little with the end of the gun barrel.

'It's heavy,' he remarked. And immediately afterwards, less calmly this time, with a perceptible note of alarm in his voice, added: 'It's a bomb. It must be a bomb.'

I had leant over to look at it too. Then I started, and we both took a step back, bumping into each other.

'It's certainly not charged, but we'd better not touch it,' said Miletti. 'Even though it's not connected to anything.' He'd now become an explosives expert. 'Obviously they were putting it under the car and were surprised by Antonio. After that, when they'd killed him and I'd turned up with the gun, they had to run for it.'

'Don Michele, haven't you realised?' I said. 'We've got to tell the police, right away.'

He looked at me without seeing me. 'It must have been a message for me, that's clear. Those crooks know perfectly well who gets in first and switches on the engine in the morning: it's Antonio. Was,' he corrected himself. 'So it was Antonio they were going to blow up. Whereas he was killed too soon and they lost the advantage of surprise.'

He left the garage, not forgetting to switch off the light, and stopped in the yard outside it, in the bright sunlight; then looked up, to the edge of the tufa ramp. Perhaps he felt exposed at that point because, without bothering to walk round it, he calmly stepped over the body and walked towards the house.

When he was on the small outer terrace he turned to me. I'd followed him.

'If I call the police now we can't talk any longer. And before you go off to Formia you must tell me about Giulia and Casali. Let's go indoors. Antonio can wait, I can't.'

'And the bomb?'

'It won't go off,' he said. The expert had spoken.

We went inside. Miletti sat, or rather flopped down, on an armchair, and I told him about Giulia, the little I had heard from Luisella on the telephone. I remained standing, feeling very much on edge.

Miletti listened, staring into space and clenching the muscles of his jaw. When I'd finished he said: 'You must now get off to Formia. At once, there's no time to lose.' Without looking at me, without adding another word.

I told him I was just setting off for Formia when he rang me.

'How on earth did my daughter meet . . . Luisella?' he asked. Once again he'd hesitated, then he'd decided to use her name. It was clear that he thought her a whore because we weren't married, and it upset him that his daughter, who was unmarried—and pregnant by some unknown man, incidentally—should know her. A moralist, clearly.

'I don't know,' I said. And wished I did. 'But there's the danger that she may not go back to Formia, if she's come back to Naples.'

'You must go all the same, because if she does go back and you don't see her I'll kill you,' he said. He still had the double-barrelled shotgun beside him, leaning against the arm of his chair, and besides, he must have loathed my guts because I knew his daughter was pregnant. Then he could no longer contain himself. 'The whore,' he muttered.

I waited for the mood to pass and said nothing. If it hadn't been for the buzzing in my ear, I'd have heard the ticking of his wrist-watch, in that silence.

Finally, although the mood certainly hadn't passed, he spoke.

'You must get those papers handed back to you,' he said. 'That reminds me, I've talked to Marullo: they've been to the office as well. They actually ripped the telephone wires out from the wall; that's why that creep hadn't rung me. In the end he got round to ringing from outside. Before that he couldn't lift his arse off the chair.' It was now Marullo he was angry with.

'So we know Casali's looking for the papers; but above all that stink you noticed was all in your imagination. He doesn't know Giulia's got them. He may find out, though, and things will get too hot for her. What did he say to you?'

'Casali?' I said, and lit a cigarette. Then I gave him a cut-down, altered version of that ridiculous lunch and of Casali's talk and demands. Nothing about the final threat, though. Or, obviously, about our final agreement.

Miletti listened without interrupting me. At last he shook himself, got up from the armchair, and spoke.

'He's a shit and he lives in cloud-cuckoo-land. But we'll talk about that later. There's no time to lose now, get off to Formia. And you've got to persuade her. In the meantime I'll think of a way of getting my own back on Casali. Then we'll see who's won.' He went over to the door. 'Which way did you come in?'

'The tradesmen's entrance.'

'And did you see Idillia? Was she in the kitchen?'

'Yes,' I said.

'Then I'll go that far with you. I've got to talk to her. You might take her along to Formia with you. Giulia sometimes listens to her, she might manage to persuade her.'

We'd both of us forgotten the body lying out there. Alone and abandoned: isn't that the phrase?

But we hadn't forgotten the bomb; I hadn't, at least. I couldn't wait to get away from that hotbed of trouble.

13

You'd have thought there was a plot to rid Miletti of all his servants. First the chauffeur, then the maid, or the housekeeper, or whatever Idillia had been.

Now, poor soul, she was just a small, shabby black corpse, limp, folded away like a black dress flung aside, on the stool beside the kitchen table; one cheek resting on the seat, the arms hanging loosely and reaching the floor, where the hands were folded over at the wrists. And if she hadn't actually died of a final shock, they'd strangled her. She must have been lifted bodily off the stool, on which I'd seen her flopped down shortly before, a prey to her own fears, by a pair of steel claws, then dropped on the floor beside it. And in that short fall she'd died.

We saw her as soon as we opened the kitchen door, and the sight of her stopped us in our tracks. A heart attack never crossed our minds. With those two monsters running loose and free in the bare, savannah-like garden of the villa, it was clear at once what Miletti and I were both thinking of: before anything else, of those two—if not four—hands of steel.

Myself, I was also thinking, straight away, that we'd got to call the police. And I told him so, first thing, and at the risk of sounding like a parrot.

Miletti didn't answer, as was usual with him now. Instead, he had a very strange reaction. He started by sending out a throaty rattle that gradually became more precise and turned into a gurgling grunt which grew and grew until it became the authentic cry of a wounded animal.

'The bastards!' he roared. 'It's not possible!'

He roused himself, and, in a sudden rage, leapt at the fridge beside the door, seized a metal fruit dish standing on top of it, and, almost foaming at the mouth, for a moment looked round for a target. He found it in the larder door and, with all the anger that had exploded in him, hurled the dish at it, breaking the glass and strewing medlars and cherries over the floor.

When the sound of broken glass was no longer heard, and the echo of that inhuman yell was quiet, I was still gazing at him, astounded and puzzled. Calmed down, his rage exhausted, Miletti went over to Idillia's body and suddenly put a hand on her thin black shoulder, as if to cheer her. It lasted only a moment, but it was a gesture of tenderness I should never have expected of him, especially after I had seen him faced with the corpse of his wife. Finally he composed himself again, and turned to me, who had stayed quite still in the doorway.

'I'll call the police. You get off, don't waste any time. They'll kill Giulia as well. Hurry. I'm sorry for this poor soul, who had nothing to do with it all.'

'They strangled her, didn't they? She's got marks on her throat,' I said.

'Don't waste any more time, Iovine. Let's not start playing detectives now. Hurry, they'll kill her.' Then he thought it over. 'Admittedly you can't do much against them—you're alone and you're in pain, I can see that. But someone must go, so get a move on. In the meantime I'll make a few phone calls and we'll see what Casali and his gang do when I turn Improta and some others like him on to them.' War had been declared.

'Are you thinking of the brothers?' I asked. To myself, I was cursing Casali. He'd gone too far, he and his two hyenas, and we could all say goodbye to any hope of an agreement with Miletti.

'Who else? D'you doubt it? They went right round and came back this way while we were talking out there. They came in and went out by that door. It's still wide open. There's no doubt about it at all. But he'll pay me for it. Far from splitting the profits, I'm going to make him spend every lire he's got in medicines.'

I thought: at this point, only the death of one or other of them would untangle the situation. It would cost me my ten thousand francs, but things would soon be settled. Whereas he was forecasting a long-drawn-out death-bed. At least for that unscrupulous oaf, the only one of the pair I'd made a clear bargain with. How was it going to end?

'What shall I do, Don Michele?' I said. 'Shall I go? Will you call the police?'

'What's this fixation you've got with the police? Yes, yes, I'll call them. You get off, it's getting dark.'

It was already sunset, in fact. From the tufa bank outside the open kitchen door came a red glow, and in that light Miletti looked like an old Red Indian chief. All he needed was a feathered headdress; he was already whirling his hatchet.

'Get away,' he ordered me.

I went. As I passed Idillia's body I looked at Miletti. He had walked round the table and was now at the larder door, quite still, staring at the inside of the larder, which could now be seen through the broken glass, its extravagant shelves loaded with packets, tins and bottles. The sight of all those goodies seemed to fascinate him.

When I was out in the road I thought he called out something, but took no notice. I was tired, exhausted and uneasy. And, above all, in a hurry.

The Alfetta was outside. I got in, manoeuvred in the narrow, empty road and set off in the direction from which I'd come; the sun behind me and the long shadow of the car ahead.

Before the crossing with via Orazio I saw one of the grey suits, parti-coloured shoes and all, crossing the road just ahead of me. Going towards a 124 parked beside the parapet. Empty, it seemed to me.

He didn't see me because I had the sun behind me and didn't hear me because I was already in fourth gear and going fast. Perhaps it was the actual speed at which I was moving or perhaps the echo, which had remained superimposed upon the now continuous buzzing in my ear, of what the old man had said about my tussle with the Twins, the bruises of which I still bore; or else my anger at the bruises themselves. Whichever it was, the fact is that I accelerated. Instinctively, too, I switched on the headlights. If I'd had a machine-gun like a plane I'd have used that too; as it was, all I did was sound the horn.

He was now in the middle of the road and I was roaring towards him, baying and blinding him. In that moment he turned to face me and the low-lying sun, and stood completely still, dazzled: it was Pasquale, the more aggressive and brutal of the pair. I accelerated harder, this time decisively and consciously, furious, tense and sweating, shouting inside myself: 'Don't move, you bastard, don't move! Stay there!'

But he didn't. His bewilderment had lasted only a second, and when the shadow of the car was just about to hit him he shot away. He made a jump worthy of a grey panther and, like a panther, landed on all fours on the narrow pavement that ran beside the low parapet. He got up again, still leaping like a great cat, and started flying in the opposite direction to me. He wasn't even limping, curse him.

I braked, swerved and slithered for some way, then went into reverse and shot backwards, the engine giving a long, unhappy moan. My hands were trembling on the wheel; I was shaking, clumsy with anxiety and zigzagging about the road.

This made me scrape the edge of the pavement with the right-hand hub-caps, and at that speed they must have sent out sparks, as well as their terrifying metallic screech. I had now increased the panther's panic a thousandfold. He must have thought I was climbing up onto the pavement and did something unexpected, like an animal blinded by fear; he made another jump, but this time over the tufa parapet, vanishing on the other side.

I braked and once again yielded to instinct. I went into first gear, set off, changing gear again and again, anxiety growing within me and rising gradually.

I went past the 124, dark and old and still empty, and at the crossing turned abruptly right into via Orazio, swaying into the middle of the road. By a whisker I avoided a car coming in the opposite direction, which pulled away, hooting loudly.

He was down there, at the bottom of the tufa slope which carried via Catullo, from the top of which, aware or unaware of the height, he had flung himself after leaping over the parapet. On all fours again, licking his wounds. When he heard the screech of my tyres in that mad swerve he turned, saw me, got up and started running downhill beside the wall, on my side of the road, where there wasn't a pavement. I rushed against him, roaring the engine and sounding the horn, by this time blinded myself by the sun which was now in front of me and by my indifference to the consequences: there was traffic and yet I wanted to mow him down, there, in full view of all those witnesses.

He realised it was a mistake to be running, slowly and clumsily, on my side of the road; he realised, that is, that salvation lay on the opposite side, on the pavement, and suddenly turned and crossed. It was a matter of seconds. I saw his careless, stupid dash, I saw the big white car coming up the hill at top speed, and finally I saw his body in the air, like a puppet blown by the wind, arms and legs waving and beating. And I heard the long, rending moan of the horn of the car that had struck him, which accompanied his flight.

He fell a few yards further on, his head hitting the edge of the pavement he had been aiming for, while I went on for a few dozen yards beyond the big white car, which had stopped at once, its bonnet dented. I braked and opened the door. Then two more things happened: I saw the flash that glittered for a second on the steep side of the hill, and heard the explosion.

Lying motionless on the ambulance stretcher, Miletti looked dead. Actually, he was asleep, and all that was wrong with him was a fractured shoulder; but the shock he had suffered, at his age, made it advisable for him to go into hospital at once. At once only in a manner of speaking, because to start with the ambulance had arrived more than half an hour after I had rung the police. Nor had the police been any quicker. In fact they had arrived together—assistance medical and judicial.

Every time the ambulance jerked Miletti's head flopped from side to side in what looked like a continuous, monotonous gesture of denial, as if even in the sleep brought on by the tranquilliser he had been injected with he couldn't believe what seemed to him a bad dream.

I'd found him lying face downwards in a pool of water, in the inner doorway of the kitchen, alive—contrary to any reasonable forecast—and conscious. The explosion had brought down the whole inner wall of the kitchen and with it Miletti's body, which was now sticking out from the larder.

'I saw it. In there, in the larder, and I called you,' he murmured when I leant over him and lifted his forehead to stop him drowning. A violent jet of water was pouring out of the broken pipe all over me, soaking everything. 'The package. Like the one in the garage.'

Later, the police hadn't found any package wrapped in black plastic in the garage. So they'd even taken the risk of recovering the parcel, the monsters. Clearly they wouldn't have slept that night if they hadn't passed on Casali's message.

Little was left of Idillia, though, and what there was was strewn about the kitchen. A complete arm, bare and torn, was floating very close to Miletti's head, and the sight of it made me try to lift the old man and put him elsewhere, where it was dry, above all. But his shriek of pain made me give up the idea and I had to stay there, swimming in water under the implacable jet and holding his heavy head up, until help arrived.

'Fifty thousand francs,' he managed to whisper to me before he plunged into sleep, after having an injection of some tranquilliser. A little earlier, he had seemed in no state to reply to the two or three carefully worded questions which the head of the Flying Squad had asked him.

But he had found his voice again, after they had lifted him and transferred him to the stretcher, putting him down to bleed on the valuable carpet, while they bandaged his shoulder, broken when the violence of the explosion had hurled him against the doorpost, and injected the tranquilliser.

'Fifty thousand francs,' he whispered. 'I'll hand them over in Switzerland if you find Giulia. Before Casali.' He was wet all over but his mouth was already dry and he found it difficult to speak. 'Find Giulia and if I survive I'll fix you up properly.' Then he grasped my arm. 'Don't mention Casali to them. If I live I'll deal with him. You find my daughter. Don't lose any time. Save her. You're the only one I trust.'

And he collapsed, as if the admission had been too much for him. The chief of the Flying Squad had approached, looking curious and suspicious, but the old man had gone.

And I was thinking of this now, in the ambulance, going to the hospital with him because I didn't feel I could send him off alone, after that revelation of trust and the prize he had promised me—the promise to fix me up for life. Now I could only hope that the old man would survive the shock and the pneumonia which he couldn't fail to have caught. The head continued to wobble in denial every time the ambulance bumped and the rest of his body looked like that of a child. He had tiny feet, which barely poked up under the blanket wrapped around him.

He opened his eyes once, but closed them again immediately with a faint moan. And I shuddered, with a feeling that for that moment they had rested on me, passing judgement.

I shook myself only when the ambulance stopped in the hospital courtyard. We had arrived. For myself, I had also arrived at a decision.

14

It was past nine and at that hour I wouldn't find him in his office, so I rang him at home. A man's voice answered, hoarse and disagreeable, and when Casali at last came to speak I was just going to put down the receiver, impatiently.

I was in a service station on the main road. I'd told them to fill up the tank and was taking the chance of ringing him, but I was panting as if I'd arrived on foot after running all the way from the hospital, where I had left Miletti.

Casali seemed to me out of breath as well: the effort of carting all that fat about. And he went straight into the attack.

'Just the man I was thinking of,' he said. 'What's this I've been hearing? You've really got yourself into trouble. What a thing to do. Who d'you think's going to control Tonino now?'

'And who's going to control Miletti, Don Nicola?' I answered. 'What a thing to do, sending him to hospital the way you did.'

This must have been news to him. 'What d'you mean, hospital?' he said, his loud voice having changed its tone slightly.

'When a bomb goes off nearby, if you're not killed at once you go to hospital, with a few bits broken if you're lucky. Don Michele was lucky, he came out of it as well as you could expect, but you didn't just blow up his house, you blew up any hope of coming to an agreement with him.' I then added a few details about the explosion.

'Bad luck, that's all it was, bad luck,' Casali said, no longer panting. 'The truth is that all they were meant to do was put a little hint under the car. Then when the chauffeur was laid out cold, they were so conscientious that, to avoid blowing up the old man if he happened to sit in the driving seat next morning, they moved the package into the kitchen. They couldn't really be expected to think he'd be poking around in there. Bad luck.'

'And the two who died were just bad luck, was that it?' I asked.

'What's that got to do with it?' said Casali. 'You wouldn't expect them just to drop the package, would you? They couldn't hand it over to the old woman or the chauffeur. These little accidents will happen. But what about the old man? Is it serious?'

I told him it wasn't, but that there was danger of complications in his lungs, they'd said at the hospital. 'Why, d'you want to send flowers?'

'Now, now, don't get scratchy,' said Casali. 'You've got enough troubles of your own. Tonino saw what happened from above. He's now watching over his brother in the mortuary, but he'll have to come out of there soon.'

'I didn't run him over,' I said. 'I just wanted to scare him.' What part of it had Tonino seen? The first or the second? Or both?

'But you chased him under the wheels of another car, and that's the sort of thing you've got to pay for. It's something you must expect.'

'How am I supposed to take that, Don Nicola? As a threat?'

'For heaven's sake, Iovine, we're in business together, aren't we? I'll try and reason with Tonino a bit.'

What I really wanted to know, though, he still hadn't got around to telling me: whether I was in any official trouble over the accident.

'D'you happen to know what the man who ran him over said in his statement?' I asked.

'Well, I know he said what had happened, and that when you got into the car again after the explosion and ran off, he took your number. You ran to the villa, I suppose. But none of that matters, it can always be smoothed out.' Everything was always easy to him. Like the bomb. 'The real trouble's Tonino,' he added.

'I told the police I'd witnessed an accident and that I'd driven off to the villa when I heard the bang. They didn't say a thing, didn't seem to think it the least bit important.'

'Because it was the traffic cops' business,' said Casali. 'In any case, you weren't in the wrong.'

He thought I was still on his side, and I mustn't make him think otherwise.

'See what you can do, Don Nicola,' I said. 'With Tonino, as well. Meantime, I'm still seeing to the papers.'

'Remember the seven days, Iovine,' he said, and I could feel him ticking them off.

'I'm remembering,' I said. 'But things are complicated now, with Don Michele in hospital.'

'It was bad luck, as I told you,' said Casali. 'In any case, we'll have no more misfortunes like that. I'll settle things connected with the accident and you see to the chances of agreement.'

This, in the midst of an all-out war and after blowing up his partner. Either so bare-faced an attitude was the result of naïvety—which suited me well enough, though I didn't really believe it of him—or else he just didn't know Don Michele. This last possibility I suggested to him.

'Money cancels out ill-feeling, you'll see,' he replied calmly. 'The only thing to hang on to is the idea that my intentions are serious, as I think I've shown they are. Let's not bring any more misfortunes on ourselves, because it's both of us or neither. That reminds me, I'll see about those francs of yours tomorrow.'

'And what about Tonino?' I said.

'Well, that does mean trouble,' said Casali.

I got into the car again and set off, pursued by the thought of Tonino. Also, Casali's calm tone had made me worried about Giulia. He hadn't mentioned her this time, but this didn't mean he didn't connect me with her, because by now he was bound to know that she'd run away from home with the papers. He must also have realised that I was ringing him long-distance, yet he hadn't asked me where I was calling from. He'd mentioned the francs, though.

Was he giving me the chance of getting them first from him, and ought I to refuse? Of course I was playing with fire, but Miletti's last words and promises had been extremely stimulating.

I'd got beyond Castel Volturno and the traffic was thinning out; I was now less blinded by the approaching headlamps and this was a relief. Before, I'd been exhausted; now, after the last blow I'd received during this dreadful evening, I was positively vapourised, a single black cloud of weariness, and couldn't have borne the continuous rhythm of those dazzling lights much longer.

Forty kilometres still lay between me and Formia, but Mondragone wasn't far and I'd make another stop there. I hadn't rung Luisella and must do so right away.

When I rang she answered at once. Another worried person with a hand on the receiver.

'What on earth have you been up to? You vanished. I tried to get you at home and at the office to tell you Giulia had telephoned.'

'Where is she?' I almost shouted.

'Here at Formia. She's at the Bellavista. We've arranged to meet after supper. She's expecting me there about ten.'

'Where is this Bellavista?' I asked, my voice almost breaking. You'd think I'd found a lost daughter.

'On the main road, before you get into Formia. Where are you now?'

'At Mondragone.'

'Well, coming into Formia, about a kilometre before it, towards the sea. What are you going to do, are you going there? What ought I to do?'

I had a clear vision of the two of them together, ranged against me. If I wanted to persuade Giulia, I had to see her alone. Luisella's Greek chorus of haughty irony would only complicate things. 'Maybe you'd better stay at home,' I told her.

'Better for who?'

Christ, she was going to be jealous again.

'Well, you mustn't come,' I told her.

'Don't worry, I won't. Who wants to see you? Manage on your own. Go on and hoodwink the poor little thing. And go to hell.' But she didn't ring off.

'Luisella. Don't ring her up, don't warn her.' She was capable of anything, that girl. 'Look, I'll call you afterwards. If we meet while she's there we'll end up fighting and that'll throw everything out.'

This time she did hang up, before I'd finished the sentence.

I'd get there by ten, but I was completely whacked. A shudder of pain was running down my second leg now. With the buzzing of the unoccupied line in my ears and a single aim—to arrive in time—I dashed out of the bar, fearing that Luisella might have one of her brilliant ideas which would make me lose Giulia at the very moment I was catching up with her. To avenge herself or, because of one of her twisted notions, to save Giulia. It was the worst half hour of those last two terrible days, but at ten past ten I reached the Bellavista.

It looked less like an hotel than like a castle taken to pieces and roughly rebuilt inside a long, high, castellated wall: towers scattered here and there, and the central part cut in two and set up at the sides. The swimming pool was in the courtyard, immediately beyond a high gate with a small luminous sign on it; round and illuminated, it must have been the old well enlarged or the moat cut down in size and embellished with blue tiles. At that hour it contained a single crazy old woman, blonde and wearing a bikini, who had evidently decided to spend the night swimming round and round.

Behind the counter, the porter was done up to match his surroundings, in an amazing red outfit which needed only a halberd to complete it. I couldn't see his legs, but he must have been wearing shorts.

When I asked him about Giulia Miletti he stared at me from head to foot, disapproving of my tieless condition and the damp, rumpled suit. Then he decided to answer my plea for help.

'Miss Miletti has just left the dining-room,' he said; but it was a very special favour, no doubt about that. 'I think I saw her going to the Open Room.'

'What's that?' I said.

'The hotel's nightclub,' he said, smug and contemptuous. 'Right there at the end, in the second courtyard.'

This turned out to be a kind of cloister, all pretty columns and lemon trees, with wrought-iron tables and chairs, painted white, scattered among them. The dance floor and the band were in a corner, behind a single very tall palm, and Giulia was in the opposite corner, sitting at a completely isolated table. A single couple was moving about on the dance-floor; two other couples, also foreign and aged, were sitting at a table together. There were more waiters than customers among the columns.

She wasn't in her denim uniform, but wore a light flowered dress, and, on the table in front of her, there was even a black handbag with something glittery on the fastening clip. Well brushed, well made up, and self-possessed, she was sitting there with her shapely legs crossed, staring into space and waiting.

Not for me, of course. When she saw me coming across to her she started and stubbed out her cigarette in the ashtray. Then she composed herself, crossed her legs again, and stared expressionlessly at me. Her eyes were light blue.

Her mother must have been lovely. Miletti had never spoken of his second wife, perhaps persuaded that Giulia's looks were all to his credit; but apart from the eyes, in him so cold and in her so fine, she was quite unlike him. Perhaps they were more or less the same in height, though she was still the taller; and that delicious smile of hers had nothing in common with her father's gloomy, haughty reserve. Not to mention the chin—in his non-existent above and all too abundant below, in her gently pronounced, a decisive touch in the sweet oval of her face. And, unlike her father, she was dark-skinned and black-haired; the hair cut like a sort of helmet. Never had I seen her so tidy; but I'd watched her blossoming these past two years, and now gazed admiringly at the result.

'May I sit down, Giulia?' I asked, pulling out a chair.

She made a vague gesture in the direction of the chair, and her foot continued to twitch. Then:

'What's this, Luisella's betrayed me?' she said.

Perhaps I needed to get my breath back. For a long time I looked at her without answering.

'Luisella hasn't betrayed you,' I said at last. 'She's done you a favour, and me one as well. I've come specially from Naples.'

She stopped staring at me, in order to light another cigarette. Then, but just to gain time, she said:

'I'm wondering why.'

'Apart from the reason you know perfectly well, there's another. Your father's in hospital. Tomorrow morning they're moving him to a private nursing home.'

She looked at me again and I couldn't see the smallest sign of alarm in those blue eyes. In fact, she smiled; and the bitterness that was still part of her expression didn't stop a pair of dimples appearing in her cheeks.

'What's happened to him?' she asked, the indifference of her tone spoiled when she suddenly cleared her throat.

'Everything. First of all they smashed up his house'—better lay it on thick—'then they blew him up. With a bomb. He was flung violently against a door and fractured his shoulder, and he's in danger of pneumonia.' I kept back the news of the two deaths, above all Idillia's, thinking that in the end it might be decisive.

'Who?' she asked. This time she managed to be detached, to sound merely curious. '*They* did all this. But who are they?'

I told her, then added that they would now be taking notice of her. That the Twins had been separated I omitted to say, though.

'Why? Because of those papers?' she said.

'Yes, because of those papers,' I replied. 'Giulia, why don't you try and see reason? Give me those papers, get yourself out of this terrible mess and come to Naples with me to see your father.'

'He can die, for all I care. I don't give a damn,' she said, and cleared her throat decisively. 'As for the papers, I haven't got them with me.'

I had calculated that my news would have a greater effect on her. Now I brought out some further news, not particularly tactfully.

'Don't you realise you're playing with fire?' I said. And she wasn't the only one, either. I went on, using words I'd already heard or thought. 'It's all getting too much for you. They've already killed Idillia. Strangled her. And the explosion blew her to pieces. What are you waiting for?'

She sat quite still, her foot came to rest at last. There was a flash across the blue sky of her eyes, and when it had disappeared I saw, through the silly, smart gloom where we found ourselves, the glitter of tears that were reluctant to fall, between her long dark lashes.

'What are you waiting for, Giulia?' I said, taking advantage of her disturbance. 'For them to land on you? For the police to find you? It would look a lot better if you just turned up, maybe after seeing a lawyer. You know they're looking for you, don't you? That it seems you were at Faito and saw those two . . . bodies? I can help you, with the police as well as the other business.' Wondering meantime who'd help me with the police, and my idiotic idea of revenge. 'Giulia, you're in an ugly mess, and on your own you're not going to get out of it.'

The tears finally flowed and with them all the despair she must have been hiding those past two days.

'Leave me in peace,' she almost sobbed. 'I might have known that if I went to Luisella I'd find you.'

'Luisella's your friend, you must believe me,' I said. 'She hasn't betrayed you, in fact she's asked me to help you. She told me everything.' I looked at the hand lying in her lap. 'I know about your other . . . trouble. And I want to help you with that too.'

Nervously, still moved, she began waggling her foot again. 'I don't give a damn for your knowing,' she said, 'or anyone else knowing either. And I don't give a damn that my father's in hospital. *He* wanted to help me, too. Force me to have an abortion.'

'Your father knew you were pregnant?' I said, perhaps even more astonished than she had been when she saw me enter that noisy little enclosure.

The waiter picked that very moment to come up to our table, smiling a little too much. Giulia already had a Coke, and I ordered a whisky for myself. The ancient couple on the dance-floor were still clinging together, to a slow rhythm now, swooping and dreaming under the bored, ironic eyes of the band.

'So your father knew?' I said, thinking of the way the old man had looked, and had been silent, and still unable to shake myself out of my surprise.

'Yes he knew—dear daddy, that little old tyrant. I told him when he decided yet again to interfere in my love life. Or rather, to get you to interfere.' She looked at me, without hatred. 'And you did interfere, obediently, subtly, creepily. What did you think you were doing, scaring Pino?'

112

'So it was him . . . Pino Gargiulo?' I asked. I was going to need that whisky, now, at once.

'Yes, I'm pregnant by him. And I don't give a damn who knows that, either. With your ridiculous, out-of-date, bullying logic, you thought you could scare him off with threats of arrest. A couple of boot-lickers, you and Inspector Lentizzi.' I was quite right to think she had looked at me without hatred; what she felt was quite clearly plain contempt.

Still more confused, but above all stunned and clumsy, I exclaimed: 'But wasn't he with your stepmother?'

Despair prevailed over her contempt and she burst into tears. Perhaps it was the first time she'd done so since she made that discovery—and exactly how horrible it must have been for her, I'd only just realised—because the tears that had hovered became a stream. Red-faced, swollen-eyed, her make-up ruined, she looked slender and defenceless; but I was more confused than ever when I heard her exclaim: 'Oh, poor Idillia!'

15

The orchestra, if you could call it that, started up at a frantic pace, having decided to rid itself of the two dancers by giving them a heart attack; but all it managed to do was attract the four odd others sitting out, onto the dance-floor, and allow them to work off their accumulated boredom.

The idle waiters had vanished in the meantime; but mine turned up again with the whisky and his smug smile, as if he'd distilled it himself.

The noise overwhelmed Giulia's last sobs. She recovered, picked up her handbag and worked away with handkerchief, small mirror and lipstick. Like a smart little lady. I drank half the whisky and wondered, mechanically, what the waiter could possibly be so proud of; any of us could add water to a bottle.

'How long had you known Pino Gargiulo?' I asked her abruptly, without realising I was prodding the wound.

Perhaps she didn't realise it herself, or else needed to vent her feelings to react in some way. Or perhaps she was ashamed of having let herself go, of having hidden her own real suffering behind her sad remark about Idillia. She pushed the hair off her face with an automatic gesture and then shook her head to fling it back; she was ready to talk.

'Since last winter,' she said. 'A couple of months before my father got to know about it and you threatened Pino.' This time she spoke without rancour: just mentioning it, that was all. Perhaps she'd stopped despising me; who knows.

'It wasn't my idea, Giulia,' I said. 'Your father made me do it. It's not my usual way of . . .'

'You obeyed him, though,' she said. 'But let's drop it. I don't love him any more, I just hate my father. But at that time I did . . . love him. He helped me a lot, especially to put up with my father. Though he came to hate him as well, later on.'

'Why, did Pino know your father?' I asked.

'Only in a manner of speaking—by repute,' she said.

'From what you told him?' I still felt curious. 'Did he hate him because of that?'

'No, he knew him before he met me,' she said.

'How?' I asked.

'I told you—by repute.'

'Where did Pino come from? From Naples?' I asked.

'No, he was born in Milan, and was brought up all over the place.' She lit a cigarette, and for a moment reminded me of her father.

'And did your father know him?' I asked.

'When I told him I was pregnant by Pino,' she said, 'and he was in convulsions of rage—real, proper convulsions—he said something that sounded as if it had just slipped out, I remember. He swore, and shouted that Pino was a bastard, though he didn't use the word. With the sick mind of an old reactionary'—those were her very words—'he attributed to him God knows what sins of his mother. He called her a whore, in other words. Obviously, he was the son of a whore.'

'How did you meet Pino?'

'Marullo introduced him.'

'Marullo?' I said, and drank the second half of that glass of whisky; then I signalled to the waiter to bring me another. I turned back to Giulia, not wanting her to regret talking or to give up her outburst, or whatever it was. 'How did Marullo come into it? Where did he introduce you?'

'In the office in via Marina, one day when my father was out of town and I went along to collect some money he'd left. He never keeps money at home and we always have to ask him and go along and fetch it at the office. Had to,' she corrected herself. 'Tina never had any money either, but that served her right, the filthy tart.' She paused a moment, then went on. 'Marullo was his cashier, as far as we were concerned. That day I found him talking to Pino. He had to introduce us, but I noticed he felt uneasy about it. When I left the office Pino came with me.'

At this point I couldn't help asking: 'And what about the four hundred thousand lire? That was in the house.'

She looked at me, but only for a moment. 'D'you know about that too?' she said. 'Did Luisella tell you?'

I looked down at her strong, shapely legs. 'I heard it from your father,' I told her.

'Well, I didn't know the money was there. I found it when I was looking for the red file. I needed it and took it. I'd decided to have an abortion.'

The file, of course. 'How did you come to know of the existence of that file?' I asked her.

'Pino told me. We'd decided to take it and run away together, and hold my father off by blackmailing him.'

Pino? So he knew about the file, the bastard. He kept popping up all over the place. I had to hurry, though, Giulia might start back-pedalling; some miracle was making her talk.

The waiter distracted me. Back at last from the distillery, where he must have been on a special trip for my whisky, he put the glass down on the table with a whole pantomime of gestures and smiles, as if he was the head waiter at least and it wasn't just an ordinary glass of whisky. As soon as he left I went on.

'You said, earlier on, that your father was trying to force you to have an abortion. Now you say you'd decided to have it yourself. I don't understand. Who persuaded you? Your father? Pino?'

'What persuaded me was finding out that he was . . . with that cow,' she said, without batting an eyelash; simply shaking her head to toss the hair back again. 'And the way he was doing it.'

'But when you took the money you still didn't know about . . . Pino and your stepmother?' I said.

'Yes, I did,' she said, and stubbed out her cigarette. Then she pushed the hair back from her face with a finger and looked at me for a long time, calm and lovely.

'You already knew it? Since when?'

She didn't answer, but looked around distractedly, biting at her painted lips: she can't have been used to lipstick, but there were other reasons for her uneasiness.

The band had given up all hope, and had begun playing slowly again; the six dancers were now shuffling around the floor, at once merry and dazed. The sky above us was still full of stars.

'You discovered it on Tuesday evening, then? Giulia, how often were you up at Faito, between yesterday and the day before?'

'On Tuesday. I discovered it on Tuesday afternoon!' She almost shouted, and I realised that all her calmness was a fake, an effort she could no longer keep up. Tears flowed again and, from that festive funeral parlour in a geriatric hotel, down at the opposite corner of the enclosure, gleams of light glittered on her bright eyes. 'He'd said we must meet there. It was the only place where my father couldn't find us, he said. We'd got to decide.'

'Decide what?' I said, beginning to feel rather like Assenza.

'Everything. About the baby, our running away, the lot. It was weeks since we'd met, because when I told him I was pregnant he vanished. Then on Monday he rang me up to arrange this grisly meeting.' She stopped and wiped her eyes with a handkerchief. 'When I got there next day I found him with that creature. They were in each other's arms on the living-room sofa. I saw them as soon as I opened the door, and I screamed. Yes, because it was worse than a fright. I had a feeling I'd fallen into a trap. Then I ran away.'

'You saw them, then . . . alive?' I said.

'Very much alive and pretty disgusting.' She was now weeping and sobbing uninhibitedly and the waiters had of course all reappeared and were peering in our direction.

I then did something Assenza would never have done: I took her hand, which was lying on the arm of the chair. She didn't withdraw it. The nails were painted: she must have spent those two days brooding, and putting on make-up. But why hadn't she telephoned Luisella sooner? I pressed her hand and she didn't object. She was wearing a man's wristwatch.

'And where did you go, when you ran away?' I said.

'I can't remember. I got into the car and drove around, thinking and crying. Like I am now.' Suddenly she withdrew her hand. Then she seemed to take control of herself and went on: 'Thinking, above all. Feeling rage and jealousy. Mad jealousy. I've never loved Tina, but at that moment I hated her with my whole soul. I'd have killed her if I could. And him as well.'

'You didn't go straight back to the house at Faito?' I said.

She looked at me as if she'd realised only then the conclusions that might be drawn from what she'd said. 'No,' she said decisively, drying her eyes for the last time. 'What are you thinking? It's monstrous. You're a snake, a monstrous snake,' she added, making it quite clear. And she looked at her hand, which she had laid down on the arm of the chair once again.

'I was only asking,' I said. 'All I want is to help.' Probably creeping along like a snake, in fact.

'Of course, just trying to help,' she said, and paused to reflect. 'Now I can see why the police are looking for me.'

'They suspect you were there on Tuesday. But they've got proof that you were there yesterday morning,' I said.

'Catello?' she asked.

'The suitcase and the bag. Apart from what Catello said—what he had to say.'

'I took them up there next morning,' she said. 'Actually I was out of my mind, I just wasn't reasoning any more. I'd decided to stay there, just to annoy them or to get them out by blackmailing Tina, or to show I didn't give a damn—I don't know what. When I got back to Naples I decided to run away from home and stay up there at Faito, for a day at least, and spoil the whole thing for them.' She'd stopped crying and was beginning to grow confused. 'I took all sorts of decisions, all of them wrong ones. I'd creep up on them . . . while they were asleep. D'you follow me? So I drove around for practically the whole night and ended up at a small hotel in Sorrento. And of all those . . . well, furious decisions, just one seemed to me right. My decision to have an abortion. I just couldn't bear the thought of having his child.' She stopped to get her breath and perhaps her desperate young thoughts into some sort of order; she'd decided to tell all, in a rush, and continued confusedly. 'I hated my father because he'd come between Pino and me and because he'd attacked me. Yes, he did. Idillia had to intervene several times. But it wasn't just that he hit me—no, he got a doctor to the house to examine me. He's always got everyone to do what he wants. He wanted me to have an abortion and he wanted it right away, without any argument. It was a long fight that went on for days. Then suddenly, after I'd seen what I saw, I decided it for myself. I was blind with hatred. I'd gone up there to talk to him, to decide how to save the . . . child—his child, d'you realise?—and I found him in the arms of that ugly bitch. Yes, I was blind with hatred. Hatred of him, of my father, of that house. And I had just one clear idea: to run away and get an abortion. I'd thought about it for hours, the whole afternoon and evening. Then I ran away. I'd decided. After realising, among other things, that he'd done it on purpose—Pino, that is.'

'Making you pregnant, you mean?'

'No, being found there with her. I've no doubt at all about it now. I felt I was in a trap and that's what it was. He knew I'd be going up there and when he rang me on Monday he must already have been up at Faito with her. Besides, they must have heard me turning up in the car. In other words, it was all set up. But why? Why, I kept wondering. And I'm still wondering.' She was silent and sat brooding, her shining eyes bluer than ever. 'And maybe getting me pregnant too. Yes, that as well. But why? Why did he do it?'

By now I'd taken a real dislike to the lad, but I couldn't think he was such an idiot, for all that long hair of his, as not to have a motive of any sort.

'You said he hated your father,' I said. 'It must have been a crazy, childish way of hurting him in some way. Making it with . . . getting at him through his wife and daughter.'

'I've thought of that too,' she said at once, shaking her head, but this time not to fling back her hair. 'And I just can't make it out. It's true that he was always talking about my father and those papers. He said that if we had them in our hands he couldn't do anything to us. It was he who suggested it to me, when we were planning our bolt. He even suggested what I should say, once I'd got them.'

'Did he know where they were?' I asked. Quite capable of it. I now thought him capable of anything.

'No, all he knew was that they were somewhere in the house. It was easy for me to guess where they were,' she said. 'But who cares about those papers?'

Well, I cared for a start, and cared a good deal. But I didn't tell her. I was thinking of that boy, who had somehow known everything. How had he done so? I thought of Marullo, too, as I shivered in that damp courtyard and those damp clothes. How many people had known of the existence of that second contract?

'You said you took the suitcase and the bag up there yesterday morning,' I said. 'So you saw them . . . once again?'

'Dead,' she replied. 'Both of them dead. He with his throat cut and she in the bath. I had cramps in my stomach when I saw them. I thought I'd go mad.'

'And you went to Catello's house to ring your father. You had a row with him. Why?' Then I suspected something. 'Did you say anything about having seen them? Dead?'

'No, I didn't. I had a row with him, yes, and I don't know why, I was even more out of my mind, then, than I'd been the previous evening. I was beyond myself. It seemed right to take it out on him.'

'And then you went back again in the evening, after bringing Luisella here,' I said. 'Weren't you tired of running around in the car like that?' Did she feel attracted by the place, or something?

'In the morning I was so bewildered and confused that I forgot the suitcase and bag. I went back to get them. I was scared they'd be found.'

'And you left them behind again,' I said. More and more like Assenza.

'While I was there I heard someone coming and ran off. I hadn't been there long and hadn't found them. I went all over the house, with those two bodies still there, it was like a nightmare. In the end I found them behind the front door. I'd left them when I went there in the morning. Before making that horrible discovery. I'd only just found them when I heard a car driving up and footsteps, and I panicked. I didn't want to be caught there in the house and my first impulse was to run away. I know, it seems incredible that I had the courage to go back there, and what for? To get a suitcase and a bag because I was scared they'd involve me, although I hadn't done anything. But that's what happened, I swear, as I swear I felt bewildered and panicked. And now I've got two reasons for staying out of Naples, because I know no one'll believe me. They'll all think what you thought at first, that I might have killed them out of revenge. You're not the only monster.' Well, that was something.

I didn't tell her that I was the person she'd heard arriving. 'Why did you come back here, then?' I asked instead. 'Without the suitcase or the bag.' And I looked at her dress. What was the meaning of that get-up—a way of dressing up, to avoid being recognised?

'When I ran off from Faito again I hadn't anywhere to go. Luisella was here. She was the only person I'd told about it and she'd promised to help me. Besides, as I said, I'd got a double lot of reasons for staying out of Naples. So I came back here to Formia. Also because I haven't any time to waste—I'm already two months pregnant.' Instinctively she looked down at her womb. Then she touched the hem of her dress, and almost raised it. 'This is Luisella's. She lent it to me yesterday morning, with some other things.'

I hadn't recognised it. As usual, Luisella must have left the house with a whole pile of suitcases. Perhaps the make-up had been her idea as well. Typical. I then asked Giulia, because I remembered it, about the other dress, the one with blood-stains on it; and as I changed position in my chair I touched her calf with my foot.

She answered at once—too quickly, just as she changed the position of her leg too quickly: 'Have they found it?' She seemed incredulous.

'Well, of course,' I replied.

'I had it on yesterday morning,' she said; her eyes glittered again, and she had to pause. 'It was terrible. I couldn't believe my eyes, I couldn't believe it really was him lying there on the floor. I was crying and trembling. At that moment I no longer hated him, I was just overwhelmed, beyond myself, desperate, and I didn't know what I was doing. I must have touched him with my hands, perhaps. I must have touched him with the courage of despair, I don't know, I don't remember. I leant over him and all I remember is that when I got up my fingers had blood on them. The tips of my fingers. And so I rubbed them on my dress. Then I found I'd stained it and ran into my bedroom. I didn't think of washing my hands right away. I ran into my room to change, put on some old pants and a shirt I'd got there. Afterwards I went to the bathroom. I looked at my hands and was filled with disgust. They weren't dirty any longer but I had to wash them. When I opened the bathroom door I had another shock. I don't know how I didn't faint. In fact, how I didn't have a miscarriage at that very moment, right on the spot.' She shut her eyes as if to cut out the memory, and two tears rolled down.

After a while, with her eyes still closed, she added: 'I don't even know why I'm answering all these questions.'

The noise had suddenly stopped. The stout elderly Germans were going back to their tables and the band, having put away its instruments, had started to yawn. It was like a signal; suddenly things happened, catching me by surprise at the very moment when I was going to return to the subject I cared so much about. Giulia rose, the waiters leapt in our direction and I was left open-mouthed, the words cut off as I spoke.

I paid the bill and ran after Giulia through the lemon trees and, further on, through the little columns of the portico. She was moving hurriedly away, her figure looking slim in high heels and Luisella's light dress, which was tight for her, I now realised admiringly, especially from behind.

When I caught up with her I took her elbow, squeezing it, and shivered as I felt the contact with her skin.

She stopped and turned. Her face wasn't exactly overwhelmed, as it had been before, but she was crying.

'Wait, Giulia. Why did you run off like that? We've still got to talk. I've come on purpose from . . .'

'Don't you realise this isn't the time for it?' she said, gazing around, but, I now realised, filled with contempt again.

'I wanted to ask you about those papers,' I had the bright idea of saying.

'It's not the right time. Tomorrow.'

'Listen,' I said. 'Wait. Just a minute.'

She had turned and freed her arm, almost snatching it away, and was moving off again. Then she stopped once more.

'One final question. We'll talk about all the rest tomorrow morning. How did you meet Luisella? And why did you turn to her, of all people?'

She looked at me. I was mistaken: I could read sadness in her eyes, but surprise as well.

'Why d'you want to know?'

'Just because,' I said. 'I'm curious.' This was true.

'I didn't know her, Pino knew her and he talked about her—quite often. He admired her. And he knew it had happened to her as well.'

'What had happened?'

'She'd had an abortion. And not so long ago, either.'

And there she left me, with the distinct impression that she'd said it in order to get at me, some way or other.

16

Pino and Don Michele, Pino and Marullo, and finally Pino and Luisella. Everywhere, always and only—Pino. Not to mention Pino and Giulia's pregnancy. The result: I hadn't shut my eyes for most of the night, in that castle of sorts at Bellavista where I'd spent the night, being absolutely incapable, the previous evening, of getting into the car and going back to Naples, then coming back to Formia in the morning.

About half a dozen other events, not all of them ordinary

but all of them happening in the past twelve hours, could have occupied my mind for part of that sleepless night, but that hairy idiot, God rest his soul, took up the whole of it.

Including the sick, painful thoughts that the memory of my meeting with Giulia aroused now and then. Towards dawn I fell asleep.

At nine I woke up with a start, worrying over just one thing. I rang and asked for Giulia's room, then waited ages with the receiver in my hand and all the relentless results of a binge I'd never been on: headache and the rest of it. The bruises had ripened like plums: they were tenderer than ever and I couldn't find the right position on the bed.

The switchboard girl spoke again at last. 'Nobody's answered, I'll give you the receptionist,' she said, and put me through.

It wasn't the one who'd been there the previous evening. This one was pleasant and helpful.

'Miss Miletti left the hotel this morning,' he told me.

'This morning? When?' I thought of that idiot doorman in the red jacket.

'Over an hour ago.'

'Why didn't you wake me?'

'Really, we didn't know that...'

'I asked to be called at seven-thirty.'

'I'm sorry, Mr Iovine, but there's nothing about it here.'

Of course, his colleague the halbadier.

'So Miss Miletti's gone?'

'She has, I'm afraid. I'm sorry.'

'So am I. But what I meant was: isn't she coming back? Has she left, or just gone out?'

'Yes, indeed. She's paid her bill and left.'

'And left no message for me?'

'She left no messages for anyone. In fact she was in a great hurry. She did just make a call from the phone box in the hall here.'

'She called an outside number, you mean?'

'That's right.'

'A Formia number, or where?'

'A Formia number.'

Luisella's, obviously. I hung up, disappointed, saddened and furiously angry, and asked the switchboard girl to get Luisella's number for me. She put me straight through.

It was Luisella's mother who answered, I think. Luisella wasn't there.

'Has she gone out or gone away?' I asked. This looked like being a day when people took off.

'Gone out. Who are you?'

'I'm Sa— ... Alessandro,' I said.

'Ah,' she said, and hung up rudely. Obviously her mother.

I was furious with Luisella; and, in my rage, blamed her for Giulia's sudden departure. And I was impatient to talk to her again, as soon as possible. But this time—if Giulia had really rung her before vanishing again—she wouldn't tell me anything, even if she did agree to come to the phone. In fact I suspected Luisella of telling her mother to say she was out. Unless she'd gone out to meet Giulia. But where? Horribly anxious about all these questions, I was shaking at the thought of setting off in pursuit of them again.

I went into the bathroom. It was so small it must have been made out of a built-in cupboard, and of course it had no bathtub, just a plastic tent with the sprinkler of the shower that had been gurgling monotonously all night long. But I didn't get under the shower: all I needed was some coffee. I washed my face, dressed and went downstairs. My beige gabardine suit was quite dry but in a pitiful state.

It was a day of arrivals as well as departures, it seemed: when I went into the hotel bar I found Assenza there. He was sitting on the only stool at the ridiculous round counter, looking out from that eminence at the comings and goings in the hall. Legs dangling, belly poking forward because of his position, he looked uncomfortable.

As soon as I saw him I stopped in the doorway and gazed at the end of the room, as if it were possible and credible that I'd failed to see him in those few square yards. But the gimlet eyes were upon me. Then I pretended to notice his very noticeable presence and, wrinkling my cheeks into a smile of pleasure it was impossible and incredible I should feel, approached him. An empty cup stood in front of him.

'Why on earth are you here?' I asked. Out of all the original things I might have said, I had to choose that.

'You mean, what favourable wind has blown me along?' Just the answer I deserved. 'Well, the same one that blew you. Will you have a coffee?'

Then, when the barman had put a steaming cup in front of me and I'd stopped looking at him, I said: 'Of course. The same wind.'

'But you've been luckier than I have, Iovine,' he said, rambling on as before. 'You got here first.'

I followed his eyes, and, looking out of the window on to the courtyard, saw the ancient blonde still swimming round the pool. Either she hadn't been satisfied with her efforts the previous evening or she hadn't been to bed. Assenza was staring so hard that I was afraid he was going to make some profound remark about her. Instead he said:

'Well, did you manage to talk to her last night?'

With dismay I realised the delicate situation I was in, and above all what an interrogation I could now expect. I couldn't deny that I'd been talking to Giulia under the eyes of all those waiters, nor, on the other hand, could I repeat all I'd heard; I could and must chance to luck, that was all. Assenza's small eyes had in the meantime started staring again: no way out, then.

'Yes, I talked to her but she wouldn't listen to reason. Poor soul, she's shaken and upset, and doesn't know what she's doing. She's now run off again.'

'Of course, because she saw the two bodies, didn't she?'

'Giulia? Oh, we didn't talk about that. She was too upset.'

He was still perched on his stool, quite still, and from up there looked owlishly down at me. 'What about, then? Upset about what?'

I pushed away the cup, which was now empty, and put an elbow on the counter. 'Well, mainly about the accident to her father. You know about it?'

'I know about it.' There was to be no getting off the point that day, and I certainly wasn't going to be allowed to wander. 'And I've found out some other things, too. First, that the woman choked to death...'

Choked? I'd been the first to mention drowning, but deep down I'd never believed it; vaguely I'd foreseen from the very first that something worse had happened. My surprise then was just another attempt to get off the point.

In a few words he foiled my efforts. 'She was choked by having her head held under water. Did you see her eyes? Almost out of their sockets. Secondly, the suitcase and bag found in the hall belong to the girl. Thirdly'—I'd forgotten he was a mathematician, among so much else—'the stains on the dress in the wardrobe were those of the young man's blood. What did she refuse to do?'

'Well... she wouldn't go back to Naples. What else would it be?'

'But wasn't she upset about the accident to her father?'

'Certainly. But you know what these youngsters are like,' I said.

A game of ping-pong. The ball was his questioning, which for quite a time I managed to return, and he sent back again, and so it went on. I managed to say nothing important, and he carried on with the game, glancing at me now and then with an ironic little smile. Then he caught me unawares.

'Why haven't you shaved?' he said.

Mechanically I ran my hand over my cheek. 'I've got nothing with me, I came without luggage.'

'Of course, you left Naples in a great hurry, didn't you?' It was a statement, not a question. The question followed quickly, though: 'How did you know Giulia Miletti was here?'

I thought: if he gets his hands on Luisella he'll squeeze her till he gets her to tell the little I've told her. 'Well, I was upset yesterday evening myself,' I said. 'After all that had happened. D'you know about the other accident, the one that took place before my very eyes? Just before the bomb went off?'

'The car accident? Of course I've heard. He's dead.'

'The man who was hit? Poor fellow.'

'Pasquale Lauria.' He had checked the name on a crumpled scrap of paper he'd taken out of his pocket. 'Yes, he's dead. He leaves a brother,' he added, looking me straight in the eye.

'Ah.' The shiver I had felt so many times since I opened my eyes that morning was now aroused by his eyes and the memory of Tonino.

'Did you know him?'

'The dead man? Never seen him. Why d'you ask?'

He'd laid down the ping-pong bat and the ball was no longer bouncing. Clearly he was tired of the game, for he went on to revelations, perhaps to set me a good example; but without getting away from the point.

'We'd put out a general alert when the girl vanished. This morning Formia told Naples, which told me, so here I am. You're right, it's a wise man that can understand these youngsters. But she should have realised that giving her name in the hotel here was like giving it to the police. And you're right, she must have been upset. But how did you say you knew she was here?'

'I didn't say. I'll tell you now. She rang me up.' It wasn't very plausible but I couldn't find anything better.

'Giulia?' he said, incredulously. 'And where, may I ask? Seeing you're always on the move.'

'In my office, yesterday afternoon. And I'd have come here at once if I hadn't first gone to her father's house, where things happened, as you know.'

'I see.' The trouble was he didn't believe me. 'But why on earth did she ring you? Did she need advice? Consolation? Was there anything between the two of you?'

'What d'you mean?'

'Anything affectionate, let's say.'

'Listen,' I said, 'Giulia's the daughter of a friend, who's in hospital at this very moment. And she's a child.'

'What's that got to do with it? You're not exactly old, even if you are a friend of her father's, and you're certainly not bad looking. Quite a lad, as you say in Naples. Dark, curly-haired, slim, the ideal of plenty of children.' Either he felt like being complimentary or else he was trying to get into my good graces. For a long time he looked at me, then added: 'Even without shaving.'

He twirled round on his stool and tried to find a dignified way of getting off it; not finding one, he took up his owl-like position again.

'You know,' he went on, 'I've been checking up on you and it appears you're a real heartbreaker.' It really was Assenza talking—using these very words. 'What do you do to make all the girls run after you? What have you got, a secret weapon? Before you were living with your present mistress you had another one, a married woman, who helped you in all kinds of ways, if I may put it so.'

'Is it a crime to have a mistress?' I said, annoyed and unnerved by his ironical grin and by what he was saying.

'No, of course not. But when the mistress commits suicide because she's been abandoned and is immediately and quite shamelessly replaced by another, then things look a bit different.'

'She was neurotic, you must have heard that as well,' I said. 'There may have been a thousand other reasons for her suicide.'

'Of course, of course. The fact that the poor creature stole three million from her husband in bonds payable to bearer was probably the reason. What's odd, though, is the fact that the three things happened so close in time: the theft, your leaving her, and the suicide. And I've a suspicion there must have been a fourth thing between the theft and your leaving her: the cashing of the cheques, for instance. By you.'

If it's clever to move like an elephant, trampling everything underfoot, then he was clever. All he needed to ask me was where I'd got the money to buy my car. Quite capable of it.

Meantime, I wished I could find out where he got all his information. Could nobody around here mind his own business?

'You haven't come all the way from Naples to question me, have you?' I said. 'Didn't you come to talk to the girl?' When it came to showing wounded dignity, I must admit I wasn't as good at it as Miletti.

'Of course. I brought all this up on account of the girl. She might—it's just an idea, of course—have a weakness for you, Iovine. Which in turn might make her . . . hand something over to you. What d'you think? You never know. Life often repeats itself.' The Thinker was now speaking.

Beyond the window, the swimmer seemed to have tired at last; she was getting out of the water and, in the harsh sunlight, her gleaming body showed all the saggings and wrinkles of age. Another fanatic. Assenza's round face was smooth and actually looked, in the half-light, as if he'd slept and rested on that intuition (or information?) about Giulia having something I was longing to get hold of. This really annoyed me.

'If you've finished I'll go,' I said. 'I'm in a hurry to get back to Naples, and if you don't mind we can carry on this conversation another time. If you want to continue insulting me you have only to whistle and I'll come crawling on all fours. But I've got to go now.'

And I left him there, with the two empty cups in front of him.

I was almost in the doorway when he caught my attention, still ironic, and not even raising his voice. 'Tonino's beside himself,' he said.

'Tonino?' I'd turned: up there on the stool, his big smiling face looked like a moon that had risen above the hill of his stomach.

'He's blinded with grief,' he said. Pleased, now, as well as smiling. 'Antonio Lauria. Haven't you understood yet? The victim's brother.' This time he hadn't consulted his piece of paper. 'The accident. You haven't forgotten it already, have you?'

'And I . . .'

'How d'you come into it? Oh, come, Iovine, what d'you take

me for? Unfortunately the only thing I haven't got is proof.'

'Proof of what?' I felt stuck there in the doorway.

'You ought to be thankful to that bomb for going off at just the right moment, or else I could have got you on the charge of at least failing to help the victim of an accident.'

'I didn't knock him down,' I said, 'and I wasn't the only motorist going by. What proof, Inspector?'

'Struck by the word, aren't you? Well, proof that what Tonino let slip may be true. But he may have been bluffing. All the same, he did mention your name. And how the hell does Tonino know you, when you don't know him or his brother?'

'I repeat,' I said. 'I don't know this Tonino and I didn't know his brother. When the accident happened, I'd left Miletti's house and was dashing here to Formia.'

'I'm only supposing, and I can tell you I'm very much amazed. I don't believe in coincidences and now I'm asked to believe in a whole string of them. You dash up to Faito and find a couple of corpses. Then you dash off to Formia and on the way you see another death, after leaving a house where there's yet another death and a bomb goes off afterwards. A real bomb, no less. What are we coming to?' He sounded almost scandalised.

'Are you saying I'm involved in all these deaths?' I said.

'Murders, don't forget,' said Assenza. 'And don't forget the woman blown to bits by the explosion. Another murder.' His small eyes flashed. 'No, I'm not saying you're involved, I'm just counting. We've got to four, if you include those at Faito and exclude the accident.' A mathematician, as I said.

Having failed to find a dignified way of doing so, he was now getting down from the stool. He stuck a leg out into space and completed the operation with a clumsy jump, landing on his heels. After which he looked stunned for a moment.

'I see no connection . . .' I said.

'Excuse my saying so, Iovine,' he interrupted, 'but what you see or know doesn't matter much, as long as you keep it to yourself, at least. In the meantime I've had to hold the Bellellas.'

'You've arrested Catello and his wife?'

'Hold on,' he said, and joined me at the door of the bar. 'I haven't got proof against them either.'

'That they killed the two up at Faito? But that's absurd.'

'You can never be too careful. Why on earth are you so worried about that wretched pair? It's not like you. Is there something I don't know? For instance, about Giulia and her comings and goings at Faito?'

He was always able to catch me unprepared. 'Comings and goings?' I said.

'I must say, your habit of answering questions with other questions is rather annoying,' he said. 'Anyway, I want you to know: Giulia's been up there more than once. I don't know what she saw or heard or did, all I know is that both times she managed to forget her suitcase and bag.' He was moving towards the entrance hall, as if to see me on my way.

I followed him, resignedly. 'You really believe the girl confided something to me yesterday evening, don't you?' I said. As if there was the least chance of shaking him in what he believed.

He didn't reply. He was busy looking around, clearly annoyed.

'She told me nothing,' I went on. 'Nothing at all. She didn't say anything about Faito. When you meet her you'll know I'm telling you the truth, Inspector. That girl can really keep things to herself.'

'Like her father?' he said suddenly, twirling round to look at me.

He walked out to the car with me, after keeping me company while I paid the hotel bill. His last question hung heavily between us.

When I shut the car door, after lowering the window, he leaned against it. Persecution.

Nightmare, rather. Because, implacable to the end, he carried on. 'You haven't answered my question,' he said.

The car had been parked in the sun and the steering wheel and seat were scorching. So that made me uncomfortable too, apart from the little eyes I could feel boring into me.

'What am I supposed to answer, Inspector?' I said. 'Whatever I say, either you don't believe it or you're ironical about it. And I really am tired, believe me.' This at least was perfectly true.

'So was Don Michele, as you call him,' he said. I'd never called him that in Assenza's presence, I was quite certain. 'He was tired as well, when I went along to see him yesterday evening, after you'd left.'

'In hospital? I can well believe it, the state he was in. You'd want a corpse to give you a statement.'

'He was awake,' Assenza went on, as if I hadn't interrupted. 'They'd put his shoulder in plaster. I don't say he was well but he was certainly able to talk. Nothing doing, he wouldn't answer a single question. Pig-headed. Like his daughter, by the sound of it.'

The engine came to life the moment I turned the ignition key, but he didn't move from where he was, his face stuck almost inside the car. I could feel his hot breath on my neck.

He continued chasing me, delaying me. 'What I say is,' he said, 'if a bomb goes off in somebody's house, the least it can do is loosen that somebody's tongue. But oh no, he was tired. Nobody'd believe it, if you told them.' Without realising he was the unbelievable one. At last he withdrew his head from the window. 'And now you're tired. First thing in the morning, soon after you've got up.'

I reversed and saw him framed in the windscreen, his image shifted on to the curved side of the glass, which seemed to make him look longer and thinner.

'As far as I'm concerned, it's true,' I said. 'Even if I've only just got up and I'm not in hospital after a bomb blew up practically in my face.' I poked out my head. 'Goodbye, I must go.'

'Go, go,' he almost shouted.

When I passed him, as I turned, he went down to his knees so that his face was framed in the window at the height of mine. To avoid missing his last chance of telling me, he spoke in a single breath.

'We freed the Bellellas early this morning. Tonino's vanished.

That reminds me, the mystery lasted less than twenty-four hours: we know he was called Giuseppe Gargiulo . . .'

The rest was drowned in the roar of the engine and lost in the distance.

That reminds me. Reminds me of what? Oh, to hell with him.

At the hotel entrance gate the uniformed porter waved me obsequiously off.

17

Mondragone was becoming a regular staging-post in my life. It wasn't far from Formia and if necessary, once I'd at last spoken to Luisella, I might even make a small effort and return there. Meantime I'd put a few miles between myself and that terrible Assenza. I stopped outside the bar I'd been in the previous evening and went in to telephone.

Alone, and obviously bored, the owner recognised me and greeted me with a broad, delighted smile. I ordered a coffee, feeling I needed rather than wanted it.

Luisella's mother answered again and this time it was clear, from the way she hesitated, that her daughter had decided not to come to the telephone ever again. Luisella was still out, she told me, and she had no idea when she'd be back. Then she asked who I was, regretted it, and put the receiver down suddenly, without waiting for a reply. In spite of the two packets of sugar, my coffee tasted bitter.

About midday Luisella still wasn't back. I called from another bar, having decided not to give up and at the same time not to give her mother any satisfaction: this time, before she could do so, I slammed down suddenly, as soon as she had asked who I was, correctly but incuriously.

When I left the bar, which was cool and shady, I was blinded by the sunshine on the long rocky slope that ran dazzlingly from the road down to Lake Patria, which lay below, glittering and blue, with a few scattered umbrella-pines around it.

Then I looked at the parking area of the service station there beside me. I'd driven all that way in the sun—in that sun—sweating and dazzled, and put only a few yards between myself and Assenza: there he was, shaded by the roof over the pumps, his hands resting on the top of the black police car which the attendant was filling up with petrol, enjoying the coolness and chatting to the policeman at the wheel, who had taken off his cap and was wiping round the inner edge of it with a handkerchief. Although talking hard to this other victim of his, he had still seen me, because he suddenly turned in my direction and, without interrupting himself, greeted me with a wave.

I stood stockstill on the step outside the bar, unable to cross the short space from there to my car for fear of being intercepted by him. But he was expecting me to go back into the bar.

'Iovine,' he called. 'Alessandro Iovine!'

So the nightmare wasn't over. I stood there, one foot in the bar, the other on the step outside it.

When he came across I saw that he wasn't smiling; in fact his face was made serious, even sinister, by the dark glasses.

'Don't worry, I'm not following you,' he said. 'Were you going in again? Shall we have another coffee?'

'Thanks, I've just had one,' I said.

'Pity. You make me give up the idea,' he said. 'But weren't you going in?'

'I was going to the loo,' I said; but if this had been true I might have burst under his very eyes, because he continued talking, quite unruffled.

'Oh, fine,' he said. 'Well, as I was saying, I'm not following you. We're just going in the same direction. I had no more reason than you had to stay on at Formia.' The glasses were very dark, a black stain like his moustache, and I couldn't make out the expression in his eyes. 'Weren't you in a hurry, though?'

'Yes, why?' I said.

'Then how did I manage to catch up with you? You left a long time before me.' As if he were talking to a friend on some weekend outing.

'You want to know everything, don't you?' I said. 'All right, this is the second time I've stopped. D'you want to know why?'

'You've already told me. At least one of the whys. You see, I was just surprised, because I saw you rush off at such a rate that I thought you hadn't heard the last thing I said.'

'About the Bellellas?' I said. 'Well, I did.'

'No, about Gargiulo. Pino.' This time I thought I could see where his eyes were resting. I could feel them on me, burning like the sun, in spite of the screen of those very dark glasses. 'It wasn't difficult to identify him, they'd got a record of him at headquarters. Drugs. I was afraid you hadn't heard.'

He was putting out his claws. I was the mouse and I started struggling.

'Yes, I'd heard it,' I said. 'But the name means nothing to me.'

'It means nothing to you,' he said carefully. Then he shot out, suddenly: 'D'you know Inspector Lentizzi?'

'Yes, why?' I almost jumped. And at the same time I wondered: if he hadn't caught up with me on the way back to Naples, when would he have dealt this card? What had he decided to do, persecute me for the rest of my life?

'You seem to like playing with "Why?"' he said. 'Well, because the charge against Gargiulo was made by Lentizzi and on Wednesday evening, after you'd found Gargiulo's body, you telephoned Lentizzi from Faito, without managing to speak to him.'

'What about it?' I said. 'Are you trying to say that as I know Lentizzi I'm supposed to know all the people he's charged, including this Gargiulo? I rang him for advice. With a couple of corpses in the house, I had no idea what to do.'

'You never told me you'd made this second phone call,' said Assenza.

'Obviously I forgot. It didn't seem to me all that important, and it still doesn't. May I go now?' Perhaps my struggles had been successful.

'To the loo?'

I could have strangled him. 'Wherever I like,' I said.

'One last thing,' said Assenza. 'As your hearing's good, you'll also have heard what I said about Tonino Lauria.'

I didn't answer; instead I pushed aside the bead curtain of the bar door.

'He was supposed to sign the document for the release of the body from the mortuary, but he didn't turn up. He's vanished. I heard on the phone.'

'And why are you telling me?' I asked.

'Because I suspect he's out looking for you.'

I dropped the bead curtain. 'Why for me?' I said.

'Why, why. I've told you, he was savage. Anyway, that's your business.' As if it wasn't enough for him to poison my existence on his own account, he had to poke the memory of that other nightmare under my nose as well. Then, catching me unawares as always, he drew out yet another claw, one that was quite unexpected and sharper than the rest. 'That reminds me,' he said, 'have you heard about Casali?'

It was the second time he'd put it that way; what thread of logic led him to think and talk about particular things? 'What reminds you?'

'Tonino does, for heaven's sake,' he replied, and with the right-hand index finger on his nose pushed the glasses up, leaving his small black eyes naked. 'Early this morning Casali's car was blown up. I heard it at Formia as well, by phone. Another bomb. Tit for tat.' This time he wasn't shocked, merely amused.

'And what about him? Casali,' I said.

'He was still in bed. An exchange of messages, obviously. Only they've got it in for the chauffeurs. This one's dead as well. You worried?'

'Me? No, not in the least,' I said.

'I thought you were,' said Assenza. 'Ever heard of the Castellammarese war? Well, maybe not. Not quite in your line, is it? Anyway, there's nothing new under the sun.' After which deep thought he moved away, returning to the black car, which had now left the petrol pump and was parked with its engine running. Assenza climbed into it and vanished, leaving me to wonder how on earth he had linked Tonino with Casali and, more importantly, Casali with me.

In spite of its name, Acacia Villa had neither a garden nor any acacias. It was a large grey building with a useless gate in front of it and a kind of tail that stretched back into a concrete-covered yard. Each time they'd added to the house, it was clear that they'd increased the size of the yard. There wasn't much room left for stretching in, though: on one side a large building rose, just like all the others that ran along that side of via Caravaggio, and on the other the windows looked out on to the blast furnaces of Bagnoli. An ideal place for invalids and convalescents.

By now, Miletti should have been transferred here from the public hospital, and when I saw the old grey 124 parked with its wheels on the pavement outside the gate I knew the transfer had taken place.

For more than a minute I hesitated. I hadn't been home or to the office, but had gone straight to the nursing home, certain that I'd thus escape Tonino. Yet there he was, waiting for me. That second bomb must have made him wilder than ever: he'd left his much-loved brother in the mortuary to come after me and had stopped taking even the smallest precautions, leaving the old crock quite recognisably there, in full view. Very likely he'd settled himself outside Miletti's door, or was even hiding behind it.

He wasn't in the road. It was almost empty, apart from occasional cars passing along it. So he was inside. For a moment I thought of rushing home; it was a good chance to shave and change. Then it struck me that if we met there things would be exactly opposite to the way they'd be here—we'd be facing each other alone. Suffering might have maddened Tonino to such an extent that he'd pull out that knife of his even in the presence of doctors and nurses. But if that did happen, first aid would be at hand, at least.

When I went in, after parking at the end of the line of cars, the hall was even emptier than the road, though. Behind the porter's abandoned counter, the switchboard was sending out metallic gurgles, accompanied by the restless flashes of winking red and green lights.

The lift was beyond a glass door, at the start of a very long passage that matched the shape of the buildings—probably going to the furthest point of its ridiculous tail-end. This passage wasn't just empty but was silent, unlike the hall. Suddenly, from the end of the stretch of shiny green linoleum, came a squeak of rubber soles: a man in a white overall was coming towards me. Automatically I raised an arm to attract his attention, but he didn't see me. He opened a door and vanished, leaving me once more anxious and alone.

Above the lift door, the illuminated square was alight at number one, and when I pressed the button a second time nothing happened, the number still stayed alight. Obviously, I thought, at this time of day they blocked the lift and all went off for lunch, leaving nobody but the patients and madmen armed with knives. I'd never find anyone to tell me where Miletti's room was, particularly there on the ground floor which, being so easy to come into, made me feel more exposed than ever.

When I turned round I saw the stairs for the first time, directly opposite the lift. I went across and as I was putting my foot on the first step the silence behind me was suddenly broken by the crash of the lift's double doors opening. For a moment I stood there, puzzled. I looked at the inside of the lift, which was waiting for me there, and then, above me on the second flight of the narrow, walled-in staircase, I saw two feet in parti-coloured shoes, black and white, coming down the top steps at that very moment. By leaping away, I was just in time to get inside the lift before the doors closed automatically. When I grazed them on my way in they stopped with a shudder; then jerked shut as soon as I pressed a button, quite haphazardly. Before they met, though, I was just in time to see, through the intersections, a pair of grey trouser legs above parti-coloured shoes, half-way down the second flight of the staircase opposite. So he hadn't seen me.

I'd only just leant panting against the grained wall of the lift when it stopped and the doors re-opened. I was on the first floor, just above the head of that blood-thirsty beast. I then pressed the top button hard, the one for the third floor, and went on up, wishing the ascent would never end, that it would carry on beyond the building's roofs and terraces, and whisk me away out of reach.

But it stopped on the third floor, after barely a minute, and this time I had to get out of it, still sweating and panting.

I found myself in another passage, much shorter than the other one and dazzlingly white in the sunshine that poured in through the wide windows along one of its walls. At the end, towards what I thought must be the front of the nursing home, was another window, also open. I went cautiously up to it and, a step away from the windowsill, bending forward and putting the weight of my body on to one leg, I leant across and peered out, careful not to poke my head too far forward. Yes, the window looked out onto the road.

And Tonino was down there immediately below me, walking alone in the sunshine up and down outside the entrance to the nursing home. When he reached the place where the old 124 was parked, he stopped undecidedly; but at that moment I heard footsteps behind me and was suddenly aware of the ridiculous position in which I found myself, perched there behind the windowsill, leaning forward on one leg.

'Are you looking for something?' said a voice: a reasonable question, in the circumstances.

When I turned, a nun who looked as if she'd just come out of a laundry, being dressed in white from head to foot, was staring at me sternly from the lift door.

'Are you looking for someone?' she asked.

'Yes, Mr Miletti's room,' I said. 'He should have come in this morning.'

'The one who was hurt in the explosion?' she said, without taking her eyes off me. Suspicious old hag.

'That's the one,' I said. How could I possibly explain that I hadn't been able to shave?

'Don't you know he's not allowed visitors?' she said. 'The room's sealed off by the police, in fact. He must be under arrest.'

'Under arrest? That's impossible,' I said. 'No, there was no one downstairs. There's no one in the whole place.'

She took no notice of this last remark, as if such a thing were absolutely normal; what's more she seemed cross with me on account of it. 'You shouldn't have come up here,' she said.

'Sister,' I said, 'I couldn't find anyone so I came up.' I'd been listening hard, but hadn't heard the car moving off.

'And who told you he was on this floor?' There must be some kind of proverb that says: a day that starts with an interrogation will continue with interrogations.

'Nobody told me, sister, I just guessed it,' I said, ready to go down on my knees and say a prayer if only it would stop her.

She did stop, thank heaven. 'Well, this Miletti's in room 308,' she said. 'Turn left at the end of the passage.' Abrupt even when she made concessions. 'But the policeman won't let you in, you'll see. Some other people came and he didn't let them in. Specially the last one. A funny fellow, that.' And she stared at me again. Then, with a flick of her hand, she ordered the lift door to open. 'We've never had people like that in here before, nor the police,' she went on. 'Who'd have thought it?' And with a rustle of her white skirts, she vanished into the lift.

I went back to the window and took up my previous position. No-one was down in the street and the 124 was still there. I went across to the other corner of the windowsill and leant further out. Tonino was down there, almost at the end of the row of cars parked half on the pavement. When he reached mine, the last car, he stopped suddenly. Then he looked around, and I drew back in a hurry. I might have guessed he wouldn't give up easily. He might even have tried to take it out on Miletti. Blinded by suffering, Assenza had been right. Old Don Michele probably owed his life to Assenza's prudence, in fact.

Then I became even more agitated, thinking the madman was going to destroy my car. Instead I heard the sound of running footsteps. I leant out again: Tonino was running towards the entrance of the nursing home. He reached it and opened the gate, holding on to one of the gateposts as he came round the bend.

For a moment I stood there, hesitating. I looked at the stairs and then opposite them, at the lift. In the illuminated square, number two had switched off. The nun had got out on the second floor. I waited another minute and when I saw number one light up I knew that someone had sent for it from below.

It was then that I made my second mistake; the first had been to leave the car outside. Instead of running downstairs and, now that the road below was empty, getting completely away, I panted down to the end of the passage, to the only other safe place which Assenza's prudence and far-sightedness offered, to me as well as Miletti.

18

I saw the policeman at once, as soon as I turned the sharp bend in the passage. He was sitting on a chair beside the door, looking bored to death, a rolled-up newspaper in his hand, with which he kept tapping the knee of his crossed leg. On the door, when I got there, I saw the number 308 in metal figures.

That windowless stretch of passage was pretty dark, so I didn't at once see the two figures sitting in a kind of waiting room where the wall was set back, exactly opposite the policeman: Marullo and Catello.

They were sitting silent and still, opposite each other on two small armchairs made of metal and green plastic, with the absorbed, regretful air of relations called out of nowhere in particular by news of a death in the family. When I greeted them with a nod they both nodded back, then sat quite still again.

I turned to the policeman. 'Is this Mr Miletti's room?' I said.

He seemed glad of a chance to talk, to be distracted; he was young and, in spite of his initially abrupt tone, polite.

'Yes, but you can't go in,' he said. 'I have definite orders.'

'I'm his financial adviser,' I said. This nearly always worked; sometimes any sort of title would do.

And in fact he seemed to hesitate. But it was only a feeling I had. 'It's impossible,' he said. 'Quite soon, at two, I'll be relieved and you can ask my colleague. Orders may be less strict by then.'

'I'm a friend of Inspector Assenza,' I said.

'I tell you, it's impossible,' he said again.

'Was it he who ordered this room to be guarded?' I asked.

'I wouldn't know, I'm from Fuorigrotta and I don't know anyone called Assenza. The order came from HQ.'

'D'you know how he is, at least?'

'A broken shoulder and a touch of pneumonia, it seems. It isn't often they put a guard on someone who isn't under arrest.'

At that moment I heard, far beyond the bend in the passage, the lift doors opening: then the sound of footsteps. They came closer.

At the same time a door beside the waiting room opened and a nun came out into the passage, making for Miletti's room. At the end of that short stretch of passage a nurse appeared, pushing a trolley. The nursing home was suddenly waking up.

When Tonino came round the bend in the passage I was

already between the nun, who was standing outside the door, and the seated policeman. He saw me at once and slowed down. I turned to the nun.

'Sister, can you tell me how Mr Miletti is?' I asked.

'When they brought him in this morning his temperature was up a little. Then it went up again. I'm going to take it again now. But he may be asleep.' She opened the door, looked in and immediately drew back and shut it. 'He's asleep. I'll take it later, that's a better idea.' And she moved off.

When she met Tonino, a few yards further on, she stopped. 'Still here?' she exclaimed. Then she turned to us. 'Officer, here's the gentleman we told you about . . . the one who tried to get into the room while you were away. It was very hard to persuade him.'

The policeman got up and went across to them. Tonino was saying: 'What's wrong with that? Can't a man visit a relation?'

Grim-faced, and with the stubborn expression of a madman: there was no doubt about him now.

'What d'you want?' asked the policeman, uptight, even stern.

The nurse had reached us, in the meantime; she left the trolley outside the door of Miletti's room and went up to the nun and the policeman. 'Yes, it's him,' she said. 'I had to drag him from the door by main force. He wouldn't listen to reason.' She turned to the policeman, who was now not only stern but astonished, and hastened to make her report. 'I was serving No. 310, when I heard this man raising his voice to two of the nuns. And this is a nursing home after all! The place itself deserves a little respect, even if the nuns don't, that's what I say. Anyway, I had to run and take his arm and drag him away from there.' She turned to indicate the door and thus lost the attention of her small audience. 'Those two gentlemen sitting there saw everything, they were there,' she went on pointlessly, indicating Marullo and Catello, who had merely turned to look.

But the policeman was taking no more notice of her, and had turned to Tonino, who now had his back to the wall and was glaring at me with hatred.

'Who are you?' he asked. 'You can't stay here.'

'Why not?' said Tonino, more stubbornly than ever, still glaring at me. 'He's here.' And he indicated me with his finger, as if pointing a pistol at me.

Prudently I moved, putting the policeman and the nurse between myself and him.

'This gentleman has only just arrived, and anyway he hasn't made a fuss about going in,' the policeman replied.

'I'm not making a fuss either,' said Tonino. 'I'll just stop here and wait.' And he squeezed even closer to the wall, thus disarming the policeman and the two others.

The nun left the group and moved away, waving her hand vaguely as if making the sign of the cross; the nurse went back to fetch her trolley, still grumbling indignantly; the policeman stayed in front of Tonino, on his own. After a while he gave up as well and returned to his chair, and the short scene ended as it had begun, quite suddenly. Silence returned to the passage, apart from the squeaking of the trolley which the nurse was pushing towards the lift, beyond the bend. The siege had begun.

There was now nobody between Tonino and me, and with a bound he could have leapt across the space that divided us. So I took myself off a couple of steps and placed myself between Marullo and Catello. At this point I could only sit down: so I took the small armchair between them.

So there I was, besieged under the very eyes of the police, with that criminal lurking at the bend in the passage, like a vulture waiting for me to die. He was further away than the policeman, admittedly, but standing and obviously, being more agile and decisive, ready to leap upon me. I couldn't move and yet, more vehemently than ever, I felt an urgent need to talk to Lentizzi, as well as Luisella.

After a while the nun came back, lowering her head in the passage as she passed Tonino, and opened the door of the room. For a moment I caught a glimpse of Miletti's form under the white sheet. That was all, because the door shut again immediately and my fifty thousand francs faded away once more.

I glanced again at Tonino, who was standing perfectly still, lit a cigarette and spoke to Catello, who was now sitting sideways on his armchair, half turned towards me. 'Been here long?' I said. As if he were an acquaintance at a wake.

'Since this morning,' he answered at once. 'You see, they freed us and I rushed over to see how Don Michele was. Because they arrested me and my wife, you know. That was all we needed—after the trouble we're going through already. But there's nothing to be done about it. As if we'd killed the pair of them. Anyway, I always do my duty, so I came along here to see how he was. Troubles never come singly. First he loses his wife the way he did, then there's this bomb.' He wanted to talk. Clearly he couldn't stand much more.

Marullo, on the other hand, could clearly stand plenty. When I asked him the same question he answered briefly and succinctly. 'Not long. I shut up the office and came here,' he said, making me realise quite suddenly that I didn't know what his voice sounded like. I'd never actually heard him speak—to me he'd always expressed himself in gestures and nods.

I glanced at the clock, then looked at the crouching hyena again and finally at the policeman. It was just before two and he'd soon be relieved. I'd thought of a way, perhaps the only way, of getting out of that situation. But in the meantime, seeing I was stuck there, I decided to make the most of it. Once again I turned to Catello.

'Would you mind leaving us on our own for a moment?' I asked him. 'I'd like a word with Mr Marullo.'

His arrest, though it had lasted only a short while, or the 'trouble' he was going through, must have brought him very low. 'Of course not,' he answered, anxious to please. 'I'm at your service.' And, with an obvious effort, he got up and moved away from us, passing Tonino without minding in the least. His long, greasy beard and shabby suit made him look even older, even more tired, than he had done before. How, even for a short while, they could ever have suspected him of being a murderer was an even greater mystery than the death of Pino and Tina.

Marullo had sat quite still, in the meantime, staring into space, as if what I'd just said had absolutely nothing to do with him. With his big head almost sunk into his hump, and his eternally sulky expression, he seemed to have managed to find there the same position in which I'd always seen him. He wasn't going to adapt himself to his surroundings, they had to transform themselves around him: all he needed was his desk. And he didn't bat an eyelash when I said to him:

'Did you know Pino Gargiulo?'

He didn't even answer, but merely turned his great head towards me, slowly, without moving a muscle, as if I'd started up some mechanism inside him that could make just that movement and no other. As for his voice, he must have lost it again.

'I've spoken to Miss Giulia, mind, and she's told me everything,' I went on.

He hadn't lost his voice, but the mechanism had jammed. His head didn't move, and his short-sighted eyes stared pointlessly at me. 'Everything about what?' he said in his rasping voice.

'That it was you who introduced him to her. In the office. What was he doing there? How did you know each other?'

'Do I have to tell you about it?' he said.

'I think you do,' I replied. 'It would be the best thing for you, otherwise you'll have to tell Don Michele about it.'

With a jerk that made even the hump shudder, the mechanism got going again, and his head gave a half turn, then suddenly stopped. I had guessed rightly: Miletti knew the boy but didn't know Marullo knew him as well. Perhaps it wouldn't be hard to guess the rest, if I asked the right questions, and, even more, if I got the right answers.

'He used to come and get the money every fortnight,' said Marullo. 'I gave him a sort of allowance.'

'An allowance from you?' I was pressing him hard; our roles

were now reversed. I no longer had to endure questioning, yet I was still worried by the slowness with which he spoke. 'Money you'd stashed away? Was Pino anything to do with you?'

'Of course not, what d'you mean?' he said. 'It was money I was given to hand over to him. That's all. That was the end of it.' Of course, Marullo the cashier. He was giving money to both of them when he introduced them, Pino and Giulia.

'Was it Don Michele who gave him this money?' It wasn't really a question, but I wanted confirmation. If I didn't get it I'd not only guessed wrong but was hardly likely to understand anything else.

'What an idea,' he said. 'No sir, I was given the money by someone you don't know, who has nothing to do with this whole business.' He was uneasy, I realised, when he actually shifted his position on the chair.

At that moment Tonino came across to stub his cigarette out in the ashtray on the table in front of us, and as he leant down he never took his eyes off me. I looked quickly at the policeman: as soon as the hyena moved from the wall he'd got up, and was now standing half a yard away from him. When Tonino went back to the wall, he stayed where he was, standing beside the chair.

My relief was short-lived: the interruption had broken the spell and Marullo was now totally quiet; clinging like a monkey with hands and feet to a tree-trunk of stubborn silence. Clearly he already regretted having spoken.

'You hate Don Michele, don't you?' I said, firing on the off-chance.

He now changed completely; there were no more mechanical movements, there was no stiffness. He bent over to one side, with a clumsy jerk typical of a cripple, and I almost felt sorry for him. 'You hate him, don't you?' I pressed on.

'What are you saying?' he exclaimed, raising his voice.

'And you used to talk to Gargiulo, didn't you? You didn't just give him the money, did you?'

'What are you saying?' he repeated. Scared.

'You used to tell him about Don Michele, about what went on in the office,' I said. 'And outside it, too.'

One side of him seemed painful. He raised a hand to the height of his ribs, on the side, and with an effort straightened up. 'I said nothing to him,' he answered at once. 'I paid him, that's all.'

'And who gave you the money? Why was it given to you?'

'That's not your business nor mine. I can't tell you. Don Michele'd got nothing to do with it, though. Not with the money, nor with the lad. He never even saw him, because I used to get him along when he wasn't there. He'd ring up and I'd tell him whether he could come or not.'

'You're sure it wasn't Don Michele's money?' I said. 'Even though Don Michele knew nothing about it?'

'Are you mad?' he cried. 'What are you saying? What are you thinking?' He could hardly manage to speak. It struck me that he seemed too agitated, too frightened, as if I'd touched some tender spot. Perhaps I really was asking the right questions.

I looked at my watch again: it was ten to two. The policeman was looking at his watch as well; he too was impatient to get away. I must hurry.

'Don Michele never saw the boy in the office,' I said. 'But he knew him, didn't he, Marullo?'

He was still agitated, but this time he thought for a long time before answering. Then he said: 'Yes sir.'

'You don't know how he knew him?'

He'd decided to keep me on tenterhooks, now, because he took even longer to answer. 'No sir,' he said at last. 'I don't know anything. I just paid out the money, that was all.'

'Which came to you from someone else? Where from? Outside Naples.'

'I don't have to tell you where the money came from,' he said.

'Well, how much money? You can tell me that, at least.'

'Not much. Just enough to carry on for the month. He didn't need much.'

'Of course, you knew him well, didn't you? So well that you talked about the COOFA to him, didn't you?'

He was as agitated as he'd been before: this was where I must press the questions: if it wasn't a wound, it was at least a bruise. 'I didn't say anything, I tell you,' he said. 'I hardly know what the COOFA is myself.'

'Marullo, you always keep your eyes and ears open,' I said, 'and you know all about the file as well.'

'What file?' he protested, but a flash in his shining, short-sighted eyes betrayed him.

'You know perfectly well,' I said, hoping I'd got it right. 'As you couldn't see it in the office you thought Don Michele must be keeping it at home. And you told the boy.'

'What are you saying?' he repeated.

'It's not what I'm saying, it's what Miss Giulia told me,' I said.

'What does she know about it? How does she come into it?' He was angry now and his shining eyes gave him an air of impotence.

'You knew the pair of them were in cahoots, don't deny it,' I said.

'I do, I do deny it,' he cried. 'I swear to God I didn't know. And what d'you mean by cahoots?'

'Lower your voice,' I said. 'You don't want everyone to hear.' In fact the policeman, who was still standing opposite us, was watching us curiously. 'Marullo,' I went on, 'whatever you said to Gargiulo, it's just as if you said it all to Miss Giulia. So there's no point in denying it.'

He'd been looking at the policeman, but now turned to me, as ramrod straight as if he'd got a stiff neck. 'I never said anything to him about the file,' he said. 'It was he who asked me where it was.' Then he nearly collapsed.

'Which means?' I said, pressing hard, well aware that I'd overcome all his resistance and was now merely fighting against time; at any moment the second policeman might turn up. 'That he knew the file existed?'

'How do I know?' said Marullo. 'Casali must have told him.'
'Casali?'

He nodded, in a way that was obviously painful to him.

Casali as well. 'Gargiulo knew him?' I said; then had a new suspicion. 'Was the money given him by Casali?'

'No, sir. I told you, the money came from someone who's got nothing to do with all this. And now don't ask me how he knew Casali, because I don't know.'

'I'm not asking you, I'm asking you how Casali came to know of the existence of the file.'

Marullo didn't answer. Instead he looked—for the first time, I think, since he'd come over to stub his cigarette out in the ashtray—at Tonino. I followed his eyes: the hyena seemed to have come closer, by creeping a few steps along the wall.

'Know him?' I asked.

He turned, still stiff-necked, towards me. 'Never seen him,' he said.

I then made the third mistake of that appalling day. 'He's one of Casali's men,' I said.

From then Marullo shut up completely, even biting his lips, as if to prevent himself quite definitely from speaking.

My only consolation was that soon afterwards I couldn't in any case have stayed to listen, because the second policeman popped up round the corner of the passage, cap in hand. I looked at my watch, automatically: five past two. Slightly late.

He went up to his colleague, putting on his cap, and the pair of them exchanged a few words. I got up suddenly and at the same time, I saw, Tonino moved away from the wall. Ready for action.

'Sergeant,' I said, going up to the pair of them and addressing the first.

'I'm not a sergeant,' he replied, but pleasantly.

'Well, whatever it is. I don't know what to call you. D'you mind asking your colleague if he can let me into the room?'

'Impossible.' Just what I expected and was hoping. 'He was saying that very thing. He's got the same orders as I had.'

'Are you leaving?' I asked him then.

'Yes, why?'

'Mind if I come along with you?'

He didn't understand, and waved his rolled-up newspaper. 'No, I don't mind. It's just that . . .'

'I'll explain later,' I said. 'Shall we go?' Puzzled, he said goodbye to the other man and with me beside him set off for the lift.

I didn't look at Tonino as I passed him; instead glanced back at Marullo. He was sitting quite still, staring into space after taking up, I think, his previous, familiar position.

While we were waiting for the lift, I glanced down to the end of the passage. Catello, in the corner, greeted me by shaking his head and bowing. The Twin, who was now beside him, looked at us with the same puzzled air as the policeman had had before. He too had been caught offguard. Then he began coming towards us, but at that moment the lift doors opened and we went inside.

'Strictly speaking, you know, the rank of sergeant exists only in the carabinieri,' the policeman was explaining to me. 'In any case, I'm just a plain copper,' he went on, showing me the sleeve of his blue shirt, which had no stripes on it. He was really a nice fellow, but I was thinking of Tonino, who must then have been running down the stairs.

'Have they come to fetch you by car?' I asked.

'Yes, they brought my colleague and they'll take me back,' he replied.

'Would it be too much to ask you to come with me as far as my car?' I said. 'I left it outside the gate.'

'Well . . . if you like. But you still haven't explained . . .'

'That bloke upstairs. Did you see him? He's a madman. You must have realised yourself. All he did was stare at me. The fact is, I'm scared.'

We were now in the entrance hall, with the switchboard still sending out red and green flashes. But there was now a uniformed man behind the counter.

Tonino was outside the gate, though, obviously out of breath. A little further on was the police car, with three blue caps behind the windows.

'Don't you think you're exaggerating?' the policeman asked me.

'See him? There he is. What was I telling you? I'm scared, I tell you.'

'Right. I'll come with you.'

And he came. Not only that, but he waited until I'd reversed and set off, waving and thanking him with frantic gestures of one hand. The moment I pressed the accelerator a bit, the car responded, with a jerk that seemed as nervous as I was. A horse that could feel its rider's moods and feelings.

19

'Fiorentini police station, fifth district,' said the voice, different this time but just as abrupt as the previous one.

'I'd like to speak to Inspector Lentizzi,' I said.

'He's out for lunch,' said the voice. 'Who's speaking?'

I didn't reply; I hung up. Lentizzi really was laying it on a bit: what with breakfast, lunch, tea, supper and all those cups of coffee, he was hardly ever in the office.

I was in mine, though it was still upside down and abandoned as ever. At home, where I'd gone to shave and change, the telephone wires had been cut, so I couldn't ring up from there. Still horribly on edge, I'd run to the office, quite literally creeping along the walls and walking the whole way, because I'd put the car into a garage in via Imbriani, hoping the bereaved, ferocious Twin wouldn't go poking his ugly snout into that, at least.

As I drove off at the nursing home, I saw him in the driving mirror running to his car and a little later the old crock was chasing after me along via Caravaggio, before the final bend in it. But I managed to shake him off quite easily and shot straight home. A cunning move, I thought, since it was the last place on earth I should have gone to, considering it was the first place he'd have gone looking for me. There or in my office. I just hoped he'd reasoned in the same way.

He must have done so; so he was either less stupid than I'd thought him, or even more so. Who could say? The fact remained that I'd been the one to behave like a madman. I'd changed and shaved and, when I'd satisfied what had by now become an obsession, I'd been faced with the nightmare of how to get away. By creeping downstairs and then along the streets, in fact. And, as if that wasn't enough, I'd now gone and hidden myself in this other trap. The five thousand lire I'd given the office porter assured me of a warning by the intercom if the creature turned up at the door, but how could I be sure he hadn't settled down opposite it?

The balcony was open. On all fours I crept ignominiously out and, actually resting my chin on the marble, peered between the bars. At three in the afternoon the street could hardly fail to be empty. On my side, at least. I repeated the operation to look at the other. The local authority building opposite had been empty for the past hour, so the other side of the street was empty too. Only slightly reassured, I crept back indoors. Better put off the problem till the last possible moment.

I went to the telephone and dialled the number. At this hour she must certainly have got back, even if she'd ever actually set foot outside the house. Engaged.

Nervously I lit a cigarette and had only just put out the match when the telephone rang. It was Luisella.

'I called you a while ago and it was engaged,' I said. 'Obviously you were ringing me.'

'No, because I'm in Naples,' she said; friendly, from the tone of voice.

'In Naples? I've been trying to get you in Formia all the morning and you're in Naples? Whereabouts?'

'At the station. Can I come to your office? I've got to talk to you.'

'No,' I said. My reaction was immediate and spontaneous, and linked with the memory of that vulture lurking outside, quite capable of perching on the balcony railings. Instinctively I turned to check.

'I see. All right, pretend I never said it.' Ready to start one of her pathetic scenes.

'What d'you see? I want to talk to you too, but you can't come here. It's dangerous.'

'The same old game? Who is it this time? The big bad wolf?'

'Luisella, don't let's start up again, please. We can't talk on the phone. If I tell you you can't, you can't. It's still the Twins, OK? Anyway you needn't be funny about them. It's just one of the Twins, in fact. The other's dead.'

'But who are these twins? And what are they up to, dying off like that? No, we can't talk on the phone. I've got to see you. It's terribly important.' Always dramatic, of course.

'Giulia?' I said, filled with hope.

'You never understand a thing. It's about me, don't you realise?' As if it had ever been possible to follow her. 'You know, I'm sorry I did what I did. Going away, that is. I . . . I just can't leave you.' Melodramatic, too.

'But what about Giulia, where is she? Did you see her this morning?'

'I talk about myself and you ask me about Giulia. Yes, yes, I saw her. And afterwards I tried to find you, at home and in the office. Forgive me for last night, I didn't know you really wanted to help her. She told me she felt sorry for you, too.'

She felt sorry for me? Well, I always thought women were at their most unpredictable around the age of thirty. I hadn't reckoned on eighteen-year-olds, obviously.

'She allows herself the luxury of pitying me,' I said, 'with the mess she's in herself?'

'You don't understand. It's as if she's changed her opinion of you. In other words, she sees you in a new light.'

'No, you're wrong, I do understand. It's that she regrets having told me about you and Pino.'

'Me and Pino?' And she allowed herself a laugh. A nervous little laugh, but a laugh all the same.

'Exactly, and that you've been through it yourself. That's exactly what she said. You've got to tell me about this Pino.'

'And you've got to tell me about all the girls you've been with in the meantime.' As usual, she was counter-attacking; she hadn't realised, though, what I really meant to say. I tried to explain it to her.

'First of all, you must tell me who he is, where he comes from, and where you met him—this fellow with a finger in every pie.'

'Right, we must meet and talk. There are people wanting to use the phone here.'

'You can't come here, I tell you. And anyway I'm leaving. Tell me about Giulia, though, right away.'

'She's left. She left Formia and then she left Naples.'

It was as if she'd given me an electric shock down the wire. 'And of course you don't know where she's gone, do you? Is that how you're trying to help her?'

'Well, I hardly know her,' said Luisella. 'She's not a friend of mine. Yes, all right, I'm sorry for her'—here we go again—'but now I've got to think mainly of myself.'

'Luisella, where has she gone? Do you know or don't you?'

She was no fool; anything but. Having decided to join me, and right away, she said the one thing that would force me to wait for her. 'I do know, but I'll tell you when we meet. I've got to stop now, there are people waiting to use the phone.'

And so she kept me there, waiting and trembling; trembling above all on account of the vulture, whom I could already see and hear rifling through the room. Once again I knew the ignominy of creeping out on to the balcony on all fours and peering down into the street, and once again felt all the anger which that infuriating girl managed to arouse in me, more and more often these days.

I went back to the phone and dialled Casali's number. The same rude, disagreeable voice replied and this time took ages coming to the phone at all. Just what you might expect, from the opening words.

'Well, I was just thinking about you,' he said. 'You vanished, and several new things have happened.'

'I know: the bomb. You might have known Miletti wouldn't take it lying down.'

'Nonsense. Forget it. We're not children and we're not touchy. I've told you, money fixes everything. Any news?'

'I went to the nursing home to talk to him this morning but I couldn't get in to see him. I saw Tonino, though, and pushed off. In any case, the police are guarding the room and no one's allowed in.'

'I know, I know. They've put a policeman on here too. What's that they say—shutting the stable door when the horse has gone.' He could even wander off the point, the casual bastard.

'Don Nicola, I've no news for you and I shan't have any so long as Tonino's after me. Have you spoken to him?'

'For today, perhaps you don't have to worry, Iovine,' he said. 'He's here beside me at the table.' So the animal was stoking up, while I'd been fasting for twenty-four hours and the last meal I'd eaten had gone down the wrong way. Anyhow, the news reassured me, of course. 'I was just talking to him,' Casali said. 'Your idea of getting away under his nose with the copper made him angrier than ever, of course. Don't do things like that in future, Iovine.' Just like a brother, giving me good advice.

'What am I supposed to do, get a knife stuck into me? And what does "for today", mean, anyway? This afternoon? All the rest of the day? Will he start up again tomorrow?'

'I told you, Tonino means trouble. And with open warfare . . .' He didn't finish the sentence, but left it hanging threateningly in the air.

'And who's declared it? I thought I had a kind of a pact with you,' I said.

'You have. There are six days left, in fact.'

'I don't understand, Don Nicola. On the one hand you agree to give me a guarantee in cash and on the other you threaten me. When the six days are up, what happens? What have I got to do with these bombings? D'you realise we may all end up with nothing at this rate? Or rather, the pair of you may, because as I've already told you I can hand the contract over to others, and those photocopies aren't going to do anyone the least bit of good.'

'I stick to what I've agreed on,' said Casali, 'and, as I told you yesterday, this morning I fixed up that payment we spoke about. Everything's in order at this end. The money's where you told me to put it, all it needs is a phone call.' I could hear he was breathless once more and felt I could see him, the fat irrational pig who was paying me, his mouth all stained with sauce. But he was dangerous too, especially now that he'd paid out the money.

'We also spoke of keeping that Twin on a leash,' I said.

'We said we'd try and we'd see. You know what twins are like, separate them and they go nuts. Anyway, I'm trying and I'm seeing to it,' he said, and then added, just to keep me anxious: 'But only as far as I can manage.'

'I see,' I said, wishing him all the ills I could think of. 'I've got to look after myself.'

'I'm afraid so.' There was no other explanation: he must have understood what I was playing at, my double game, if you like. But what about the money, then? Not only that, but he must have guessed or got to know something else, because he thundered at me: 'So, get on with your side of it now. Get busy looking for those papers and that girl.'

Then: 'Iovine,' he burst out, a little later, 'did you hear?'

'I heard, Don Nicola,' I said. 'Will you tell me what you mean?'

'There's nothing to tell,' said Casali. 'Did you think I was asleep?'

'No, I realise you've been awake quite a while,' I said. 'Because you set that Pino Gargiulo against Don Michele, didn't you?'

'So you haven't been asleep, either,' he said, 'as far as I can see. But you're wrong, there was no need to do it, it was already done. When the lad came to me he already loathed the old man.'

'Came to see you? Was that how you met him? Who sent him? Marullo?' Perhaps I was beginning to get the hang of things. All that worried me was his remark about Giulia. 'So you know he was carrying on with Don Michele's daughter?'

'It was I who suggested what you might call that marriage,' he said, in the satisfied tone of a professional pimp. 'He was a pretty wideawake fellow and grasped the situation at once. But I don't know why he loathed the old man so much. And I don't know if Marullo sent him to me, either, he didn't say that.' He was admitting everything quite calmly, as if discussing some good piece of business transacted. Could he be as lacking in judgement as all that? What else was there, underneath?

'You'd never seen him before? He just turned up to see you?'

'But what's it all got to do with our little business?' Casali asked. 'And what is this, an interrogation? That fellow Assenza has really infected you with it.' How did he know about Assenza? Even that? 'Anyway, no sir, I never saw him before that and yes sir, he did come along and see me. But the poor wretch is dead now and there's no point in poking about in our memories, especially with my meal getting cold on the table. Keep well, Iovine, and look after yourself.' And he hung up without having told me anything, after having told me everything; and left me there with the receiver burning in my hand.

Luisella arrived a little later, out of breath, wearing a light linen shirt-waister and carrying the smallest of the set of suitcases she had to match her handbag.

'Remember to pay back the porter, he paid for my taxi,' she

said at once. 'My hands were full. How are you?' She kissed me on the cheek and immediately took over my office.

That was one of her qualities: wherever she happened to be, she was immediately at ease. Another quality, if it was a quality: she always forgot everything. Nothing seemed to leave its mark on her; she always managed to stay dry, like a duck. Only she hadn't a duck's small brain.

She was thirty, two years younger than me and two years older than when I first met her; and that day she looked younger than ever, like a contemporary of Giulia's. I made the comparison at once, and automatically, for Giulia had become my obsession. But she didn't wear her hair in a cap over her head, she wore it in all kinds of ways: that day, it was long and flowing. And unlike Giulia's it was brown, like her eyes. And in her whole life she'd never worn a pair of cloth pants.

'What the hell's been going on here?' she cried, going into the room ahead of me, after leaving her suitcase in the hall. 'The twins? Do they exist, then? You didn't invent them?'

She went up to the pile of rubble and rubbish in the middle of the room and bent over it. 'My art deco ashtray,' she said. It was in pieces, and she'd seen it at once. I hadn't even noticed. She was slimmer than Giulia, a few pounds lighter and a little broader, and if she'd known the comparisons I was making she'd have dug my eyes out.

'Stop worrying about the ashtray and tell me about Giulia,' I said.

'Is that how you treat my presents?' she said. 'And I can't stand this Giulia-Giulia business any longer.'

You'd think I'd broken the ashtray myself. But I no longer took any notice of her nonsense. 'I've already told you why I'm so interested in the wretched girl. Whereas you haven't explained a thing. She's left. God knows what you told her when she rang you this morning. You persuaded her to run away again, didn't you?'

'When she rang me she was already going. I tried to persuade her not to, if you must know. I insisted on seeing her, and when we met she wouldn't listen to me. She's pretty stubborn, I must say, that girl.'

'You said you knew where she'd gone,' I said.

'I think I know, but she didn't tell me straight out. In fact she refused to tell me, for fear I'd tell you. On the phone, though, she mentioned her stepmother. She said she was the only person she could turn to now for help.'

'So she's gone to her stepmother?' I said. 'In Milan?'

'I don't know where this stepmother is. In fact I thought she was dead. Wasn't she drowned in the bath?'

'That was the second stepmother. The one she must have told you about was the first, and she lives in Milan.'

'It's too complicated, I don't understand a thing. But aren't you going to tidy up a bit in here?' She was wandering round the room, looking at everything. God knows what she was looking for. I was trying to reach a decision.

'Forget it, this isn't the time for it. Tell me the rest about Giulia,' I said.

She looked round at me, her eyes wide. 'I've told you everything, there's nothing else. I tried to stop her but it was no good. She agreed to see me, she had to give back some things and the suitcase I'd lent her last night, but as she had only an old pair of pants on and a T-shirt I told her to keep them. She came to the house, I went down and we talked in the car. After which she left. But she said she wasn't even going through Naples.'

'Couldn't you have rung me after she rang you?' I said.

'Where? You didn't answer at home or in the office.'

'There, in the hotel, at Formia.'

She looked at me with sudden suspicion. Here we are again, I thought. 'Why, were you at the Bellavista too? Did you spend the night together? You're perfectly capable of it. That explains all this interest. Where's she gone! Why did she go! What did she say! And to think I even apologised. I'm an idiot, that's what I am, not to have realised a thing.'

'You haven't realised a thing,' I said. 'Luisella, please don't be a prize pest just now, it's not the right moment.'

She didn't even hear, but went on quite unruffled. 'Now I see why she changed her mind about you. She felt sorry for you, so she seduced and abandoned you.'

The waiting, the anger that had built up inside me in the meantime, my phone call to Casali, the wretched girl who'd complicated everything with her mania for running away and this other wretched girl with her misplaced jealousy, all came together to make me explode. I gave her a slap, putting a brake on my own violence at the very last minute, so that it can't have hurt her much. But you'd have thought I'd fired point-blank at her. She looked at me, holding her hand to her reddened cheek, amazed and bewildered—if not by pain, at least by incredulity. Of course, because before that I'd hardly ever given way to feeling when I was with her.

'What the hell d'you mean, seduced and abandoned?' I exclaimed, not regretting it but trying to make amends in some way. 'Cuckolded and poleaxed is more like it. Don't make me laugh. Who are you to talk? After that business with Pino.'

She didn't answer, but kept looking at me with shining eyes.

'So you've nothing to say? How did you meet him? D'you mind telling me?'

I was the one who was making a scene now.

At last she decided to talk, but not to answer my questions. Instead she rambled on, in a 'We've-spoilt-these-two-years-and-we-might-have-been-happy' vein. Like an accusation.

'What are you talking about? Is it my fault? I slave away . . .'

'Yes, it is your fault. You slave away only to make money. Some here, some there, and some left over for you. But anyone who's close to you, you lose. Look around you. You wanted an office to set up as a respectable businessman, you said, and look what it's come to. And what for? Just because you chased after money and business. Always business, and nothing else. The Twins, Miletti, Miletti's daughter and those terribly important documents. You're ridiculous. What documents? What's it all about? Another of your plans? Millions? All I've heard you talk about is millions. Always. And you've never noticed that

I love you, that I'd stay with you whatever happened, if you only took some notice of me. But no. You're as shut in and unfeeling as a sea urchin. And, like an idiot, I've come back, only to hear you nattering on about Giulia again, asking where she's gone and what she said. What are you after? What dreams? What fortunes? You're losing everything. You've never asked me a thing about those other two men. Now suddenly you want to know everything about Pino. If you'd only asked me about the first one, if you'd only shown a bit of pride—I'm not saying suffering—there wouldn't have been anyone else. Don't you realise I was trying to get away from you?'

As an alibi, this seemed to me the height of fantasy. But I didn't say so, I let her carry on, seeing she'd started and she'd never got this far before and I was learning all kinds of new things. I merely looked at my watch.

'What does it matter how I met him?'

I wasn't going to take this as a purely rhetorical question, so I broke in.

'It does matter,' I told her. 'So you'd better tell me.'

'Of course, because Giulia comes into it, doesn't she? Your plans come into it.' Oh, she was no fool, as I said. Perhaps she could read me all too well.

Her outburst was awakening echoes in me, mixed with the buzzing that had started up again in my ear: millions, Swiss francs, sums and accounts that worked out on paper but wouldn't work in real life, my rushing about, the bruises I'd got used to but which still hurt and, finally, that promise of a settlement that now urged me to carry on running, this time to Milan, to get an immediate advance of fifty thousand francs. I shook myself suddenly. With shining eyes and, in that moment of real feeling, the pain shown in her face, Luisella was meltingly lovely; but anxiety was stronger than tenderness in me, and suddenly I wasn't even interested in Pino. All I had to do, right away, was rush off to Milan. I'd looked at my watch a few minutes earlier and the last flight to Milan would probably take place quite soon.

I went to the phone to find out. Luisella watched me as I did so, astonished, filled with surprise at my sudden, obvious indifference, and when I put down the receiver she exclaimed:

'You're a pig.' At the same time, the two gleaming tears that had gathered before overflowed and spilled down her cheeks, where they left a bright, shining furrow across her make-up.

The plane had left in the meantime. All that remained was the evening train, with sleeping-car.

Quite honestly, I don't remember much about the rest of that evening. The fact was, perhaps, that I was getting used to things happening, and that was a perfectly ordinary afternoon: nothing happened.

Yes, it's true. I made my peace with Luisella, but it was a hasty peace-making, linked in a way to the mechanics of the quarrel, which had been a hasty one too. Besides, as I said, she forgot things easily. All I had to do was try to explain why I was anxious and she made up her mind to understand.

As for Tonino, the siege was for the time being lifted, he'd been having a meal with his master not long before. But as a precaution, since I didn't place too much confidence in the leash he was on, I decided to have a meal myself. And so, with all the other matching suitcases, which Luisella had left with the porter, we loaded up a taxi and went to the furthest pizzeria we could find, the one where it was least likely the beast would run us to earth. And there, the only scene I remember properly took place.

After the meal I made a move to rise, and Luisella said: 'Where are you going?'

'To telephone,' I said. 'I've got to book a seat on the train. Then I'll pick the ticket up later.'

'Why, are you leaving? Of course, of course, you've got to go to Milan.' Her tone was openly ironic.

'Luisella, I explained to you . . .'

'Yes, all right, I agree. But I'm coming too.'

'What d'you mean? Haven't you understood a thing?'

'I've understood, oh yes, that's just it.' We all understood, it was a real festival of understanding. 'But I shouldn't like to stay here and fall into the clutches of that Twin.'

'You'll go back to your mother at Formia,' I said.

'Wouldn't dream of it. I've had another row with her. Your fault again.' Of course. If she was orphaned at any time within the next century or so, she'd blame me. 'She didn't want me to go back to you in Naples. Why can't I come? I won't be a nuisance, you'll see. Let's stay together, let's not be separated just now.'

I glanced at the suitcases heaped up round the table, all of them the same except in size, and sat down again.

'I'll see to everything, you'll see. I'll go and ring up now and then get the tickets. You wait for me here, where you'll be safe. And if we find Giulia again, together, then I agree we'll persuade her more easily.'

'What d'you mean, if? Hasn't she gone to Milan?'

'She said she was going to her stepmother. If her stepmother's in Milan, then she'll have gone to Milan,' said Luisella.

She saw to everything, and even had money for the tickets, which I hadn't got with me, and perhaps hadn't even got in the bank. I waited for her there in the pizza shop, and around me were all those suitcases which later, when we were on the train, took up a whole compartment. All I had was a small suitcase, which she'd gone to fetch from the flat. She'd also remembered to tell the porter to get the telephone reconnected.

What with the suitcases and the heat, we couldn't move, and I was beginning to worry. Perhaps I was sorry, and feeling I wasn't treating the whole thing seriously enough. Even Tonino's threat seemed less overpowering, in fact quite non-existent; and really this was the only cheering thing about it all. Before getting on the train, I'd only just remembered to look carefully around. He wasn't there, of course. But once I'd found a small space to sit down in among all that luggage, I remembered what Casali had said about Giulia: if he knew she'd vanished and I was looking for her, he also knew she had the documents and, above all, that she might have run off to Milan. And this aroused or increased my worries.

Luisella, in the meantime, was settling down comfortably; and finally, having made me uncomfortable, she sat down on the edge of the bed beside me, and stayed there looking at me, waiting.

'Are you prepared to talk about Pino, now?' I asked her.

'Yes,' she said, as unpredictable as ever. 'It's like a frog in my throat, I want to get rid of it.'

'On the 'phone, the first time, when we spoke indirectly of his death, you didn't seem to mind at all. So I came a terrible cropper when I found you . . . knew him.'

'You don't see,' she replied. 'Of course I was terribly sorry, poor boy, and I'm still upset. But what you call minding has to do with you and me, with the two of us, above all.'

I understood less and less, and told her so. Then she began telling me about it. There'd been nothing between them but simple friendship, that's exactly what she called it. At that time she was pregnant—by me, she maintained, and repeated it several times—but above all she was proudly and intransigently puzzled. She was going through one of her crises of unhappy insecurity, caused by my lack of feeling, and here she repeated her comparison with the sea-urchin, which she obviously found an apt one. Her pride and intransigence, within her perplexity, were caused by the fact that she was afraid I'd think she wanted to hold on to me at any price. The perplexity, on the other hand, came from the only solution that the pride and intransigence forced upon her. In other words, she wanted, and yet didn't want, an abortion, but above all she didn't want to tell me about it. All this had aroused the admiration of the young man in whom she was now confiding, who'd done all he could to make her accept the inevitability of an abortion and to prevent her bringing another unhappy being into the world. The expression isn't mine; it was hers, or rather her persuader's. In other words, if I understood her tedious speech correctly, he was a supporter of the normal, legally constituted family, and felt anyone born outside it was destined to be miserable.

'I felt it was a real obsession with him,' she said. 'The subject made him so worked up that sometimes I felt he was just getting it all off his chest. I found it hard to follow him sometimes, I remember.' But it hadn't been hard to persuade her.

'Yes, but when did it happen?' I asked. 'And where was I, in the meantime?' I added quickly.

'It happened, as you put it, in February. As for where you were, I wish I knew. Where you were then and where you always are. Completely absent. Taken up with your big business, not noticing a thing.'

I took my finger off that particular switch but couldn't help pressing another. 'But immediately afterwards he set about conceiving another unhappy creature himself,' I said. 'With Giulia. Full marks for consistency.'

The train had been moving for some time, and the remains of daylight had vanished. We must now have been near Formia, and she was looking out, through the half-lowered window, at the alternating lights flying past in the darkness, which gave a rhythm and a meaning to our own flight along the rails. And suddenly everything seemed to me quite meaningless.

'You still haven't told me how you met him,' I said. I was now irritated, not with her but, even more than I had been before, with Pino, who had done and undone everything, known and not known everything. And Giulia had called me a snake. After going to bed with that boa-constrictor.

'In a very ordinary way,' said Luisella. What did she mean? In a way that wasn't quite up to his highness, was that it? 'I was introduced to him by Lucia. You remember her at least, don't you? She introduced us to each other, as well.'

'Yes, I remember her,' I said, thinking of this chain of introductions. It wasn't just Tonino's siege. If he hadn't been dead, where else would that creep Pino have turned up in my life? In bed with me? What was I feeling, anyway? Envy? Jealousy?

As if she'd read my thoughts, Luisella added: 'Yes, he'd been with Lucia. With *your* Lucia.' Just to make me like that son of a whore a little better: old Miletti was right.

I was shaken by her unpredictable logic. 'You know,' she went on, 'I was never jealous of her; in fact we stayed friends, Lucia and I. But the way you're so agitated now makes me wild. Whatever I told you about myself, you didn't give a damn. You didn't even wonder whether the child was yours.' And this, as a conclusion, seemed typical of her.

We were rushing, I was rushing, through the darkness now, and the flying lights outside meant nothing, they were just an illusion. Everything was more meaningless than ever.

When I put a hand on her shoulder Luisella turned to me and suddenly flung herself into my arms. There we stayed, saying nothing. Then she moved away, touched the switch above the door and came back to the bed, this time lying down on it. Soon afterwards the feeble blue gleam of the nightlight seemed suddenly to light up the compartment, and the darkness was left outside.

20

Elena Miletti lived, alone and presumably on the alimony sent by her ex-husband, in Milan, in via Macedonio Melloni. The names they give the streets there.

I'd telephoned her as soon as we got to the hotel and now, less than half an hour later, I was knocking at her door. It wasn't yet ten in the morning and I'd left Luisella and the luggage piled up together in the hotel room.

She came to open the door herself and, obviously hesitating, asked me in. She was much taller than Miletti, and must have been worn out, frustrated and burned up by a pointless fifteen-year-long effort at least to keep her end up, if not to dominate him from her superior height. I don't know why I thought this; perhaps it was suggested to me not just by her height but by her thinness, grey hair and emaciated face, or perhaps by the impression I had of seeing a beautiful woman who had suddenly grown old, from one day to the next, in a life which had unexpectedly shown itself to be too difficult. Her eyes, which were very dark and shy, kept searching for things to hold on to in order to avoid mine.

'Mr Iovine? I told you on the phone there was no point in your coming,' she said, and then added, poor prophetess that she was: 'I've absolutely nothing to tell you.'

She had gone ahead of me in the meantime, into a sitting-room that was also furnished as a dining-room, a simple, almost bare place, in spite of its dual purpose. As I went in, I caught a glimpse of a narrow kitchen, through a door left ajar.

'I've come on purpose from Naples . . .' I began.

'And you were wrong,' she said. 'You could have rung up from there and saved yourself the journey. Well, as you're here, sit down.' She indicated a low, armless sofa that, with two armchairs of the same design, made up the sitting-room corner. 'May I give you some coffee?' she said decisively. A Miletti-style woman.

'Thank you,' I said, but with the feeling that she was giving herself a reason to get away, rather than anything else.

When she pushed open the kitchen door I saw the end of a suitcase standing just behind it, as if hidden there hastily. It was only for a moment, because she closed the door again at once, but it was enough for me to recognise one of the many packages that had made our simple trip to Milan seem like emigration. It was, in fact, one of Luisella's suitcases; different shape, same series. If Giulia wasn't in the house at that very moment, she'd passed through it quite recently. She had a way of strewing bags and suitcases about. Borrowed ones, too.

At last I had a sudden feeling of serenity, settled down on the sofa and waited quietly for Elena to return.

She was out a long time, rather too long, and when she came back she was holding a tray with a breakfast cup, or something of the kind, upon it. She shut the door behind her, came and put the tray down on the glass coffee table in front of me and sat down in one of the armchairs. The cup was full of pale coffee.

I took it, cleared my throat and spoke.

'Signora, it's no good denying it,' I said. 'Giulia's here. I'm sorry for your sake, but I saw her suitcase out there in the kitchen.' After which I noticed that her eyes weren't merely anxious but glittering. It was my fate, I thought, I was going to get more tears.

She didn't even try to deny it, in fact she seemed to be waiting for a way to confess; completely if, given the circumstances, unexpectedly.

'Right. Yes. I hid it there when you knocked at the door. She'd left it here . . .'

'Giulia?'

'Yes, Giulia. She arrived this morning, after driving all night. Early this morning. If only she'd never come. I don't read the papers, so I heard the news from her.'

'About the accident that happened to Don . . . to your husband?'

'What accident? No, no, I don't know anything about that. Nor am I interested in it. Can you imagine . . .' And she burst into tears.

She was sitting there, composed, with her legs and feet together, her hands folded in her lap, crying, shaking with sobs, as if she'd been waiting for my arrival in order to give way to those tears.

I moved to put the cup back on the tray, its contents untouched and by now undrinkable, and tried, resignedly, to say something.

'Please don't . . .' I said, but embarrassment and perplexity made me stop suddenly. I was prepared, but not for all this.

'I've been wandering round the house for two hours like a

ghost, not knowing what to do, what to decide, who to turn to . . . If only she hadn't come,' she repeated, still dignified, still weeping. 'Poor darling, she couldn't have known. But she told me quite abruptly and then . . . then . . . she left. Like that, suddenly. She left me all alone . . .'

'But signora, what's happened?' I said.

'My son. My son's dead. Murdered. And she was the one to bring me the news. To think of her being that much involved.'

Now this was something I really hadn't been prepared for. 'Pino . . . Gargiulo? Pino's your son?' I said.

She moved her head repeatedly, nodding in such terrible pain that she could now no longer speak and merely shook all over. Then she turned round on the armchair, laid her arm and head on the back of it and stayed like that, abandoned to her despair.

I don't know how long we sat there, she flung down like that and I as much overwhelmed with embarrassment, surprise and curiosity as she was by suffering. Above all, what had I understood her to say? How far was Giulia involved? And in what? At last, she felt the need to talk again, to carry on with her outburst. Without taking her head from the back of the chair, she turned to me.

'I always thought that Tina was no good,' she said. 'I never knew her, but from what I heard about her I'd got a pretty clear idea. She was the reason for it.'

I wasn't at all sure of this, but I didn't say so. I couldn't tell the mother, particularly at that moment, that it was her son who was no good. Instead I asked her why Giulia had left, and—with no great tact, considering the occasion—above all, if she knew where she'd gone.

'I don't know,' she replied. 'She left suddenly. When I told her that Pino was my son, she more or less ran away. She didn't know, you see. No one knew it, in fact . . .'

'Except Marullo,' I said. 'Isn't that so?' It was too strong for me, I had to interrupt, I had to ask it.

She raised her head from the back of the chair and looked at me. 'Yes, except for him,' she said. 'How do you come to . . .'

but she didn't finish. She wasn't interested in knowing. Without being prompted, she went back to Giulia. 'Poor darling, she was telling me about the terrible discovery she'd made, and saw me turn pale and burst into tears. And when I told her Pino was my son, she said nothing at all, then burst into tears herself and a little later ran off. She rushed out of the door and disappeared. Now I shall never see her again. And she's carrying my son's child in her womb.'

'Because . . . because she was the first to tell you, wasn't she? You didn't know it already?' I said.

She looked at me again, as if only then realising she was talking to a nosey, devious stranger. Then she shrugged: even that didn't matter to her. 'I don't see—I mean, I haven't seen Pino for years,' she went on. 'He'd already gone to Naples before I came back here to Milan. To study. He was studying biology. He was clever, did you know? But already I wasn't seeing him. He had . . . repudiated me as his mother.' He hadn't minded taking her money, though. The money she sent him through Marullo, the cashier.

'But you supported him while he studied, I imagine,' I said. Then, as if it was the right thing to say at that moment I added, lying: 'Marullo told me you sent him money every month, through him.' I continued to look at her. Her beautiful, tear-filled eyes had lost all their uneasiness.

'He kept back part of the alimony my husband sent me and gave it to Pino. Half that wretched sum. I don't know why I'm telling you all this, since you're a friend of the old monster.'

Monster seemed a bit excessive, considering what she had just come out with, in bits and pieces. What had happened was that the intransigent Don Michele, after about fifteen years of marriage, had suddenly learnt that the woman he'd married as his third wife was, when he married her, already the mother of a ten-year-old son, that little marvel of hers. In other words, that for a good fifteen years this wife had kept the secret to herself. Let's be objective, the whole business couldn't have been easy to swallow, above all for an intolerant old bastard like him. It was logical that, having already been unfortunate in his marriages, he should have blown his top and divorced her. You didn't have to be an old-fashioned reactionary, as Giulia would have put it, to work that one out.

On the other hand, still looking at it objectively, I couldn't fail to understand the poor woman. She'd suffered: the father, Gargiulo, was killed in a car accident before they'd got married and the little monster—yes, he really was one—was born; so, sacrifices, working to support him with a nurse, and dreams. Only to find herself repudiated as a mother in the end.

'Yes I know, it was enormously naïve of me, and I paid dearly for it,' she said. 'Above all with that marriage, which I accepted for Pino's sake. I was alone and this mature man, who'd also been unhappy, seemed to me . . . I don't know how to say it, I only know that whatever I say now seems incredible and absurd. In other words, I hadn't the courage to tell him right away, I was too worried about Pino's future, he was already ten and had to be taken from his nurse, he couldn't go on forever living in that mountain village . . . I thought that once I'd married him, immediately afterwards, I could do it more safely. But instead after a few weeks—what am I saying?—after a few days—I realised that I'd deluded myself: the man would simply explode, the way he did fifteen years later when he found out.'

'How did he find out?' I asked. After fifteen years. The shadow of Assenza was still there, sitting beside me on the sofa.

She had composed herself again and was sitting up stiffly on the armchair, facing me. In her need to get it off her chest, she'd forgotten I was a friend of the monster. 'He told him—Pino did,' she said.

The boy had stayed in Milan, supported from a distance by his mother, who sent money, and cared for at close quarters by the nurse who, for his sake, had left her mountain village and cashed the cheques Marullo sent her. In other words, Don Michele had adopted and maintained a son without knowing it, and that dear little snake had grown up in the bosom of the family. And when enough time had passed for him to gather enough poison, he'd turned up one fine day in Naples and gone to Miletti's office to bite at one and the same time the hand that had fed him and the naïve mother who, he believed, had given him neither milk as a baby nor a father as an adult; in other words, he'd sadistically blurted out everything . . .

I now understood two things clearly: the young man's outburst to Luisella about illegitimate children, and Miletti's reluctance to tell his ex-wife about the death of a certain Pino Gargiulo. But Pino's passionate, deep-rooted, secret wish to avenge himself on the old man by striking at his mother I couldn't really understand. What did he want, to be adopted? To be included in Miletti's will? What was he up to, a challenge, a show-down? To be more effectively avenged, he'd even picked a partner: I remembered what Casali had said. So, he'd turned up at Casali's with his claws out to ask him to collaborate. And had got ideas and advice from him. But how did he come to know that Casali hated his partner? Through Marullo, was it? But who was Marullo? At this point, I had to admit that Don Michele certainly had a talent for surrounding himself with enemies: his employee Marullo, his business partner, his third wife, and even his fourth. And finally his daughter. Not at all bad. With fifteen thousand francs and an additional promise, though, he'd gained an ally.

'I'll go to the police,' the mother was now saying, desperate and desolate. 'I'll go and tell them everything.'

'Do you know who killed your son and his . . . mistress?' I asked her.

'I have no proof but I'm certain of it,' she said, after which, at the most vital point, she shut up and there was no way of getting her to say more. She had put on the brakes, her outburst was over.

'Have you thought of Giulia?' I said, after a while.

'What's Giulia got to do with it? They don't suspect her, I hope? Of course I'm thinking of her. And I'm terribly sorry for her, if I can be sorry for anyone in my present state. But you're thinking of her as well, I can see. All you've done is ask me about Giulia. You've come all this way . . . Did her father send you?'

'Yes and no. The initiative was mainly mine. I want to help her. She's in so much trouble.'

'Help her in what way?'

'Well, in every way,' I said. 'With the police, among other things, because they do suspect her. Do you really not know where she may have gone?'

'No, as I told you, she ran off.' That certainly wasn't anything new. 'Do they really suspect her? But it's ridiculous.' And she shook her head, suffering.

With what I then said I managed to double this suffering. 'Was she in time to tell you she was planning to have an abortion?' I said, and could have cut out my tongue at once, when I'd said it.

'Going to have an abortion?' she exclaimed, but that was all; and it was followed by a burst of sobbing. For a long time she wept desperately. Then, following an inevitable train of thought she exclaimed: 'Poor Pino' through her tears.

I was thinking of old Miletti.

When I was down in the street I looked round and found it impossible to breath the sigh of relief I felt I had a right to. Via Macedonio Melloni, a long, straight, grey street washed by that Milanese early-summer rain, struck me as having the desolate air of a place suited to nothing so well as funeral processions. There was no cemetery at the end: only a traffic roundabout that was busy but silent, towards which I felt myself being sucked. On the corner of viale Piceno I hailed a passing taxi and went back to the hotel.

Luisella wasn't in the bedroom waiting for me. She hadn't been able to resist going out. All I could hope was that she wasn't buying up half Milan. I asked the switchboard to get me Naples and gave the number of the nursing home. When they replied I gave them the number of Miletti's room and when he replied at last I heard not the grunts I expected but a long uninterrupted sigh: 'Hullo-who's-there?'

'Don Michele, this is Iovine,' I said. 'How are you?'

'I've got pneumonia and a shoulder in plaster,' he said. But at least you can see the sunshine through the window, I thought. 'Where are you calling from?'

'From Milan,' I said. 'I've been to see Signora Elena.'

'Ah,' he sighed.

I said nothing about my meeting with Giulia two days before and never mentioned Pino at all; I told him merely that his daughter had swept through her stepmother's house and then vanished again. He listened without interrupting me, and still remained silent when I'd finished.

'Don Michele, are you all right?' I asked.

'I've told you, I've got pneumonia.' That was obvious. What was he thinking? Me, I was thinking of those papers, which I could see escaping me more and more, while he was now so clearly detached and uninterested; and of the girl who was carrying them away from me, and with them my reward for getting her home, with or without them. Miletti gave me time to think of all this, before starting to sigh again. 'What else did that woman tell you?' he said at last.

'Well ... everything, Don Michele,' I said.

'Just as well. Now you know. Just as well, just as well. It's all very dirty linen but I couldn't go on keeping it to myself. Good, good.' As if he'd been the one to confide in me, to tell me all.

'These things happen, Don Michele, don't take it too hard. You've got nothing to blame yourself for, nothing at all. Now you've just got to think of getting better.'

'I'm thinking of all sorts of things,' he said. 'Among them that shit Casali. Have you heard?' He seemed to be on another tack, changing the subject. I couldn't blame him.

'Yes, I heard.' I now knew all about everything, except what worried me most. Where could she be hiding? I asked him, while Luisella came bursting into the room, so that I didn't hear his sighing reply.

'I didn't hear that, Don Michele,' I said, looking at Luisella; she hadn't many packages with her, thank God. Now she'd flung herself down on the bed, exhausted, and was looking at me and listening.

'I told you I had no idea,' he said. Discouraging old devil. 'But as you're up there there's another place you might try. It's just an idea, mind.'

'Go on, Don Michele,' I said, trembling with anxiety, and he continued slowly.

'That woman had an old nurse, called Carlinda or some such name . . . Well, she lives in a mountain village. Santa Maria Maggiore, I think it is.'

'You think? Aren't you sure?' What was he hatching out for me? Another trip into space?

'Yes, I think it was Santa Maria Maggiore. It's important. This old woman had her staying with her several times and Giulia's been up there with her, a couple of summers, as well. This was after she was left on her own.' He spoke with difficulty but had now decided to have a little outburst of his own. 'Because that little shit had left her on her own in Milan. She brought him up, you know that, don't you?' I grunted in agreement. 'Well, it may be—anything's possible. Anyway, as you're there you may as well try this. What else did she tell you?'

'What?'

'Did she talk about anything else?—that woman, I mean. In other words, what are her intentions?'

'What can they be?' I said. What an odd question. 'The state she's in, poor . . . Well, yes, she said she thought of going to the police. But it just meant she thought of turning to someone; she was in such a state.'

'All she wants is to throw shit in my face,' he said, unexpectedly. 'And you felt sorry for her, didn't you? Oh, let's drop it. Have you understood? Try this other thing.'

'I'll do it, Don Michele, but can you tell me where this Santa Maria is?'

'Maggiore,' he corrected me. 'I don't know exactly. But it

isn't hard to find. Around Domodossola, I think. Giulia knows the place and that old woman might help her in her present state. You know, she wants to . . .'

'Have an abortion?' On a mountain peak? I didn't believe it. 'I thought she might,' I lied.

'You're not unimaginative, Iovine,' said the sibyl with pneumonia. 'In any case, get a few other ideas. You know, that fellow Tonino's left Naples and is looking for you both, you and Giulia. Get her out of this dangerous situation for me. And don't forget that I keep my promises.'

When I'd put down the receiver, Luisella said at once: 'Well?'

'Well, our Twin's on his way here, to Milan.'

'Right, then we'll go back to Naples,' she said. 'This is a crazy city.' She liked exaggerating. 'Anyway, I always thought it a pointless trip. I always thought you wouldn't get anything out of the stepmother.'

'We're making another trip, though. To the mountains,' I said.

'In this rain?'

She was already unwrapping her purchases to show them to me, but I went back to the phone. This time I asked for a number in Lugano and the girl put me through almost at once.

'Mr Benetti, this is Iovine, from Naples,' I said. It was the converter, as he was called; that is, the chap who looked after exchanges and payments. With a smiling prosperous office in that smiling, prosperous little town. I'd often had contact with him on other people's behalf; this time it was about my own money. But this time he knew nothing about it.

'Haven't you had an order to pay ten thousand francs to my credit?' I asked him.

'From Naples? No, I haven't heard anything,' he said.

'Hasn't Casali rung you? Nicola Casali. You know him, don't you?'

'Yes, I know him well, but I haven't heard from him for a while. Ten thousand, was it? I'm amazed.'

I was even more amazed, having dropped from my dizzy delusions, to realise that Casali wasn't going to pay me, he was merely the swine I'd thought him. I looked at Luisella, and at her packages lying open on the bed, and saw, or thought I saw, the irony of her expression. At least I shan't be playing a double game, I thought, to console myself. But after a moment I muttered:

'Well, we're going to leave those bloody suitcases here in the hotel.'

21

It was like looking for a needle in a haystack. Only after we'd started on our journey did I realise that I didn't even know the old woman's surname. Admittedly I hadn't asked it, but even if he knew it my good friend Don Michele had been careful not to tell me. And the haystack was a lot more than a hundred kilometres away. All because of that blasted Giulia.

Luisella meantime was sitting silently beside me, bored. She'd had no choice. The alternative would have been to stay at the hotel, besieged by the rain, for the rest of the afternoon and evening, and heaven knows how long the following day, waiting for my return.

The car was behaving beautifully on the wet surface of the road; even with the rain pelting down in torrents it went smoothly along the straight motorway at a hundred and ten. I've got my fixations like everyone else and I'd told the porter at the hotel that I wouldn't hire any car but an Alfetta. And he'd managed to get me one, even though he'd had to scrape around. Double tip, that is.

'Just tell me if it's possible,' Luisella exclaimed at one point.

'What is?' I said. I was thinking of old Miletti, of what he'd said and hadn't said.

'This rain. This idiotic, out-of-season rain.' When she was annoyed she said things like that, and more. 'That Don Michele of yours is a real old creep. How can he possibly think of sending someone to a village lost in the mountains to see an old woman whose address he doesn't even know? And in this rain too.'

'How could he know it was raining? And anyway, it's just a try-out.'

'Of course, of course, it's such an important business you've even got to go scouring round the mountains just in case. Why can't you leave the poor girl in peace,' she concluded, with her usual cast-iron logic.

'So you think we should have gone back to Naples after coming all the way here, just to spare ourselves a couple of hours' driving?'

'Two and a half to three hours, the porter said.'

'Right, two and a half. We'll get there before evening. We left at four.'

'While he's down there in the sun.'

'In bed,' I pointed out. 'After being blown up by a bomb. And all that damn girl's fault.'

'She's got nothing to do with the bomb. If he'd only acknowledged Pino and not separated him from his mother, none of this would have happened. Nothing would have happened.'

'Yes, it wouldn't have rained today either. Was he the one who was so devious that he never said a word to his wife for fifteen years on end?'

'Well, why did he have to make such a tragedy out of it?' she said, in her usual way. 'After all, she'd had the boy ten years before she met him. I feel sorry for the poor soul. And God knows what sort of tactless things you probably said to her,' she added, just to keep in training.

'Luisella, love, let me drive in peace. What d'you know about it? Were you there? Did you have to listen to her wailing?'

'Wailing. Have you no respect for anything? To think of that poor soul telling you all that, practically confessing her whole life story, at that very moment and in shock after hearing the news—telling you of all people, her hateful husband's friend.'

It really was the old man's fate: nobody liked him. Was I the only one? I thought of my earlier view of him, then of the Swiss francs, and, as a result, of Giulia.

'Giulia told me a whole lot of things too,' I said. 'She confessed, as you put it. To me of all people. But I understand her, at least. At a certain point it's only human to let it all out. It's just that afterwards she cheated me . . .'

'We'd better not talk about that little evening of yours. Call it the need to let it all out if you like.' I glanced in her direction: she was frowning hard. 'You can tell Don Michele whatever you like, though, and he'll never let it out.'

'What's that got to do with it?' I said. 'He's a man.'

She took no notice. 'A dirty old man, you mean. You tell him his wife's dead and he doesn't bat an eyelash. He sees her corpse and hardly acknowledges it. His pregnant daughter, ditto.'

'He'd already raised merry hell. When I told him he already knew.'

'But he sent you to look for her.'

'What else could he do? That bastard Pino . . .'

'Remember he's dead.'

'. . . right, that darling boy mucked up his marriage, made his daughter pregnant, and got off with his wife . . .'

'When he sent you after Giulia he didn't yet know that Pino was . . . cuckolding him, with his wife and daughter.' As a rule she didn't express herself like that. Not only that, but she also forgot that Pino was dead and added at once: 'He was a shit as well.'

'A lot shittier,' I said. 'What could Miletti do? Go down on his knees to his daughter and beg her forgiveness? And to Pino as well? Thank God you've realised at last what a shit he was. I'd call him something else, but anyway, things went badly for him.'

'That reminds me, so far I've heard you talk about everything and everybody, about these blasted papers, about Giulia, Miletti, Casali, the Twins, the whole bunch, but you've never mentioned the two of them. Since they died, I mean. Who killed them? Because you did tell me, and it must have cost you an enormous effort, that Tina choked to death. But who did it?'

'Assenza can get on with that. I've other things to worry about.'

'Of course, business for you, crimes for him. But he's chasing after you.'

We left the motorway and after Sesto Calende, on the iron bridge, we saw the lake, looking dark and angry. At Arona the rain came down even harder. Luisella sat with her legs tucked under her and her arms crossed, as if she was cold. 'Jesus Christ,' she grumbled at one point. We'd been silent for a while and continued so along the lakeside as far as Stresa and beyond it. The traffic was as heavy as the rain and we went slowly, so that when we started to go up and then, at last, to enter the Val Vigozzo, although it had by then stopped raining, neither of us felt like admiring the landscape that popped up at every bend in the road. But when, just before Santa Maria, the road straightened out, we purred with relief, like the engine.

The village was a little further ahead but I didn't notice the turning and kept straight on. We found ourselves, under the lowering sky, in a green valley between two opposite slopes which, at the end of it, became spurs; and the road went across the whole of it. I stopped and turned back towards the houses, which were a little to one side beyond the railway line. From that side, I noticed at once with relief, it could be seen completely, and it was very small: not a very large haystack, then, in which to look for a needle called Carlinda.

Everyone there must have known her, in fact. Having crossed the railway lines, all I had to do was ask an old man who was leaning on a stick enjoying the invisible sunset in the station yard, to get the name of the tiny road in which she lived; and then we set off to find it.

But the Alfetta couldn't get down it and I went on alone, on foot, Luisella preferring to stay in the car; in the warmth, she said. Admittedly it didn't feel like June, but she'd never been so tiresome in the past.

At the number he'd given me the small green door was shut and looked as if it had been bolted for years. A neighbour told me that Carlinda was up on the Piana grazing the animals, and pointed to the sky. There were places higher than this, then; I thought I'd climbed up to the sky myself.

When I came out of the alleyway, I saw two mountain peaks facing each other, with the valley between them, green below and rocky higher up. In the dying light, and against that leaden sky, I thought I could see splashes of white here and there on the distant summits.

'Oh no. Climbing's out,' exclaimed Luisella when I came back to ask what she thought. 'At this hour? When we were on the road in the valley I saw an hotel. Let's go there and wait. You're really overdoing things a bit now, you know.'

'But it's just a run up in the cable car,' I said. The neighbour had explained it all to me.

'Let her come down, then. It'll soon be dark. You can put off our journey home for a bit. What's the rush? We can't get back to Milan now, anyway.'

The hotel, which was large and half made of wood, welcomed us with obvious delight, which just as obviously decreased when we took only two small suitcases out of the car. But at least we didn't fill the room—the second one that day, a large one with a window looking out over the valley, and with the mountains in the background—with all Luisella's matching luggage. We'd left that in the hotel in Milan.

We then decided to have a meal. It wasn't quite our usual hour for supper, but we had some time to kill, although I had a feeling Carlinda's animals must have gone to sleep quite a while ago and was beginning to fear she'd follow suit herself the moment she got home.

Before we went into the dining-room, though, I suddenly felt uneasy.

'I'll just go along and see if she's got back,' I told Luisella.

She seemed resigned. 'Go along, if you like. I'll wait here. But I'll eat in the meantime.'

So I went along, and found myself outside the small, still shut front door again. The shadow of the mountain now filled the valley, and particularly this alley-way, which was now quite dark, apart from the light that came over the garden opposite from the neighbour's windows. When she heard me knock on the door the woman appeared again at her own doorway, less than a couple of yards away.

'You haven't seen Signora Carlinda come back?' I asked her.

'No, I haven't; she must have stayed up on the Piana,' she said, and came out into the road to close the shutters of her house from the outside.

'Why, can this happen? I mean, does she sometimes stay up there?'

'Yes, if she gets late,' said the woman. 'You see, she never takes the cable car down, not even for the last lap, and at her age it's dangerous in the dark. She has a hut up on the Piana and stays there. She's old now, you see.' And if she's old, I thought, why doesn't she stop at home? But there are some things you can't quite say.

Instead I asked her if there was a tobacconist nearby; I was out of cigarettes.

'Yes, in the square,' she told me. 'Turn left at the bottom of this road and then right.' I'd have called it an alley, myself.

At eight in the evening the village was already empty and the small square was the brightest corner of that dark little world; it had a garden along one side and railings on which two lamps were gleaming. The tobacconist's shop was there and even had my brand of cigarettes; but no sooner had I left and gone down the steps than I was back again.

'That car outside, with the Naples number plate,' I asked anxiously. 'Has it been there long?'

'What's that?' said the man.

My heart had turned right over when I saw it, outlined

against the railings with a few other cars. I didn't know its number, but as far as I was concerned there was only one Mini with a Naples number-plate. Up there at the top of the world, what's more. I repeated my question less hurriedly and this time the man understood.

'I don't know, I haven't seen it,' he said. 'But my wife must have noticed it because this very afternoon, when I came to take over from her in the shop, she said something about holiday-makers, and how they were starting to come from as far as Naples this summer.'

No, his wife wasn't there just then. She was in the shop in the morning, till the early afternoon, but if I came back in about an hour I could talk to her myself, because she came and fetched him when it was time to shut up shop. Yes, people who lived nearby generally left their cars there, sometimes for several days on end.

He was old and, if not exactly lively, at least anxious to please. I thanked him and went back to the alley. As soon as I came into it, I could see the bright flashes of a television set on the ground floor of one of the houses, coming through a single lace-curtained window with the outer shutters still undone. But the feeble halo of light lasted only a few yards, and when I'd passed it I had to creep forward to the front door, which was just as black as its surroundings. Before knocking I hesitated, thinking I might have got the wrong door; then I lit a match, checked the number on the side and knocked. Silence. And silence too from the neighbour's house, which was as dark as the rest. Was everyone already in bed? I knocked again. In the end I gave up and went back to the hotel to fetch Luisella.

I found her in an armchair in the empty lounge, leafing through a magazine with her back to the switched-on television set. She'd already had her meal. I told her what I'd found.

'Suppose it isn't Giulia's Mini?' she said. 'Couldn't it be a coincidence?' She was beginning to take an interest in it all.

'The wretched girl's got a Mini and she ran away from Milan, possibly to come here. If I see a Mini with a Naples number-plate up in these mountains, why should I think it a coincidence?'

'What can I say, then?' said Luisella. 'She must have joined the old girl up on the mountain and stayed with her in the hut. Most likely she's gone out grazing the animals herself. Anything's possible at this stage.' No, she wasn't the least bit involved.

'She left her stepmother's house very early,' I said, 'so she must have got here late in the morning or early this afternoon. Anyway, before the tobacconist's wife left the shop, early in the afternoon.'

'If her car's here and she's not in the house, she'll be up there.'

'Suppose she hasn't gone up? Suppose she's wandering around here, in the village?' I already regretted having come away, I ought to have stuck it out there, waiting outside the door.

'Oh yes, she's gone to bet in the casino,' said Luisella.

I almost hated her. 'Come on. You come as well. You can keep an eye on the car while I go and knock again.'

She came, and not even reluctantly; perhaps the little mystery was distracting her from that dreary evening and, above all, from this trip which she hadn't liked from the very first. She went up to the bedroom for a moment to fetch a pullover. I was still in my light grey suit, I hadn't brought anything else. But now I wished I'd been more far-sighted: I got the hotel porter to get me an electric torch, a thing quite common up there on the mountain.

And so, preceded by its feeble gleam, we went along in darkness and silence. We reached the little lit square by the short, straight road leading to it, and when we arrived it was like coming out of a dark tunnel into daylight. The Mini was still there, and we went across to it.

'Is it hers or not?' I asked Luisella. 'D'you recognise it?'

'I don't know. I think it is.'

'What d'you mean, you don't know? You've been from

Naples to Formia in it, you saw it again next day outside your mother's house, at least you can tell me if it was that colour. No?' A very recognisable colour, too: dirty green, with a cream roof.

'Well, I didn't notice,' she replied, making me furious. Typical of her not to notice details. All details. 'I didn't look at it the way you look at your Alfetta, of course.'

'Witty as well,' I said. But there was no doubt about it: in comparison with the other cars parked there it was filthy, its wheels looked as if they were made of mud. It must have travelled a long time in the rain, and recently. 'In any case, this is her Mini, I'd bet my life on it.'

'You're the car expert,' said Luisella.

I took no notice. 'There's just one thing. She can't have got here before eleven, and the old woman up on the Piana must have gone there at dawn, at least. Did Giulia know where to find her, if she did find her?'

'But didn't you want to go yourself?' said Luisella. 'Didn't you mean to go up in the cable car?'

'I just meant to go up onto the Piana, not out to the pastures. But Giulia must have gone right on to the hut. Why should she have stayed up there? No, I think she went and came back again. She's here in the village, I know, I can feel it.'

'If you say so,' said Luisella. 'After all, you were right about coming here.' Maybe she'd given up that blasted irony of hers. 'I think it'd be odd for her to stay up there,' she went on. 'But suppose she's barricaded herself inside the house? She may have seen you from the window and taken pretty good care not to open up. Did you ask the neighbour? Hadn't she seen anyone coming?'

'No, because she's been out all day herself. What's up, aren't we lovers any longer? She sees me and barricades herself inside the house? Well, I'll go back there and in the meantime you see if the tobacconist's wife's arrived. And don't lose sight of the car. What colour is it?' Once more I plunged into the tunnel. The darkness that awaited me at the end of it was now even denser; and I'm not talking of the darkness outside.

With the help of the torch I found the little door and knocked, decisively this time; I was quite prepared to kick it, in fact. The knocks echoed round the inside; obviously there must have been a small entrance hall. I didn't wait for the echo to die down, but banged again with my open hand, not caring about the row but making the palm sting. After which I carried on banging, but with my clenched fist. My decision produced what seemed like a miracle, because after a bit I heard footsteps in the hall: someone was cautiously approaching the door. There were no strips of light, though, in the cracks of the door. Then the shuffling footsteps stopped, very close to my nose, and I began knocking again. Whoever it was must have had his face stuck to the door, because the voice, though muffled, reached me quite clearly from close by.

'Tonino?' it asked. It was hoarse and disagreeable and I thought I recognised it. Anyway, the accent was unmistakably Neapolitan.

'Open up,' I said softly, without a moment's hesitation.

And he opened the door. Or rather he half opened it and, still without hesitating a moment, I put my right foot and knee against it and pushed it open with my shoulder. At the same time I switched on the torch, and pointed its feeble yellow light on the man's face, feeling, as an immediate reaction, a long shudder all the way down my spine. The man, on the other hand, was obviously unmoved, as if the surprise and break-in had taken place in my house, and had nothing to do with him. And this he could well afford because—and it explains my shudder—he was truly enormous. In that dim light I saw standing before me the wicked giant of all the fairy tales I'd ever read as a child. As ugly as sin, with a low forehead, the pop-eyes of a hippopotamus and a face covered in boils, he was so huge that at times the top of his head almost grazed the ceiling.

Without changing expression, he put out an arm like a girder, with an octopus on the end instead of a hand. Then slowly he put out another girder with another octopus on the end of it. I felt myself gripped round the hips and lifted off the floor in a slow continuous movement: he was doing a *pas de deux* and I was his ballerina, his Margot Fonteyn. Slowly I travelled through the air, in that constant, suffocating upward twirl, and in the end found myself only at the level of that phenomenon of nature's face.

I hadn't dropped the torch, so the loathesome creature was fully lit by its feeble reflector. His mouth was wide open and out of it came a cavernous roar, and a foul stink of rotten teeth. It was his way of grunting and frightening people. And I could fit down his gullet in one piece.

Then he put me down suddenly and I dropped on to my heels. The bump thundered through my head, and as I fell all the unawakened aches of all my well-matured bruises came to life again and the buzzing in my ear broke out too. I dropped the torch, which fell on the floor and stayed there, still switched on, its ray pointing towards the monster's feet, which were encased in the biggest pair of ugly old shoes I'd ever seen in my life.

Then a great thunderbolt of a blow floored me, coming from the darkness around those feet. The octopus which hit me must have turned into a hammer, and I nearly lost my senses.

I heard the door slam and was gripped under the armpits. He was carrying me away as a gigantic, indignant policeman might carry off a mischievous boy he'd caught with his hand in someone's pocket. He crossed the little hall, lit from below by the torch on the floor, flung open a door at the end of it and pushed me through it. Then he shut the door, crossed a dark room and, still holding me up by the arm, guided by the light that came from another room beyond, he pushed me into this one.

Giulia was there, sitting in the middle of the room, wearing trousers and a T-shirt. I then realised that her hands and feet were tied behind the back and legs of the chair, which stood there on its own. When she heard us come in she turned her head and a gleam of hope lit up the glorious blue of her eyes.

'Shut up, not a word,' the giant whispered hoarsely behind me. 'I've brought your Sasà along, see, but you're not to talk, you mustn't say a word. The neighbours mustn't hear. Remember?'

So we continued to look at each other in silence. Frowning and angry, hiding all sorts of mysterious rages inside her, Giulia was lovelier than ever. But it lasted only a moment. Her eyes flashed again and she suddenly opened her mouth. I don't know what she said, though (if the fright I suddenly saw in her face did in fact make her talk), because this time the hammer-blow flung me down on the back of my head. Stronger than before, fiercer than before. And this time, yes, I lost consciousness.

22

I woke up with the most splitting headache of all time, and one of my shoes missing. I knew what I owed the first to, but where the shoe had gone I'd no idea. Every throb in my temples was a roar of pain that thundered through the back half of my skull. So there was no point in trying to think.

The man, if you can call him that, who'd beaten me up had disappeared. Only Giulia was left, sitting in the middle of the room, her head hanging, flopped forward as far as her arms tied behind the chair would allow, and with her mouth open. She was asleep. I was lying on the floor on my right side between her and the door, and I'd already been asleep, in a manner of speaking. How many hours, though, I couldn't work out; between one rumble and the next inside my brain, and above the familiar buzzing, I could hear, muffled by the window panes and the closed shutters, a continuous chirping. It must already be dawn, and the window must face out on to a garden.

The painful roaring in my head brought about by the throbbing was accompanied by sharper pain at my wrists and ankles, which were tied with wire that cut into me every time I moved. Besides this, my hands were behind my back and I had to lie bent almost double on my side. I looked at my left foot again, pressed tight against the right foot: the big toe stared at me, clear and stark, from a hole in the dark sock. I must have lost the shoe while we were doing that little dance, when he'd lifted me up and I'd struggled in the air: it certainly couldn't be called a fight. Or when he'd dragged me away. The monster.

There was no doubt about it, it was he who'd answered the phone when I rang Casali; the voice was unmistakable. The last time had been on Friday afternoon, when I'd rung from my office, and Casali, the swine, had revealed that he knew Giulia had the papers. So he's sent this giant after her, with plenty of time to get to Milan and then up to the mountains. But how had he managed to get on her track?

I couldn't stand it any longer in that position. I pushed even harder with my knees and, with a jerk to the side, tried to get into a sitting position. At the third attempt I managed it, with a groan, and looked around me.

It was a dining-room that I was in, with the table pushed up against the window, two sideboards, and, in a corner, a radiogram that was almost an antique. On top of one of the sideboards a bronze Roman chariot stood on a lace mat, on the other was a collection of knickknacks and keepsakes as modest as the rest of the rustic furniture, and, in front of them all, right in front, the unappealing face of Pino Gargiulo smiled at me from a dark wooden frame. A young, beardless Pino, but recognisable.

The chair to which Giulia was tied was in the exact middle of the room, where the table which the monster must have moved aside had stood, and just above her head a small light, which was switched on, hung from the ceiling, bringing out the coppery gleams in her hair. My groan must have awakened her: she shook herself in that stiff-necked position and raised her head. Then she saw me, sitting on the floor like an armless beggar, and said:

'What happened?'

'I ought to ask you,' I said. 'You saw him: what did he hit me with? A strong box?'

'His fist,' said Giulia. 'Well, what I meant to say was, how on earth are you here?'

'That's another thing I ought to be asking you,' I said. We were talking in whispers. Then I whispered a brief summary of all that concerned her in what had happened to me during the past forty-eight hours. 'What about you?' I asked her at the end, as if we were at a smart tea-party. 'How long have you been here? In this state, I mean.' Then I became aware of myself again: still sitting on the floor, with a shoe missing, tied with a double length of wire, head boiling, stomach empty. I hadn't eaten since the previous day, I realised. In Milan.

'Since yesterday afternoon. And I can't stand much more,' she said.

'Where did that giant spring from?' I asked.

'I don't know, I found him suddenly beside me while I was opening the door. Terrifying. He grabbed me and dragged me inside, covering my mouth with that great paw of his.'

'Wasn't there anyone in the road? Didn't the neighbours see anything?'

'Of course not, there wasn't a soul about. He dragged me inside and flung me down on this chair, saying he'd kill me if I moved or screamed. I'm used to frights by now but this was the worst one of all. No question of moving or screaming, I was paralysed. Then he started looking around, flinging everything about. He was trying to find a rope and in the end he found this sort of string which is round my wrists and ankles.' She was delighted to be able to talk, but without noticing had raised her voice. So she stopped and looked at the open door.

'But didn't he say anything? Didn't you do anything?'

'What could I do? When the first panic was over, I was still terrified. He's a madman, or rather he's demented. Haven't you seen him? Besides, I was bound and gagged. He put a rag in my mouth as well, but took it out afterwards. Nothing, he said nothing to me. All he did was grunt, which frightened me even more. At one point he said we were expecting a friend, but he may have been talking to himself. He did seem to be waiting for someone, though, prowling round the house like an impatient animal. Yesterday evening someone came and knocked at the door several times and he was waiting beside the door, listening. I heard voices outside too, then nothing. Not much later, someone banged very hard and he looked at me and said: "This time it's him". After which he came in again with you.'

So that other beast had been expected: he was merely late. I didn't want to think about it. 'You said you were opening the door,' I said. 'With what key?'

'I got here about midday and went up to Carlinda's hut,' she replied. 'She gave me the key so that I could wait for her down here. She'll be down this morning because it's Sunday, and I'm already afraid of the fright she'll get as soon as she arrives. At her age.'

'Let's see if we can get away first, and prevent it,' I said, with a confidence I was far from feeling. 'Giulia, why did you run away again? Why did you leave your stepmother? In that state, too.'

'Yes, I know,' she said. 'It must have been another blow for her, and I'm terribly sorry. But just then it was stronger than me. She told me something that stunned me. Suddenly I saw her as responsible for everything that had happened to me. She's Pino's mother, d'you understand?'

I understood, partly because I already knew it. Luisella wouldn't have, she'd probably have needed a more rational explanation. So would Assenza. Come to think of it I'd have given my fifty thousand francs to have him there, him and his men. And the ten thousand too. This led me to ask her, automatically:

'And what about the papers? Did he ask you about them? Where have you put them, Giulia?'

'No, he didn't ask me about any papers,' she replied. 'He just grunted. Listen, I didn't manage to tell you that evening in Formia, I couldn't or I didn't want to, I can't remember which it was now. You seemed to me so dodgy and at the same time so ingenuous, both interested and disinterested. I don't know, I told you practically everything, whereas I'd have liked to turn my back on you and run away, like I did the next morning. But there was one detail I didn't want to tell you.'

'What detail? Don't keep me waiting,' I said.

'That I haven't got those papers any longer.'

It was like getting another blow. On the back half of my skull this time. The physical effect I can't describe; in fact I can't distinguish it from all the others I'd had so far. All I know is that I thought at once of Assenza, of his allusions, his jokey smiles. Exactly what we wanted to avoid had happened, and had happened from the very first. I understood, I realised it at once: he'd had the papers in his hands all the time, the wretch. To hell with fifty thousand francs, I'd make that monster tear him to pieces.

'You'd hidden them in the suitcase?' I said, with an effort.

'Yes. When I went back to Faito next evening I put them in a suitcase so as not to take the file up with me. But I heard those footsteps and ran off, leaving everything there.'

'It was me,' I said, wanting, this time, to tell her everything. 'The footsteps you heard were mine. I'd come to look for you there—you and the papers. You got away from me, but the papers were there under my nose. If I'd had a minute longer I might have found them, but I was interrupted too. By the police, whom I'd sent for myself.'

'And what about this time?' she said. 'Have you come up this mountain still looking for the papers? Aren't you my . . . saviour?' she added, with I don't know what degree of irony.

'No, this time I was looking for you. As for the papers, well, I've realised that they're an open secret.'

What was happening? Was I saying goodbye to all my millions? Was I being carried away by those blue eyes? I don't know. Certainly my thoughts ran—inevitably—to Don Michele's promises, but I felt I'd got down to one last hope. If anyone else had got hold of those wretched papers—Casali, Tonino, the man who kept an eye on my car, the whole of Naples—it wouldn't have been a definite obstacle to the conclusion of the whole business. Anyone else. But Assenza meant the end of the whole dream, and, if they didn't actually go to prison, some of the smaller fry on that corrupt council would lose their jobs. As for me, I might lose face and therefore the chance of dreaming up anything else, at least in that way. But that was just a probability: what was certain was the loss of the money we'd expected.

Giulia was looking oddly at me. I now felt I had to say: 'It's true, I came here just for your sake.' But not to mention my final hope of those fifty thousand francs. Hope? Not even that, perhaps, we'd have to get out of this desperate situation first. With Tonino turning up at any moment. 'Where's the creature got to?' I asked.

'In there, asleep. He must have changed his position just now, but he was snoring till a while ago. Didn't you hear him?'

No. I'd been in heaven and all I'd heard was the twittering of the birds. Giulia listened for the snores again and heard only silence. Then she added, in another whisper: 'He's a very heavy sleeper, the beast, but we'd better talk more quietly.'

But I no longer wanted to talk. I was thinking of Luisella, who'd stayed outside. She must be doing something. I'd vanished, almost under her nose. My glance fell again on that unattractive Pino and I wished him all the pains of hell; then I looked at Giulia. She understood.

'Yes, I've seen him, I've been looking at him since yesterday. D'you know something?' We were exchanging confidences; I sitting on the floor, half dead with the blows I'd had and the news I'd heard, she on her chair, both of us bound and aching, with the monster asleep in the next room. 'I don't feel anything for him any longer.'

That creep in the photograph was the cause of everything, and she no longer felt anything for him. 'Not even hatred?' I said.

'That's what I meant. I don't hate him any more. I know now that he wanted to be revenged on my father. You were right: he got at him through his wife and daughter.' And through the papers, I thought. 'I was the idiot, for not realising it at once. When I think of some of the things he said . . .'

'Forget it. Don't think of anything, Giulia. Or rather, think of the beast who'll soon be waking up while we sit here chatting.' I didn't remind her that the other beast might turn up at any moment; perhaps she'd forgotten.

'But what can we do?' she said.

'I'll try and drag myself across to you, and your hands are free. D'you think you could free mine? There aren't any knots to untie, you just need to loosen the twisted wire.'

'Let's try,' she said, whispering even more softly.

We tried, or rather I tried, creeping along like a snake, twisting like an epileptic, pressing on the heel of my single shoe, bearing down on it and thus rubbing my buttocks along the floor. Every movement made the burning wire sink into my flesh. But in the end I reached the chair. Giulia followed every movement of mine with a grimace, automatically mimicking each painful effort I made. Then I came to the hardest and certainly the most awkward part: getting on to my feet. I laid my head first on her thigh and then, arching my whole body with an enormous effort, on her lap. I felt the warmth and smell of her body and lingered there. Only for a moment: immediately afterwards I bore down on my neck and heaved my seat off the floor; then, dragging my head on her lap, I managed to press my right shoulder against her thigh. I wriggled on and in the end found myself with my trunk leaning against her legs and my feet placed feebly on the floor. I was in her lap like a child and, considering all I was feeling both inside and out, I might have started crying. But I could now feel her breath, her warm breath on my ear and cheek: she was bending over me, held back only because her arms were tied to the back of the chair. I didn't move.

At this point we both heard the noise and stayed quite still in that odd position. The giant must have done something next door—moved a chair, a table, a wardrobe; then we realised he was just farting, having started timidly and feebly, and ending up in a roar. Just enjoying his sleep, the swine. Giulia started laughing silently, shaking with laughter, and those shivers in her tummy made me realise how unaware of our danger she was. I kept quiet too, biting my lips and stifling my indecorous laughter by burying my head in her lap, in the cloth of her trousers.

But the nightmare suddenly began again. Our two silent bursts of laughter ceased and we listened. There were no further noises, he really was asleep. The silence seemed like a continuous buzzing in the room, all over the house; then the birds outside started up singing again and I redoubled my efforts. Finally I found myself sitting on Giulia's knees. My head was now an anvil with a thousand hammers beating on it, the sharp wire felt as if it had cut off my hands and feet, and yet I felt relieved: the ridiculous position we had achieved, the previous contortions, our joint efforts and anxieties, had established a feeling of intimacy between us. I turned: she was looking at me, and her eyes smiled into mine.

'Shall I try and stand up? Now?' I whispered.

'Try, Sasà,' she said, able to address me so now.

I set my feet squarely on the floor and tried again. Then I was standing, and then, once again, sitting on her knees. Then on my feet again, then, with the side of my leg against the chair, I took my first small jump. A wave of blinding pain swept up from my ankles; but the chair, with Giulia's weight on it, held me up when I fell again on both heels—the shod and the unshod—my already painful head shot through with further throbs.

When I was behind the chair-back, back to back with Giulia, I said: 'Now I'll try and lower myself till our hands meet. I can't stay in that position for long, so hurry.'

And I crouched down. Our hands met. I leant harder against

the back of the chair, and she fiddled at my wrists and found the twisted ends of wire. I could feel her working at a single point. Before she managed to loosen the two ends I had to pull myself up several times, and I don't know where the pain was worst, at my knees, my ankles or my wrists. Not to mention my head again. In the end she took hold of one of the ends of wire she had just undone and, by raising and lowering her arms, managed to undo the whole thing. My hands were free.

When my feet were free as well I had to wait for the pins and needles and stiffness to leave my arms and legs. Then I freed Giulia. And at that very moment, on the dot, the monster awoke.

At that sudden burst of noise, which only a stallion waking suddenly in a china shop instead of his usual box in the stable could have made, even the birds fell silent all at once. We remained frozen and still, I standing beside the chair, Giulia still sitting. The giant was in the bedroom next door, which was dark because the shutters were closed, and had suddenly woken and left the bed, knocking over everything in his way. Then we realised he was going away from the door of our room, towards the hall. And he must have remembered the neighbours, because he suddenly stopped crashing against the furniture loaded with fragile objects and tiptoed out of the room.

'He must have gone to the loo,' whispered Giulia. 'It's beyond the hall, towards the courtyard.'

I rushed to the window, and opened it and the shutters. It looked out on to a small inner garden that must have communicated at the end with the courtyard where the lavatory was. It was already day and the only tree in the middle of the garden was full of birds recovering from their fright. I looked round the inside of the room, perplexed. Giulia was now on her feet and had begun rubbing her arms and legs frantically. Then we heard the shuffle of footsteps once again in the hall and she ran to me, grabbed one of my arms and whined like a frightened puppy. For a moment I looked around, no less bewildered. My eyes met Pino's ill-omened eyes and I looked away to the sideboard opposite and the one object that might be useful sometime as a defensive weapon: the bronze chariot.

The giant was now entering the room next door and it was then that Giulia began screaming at the top of her voice with all the breath in her body, still clinging to my arm, in fact squeezing it harder.

Like a bison frightened by a sudden noise, the giant charged at once. Like a fury he crossed the other room and burst into ours at the very moment when, jerking my arm free, I leapt towards the chariot. We met in the middle and I banged my head against his chest. It was like hitting a rock: my skull seemed to explode. Then I began shaking all over. I hadn't decided it myself, no orders had gone out to my torpid limbs from my stupified brain: it was he who was shaking me like a rag doll, squeezing my throat between fingers that couldn't have been human and pushing me further into unconsciousness, although I was struggling and screeching at the electric shocks of the pain and spasms running through me, as if I'd run into some high-voltage wires.

Then his hands left my throat, twisted me right round, and, like the grab on an excavator given its orders from a distance, grabbed me by a shoulder and a buttock and lifted me up into the air. I was like any odd parcel, waiting to be carried off God knows where—certainly I didn't know, being completely unconscious by then. All I know is that at some point I was restored to life, in a manner of speaking, by a blow at the back of the pelvis that should by rights have finished me off.

I found myself sitting on the floor with the giant, who, having suddenly dropped me, was drooping over me like a mountain slowly disintegrating through some landslide in the bowels of the earth. In the end he crumbled completely, squashing me under his enormous weight.

23

Giulia had been yelling throughout the whole terrible encounter —that was the only thing I could remember—and in the final moments those howls had fused with a single high-pitched screech that suddenly ceased at the final thump, when that great inanimate mass heaved over and fell. She was now calling me.

'Sasà, Sasà.' In a whisper once again.

She helped me to get out from under him and then, swaying and stumbling, to reach the chair. To put it mildly, I was completely done in. I looked at her and felt a wave of vitality in her. She seemed full of zip and excitement, kept getting up and crouching beside the chair, uncertain what to do, like a mother who's just seen her child escape from a horrifying danger. But, in particular, I saw that she was clutching the bronze chariot in her hand. The great mass lying between us and the door was quite still, and there seemed a definite connection between the two facts.

'Is he dead?' Giulia asked in a worried voice. 'You look, I don't dare to.' She had her back to him.

I looked again at the latest disaster in my life and saw nothing but his stillness; all I could make out was a red stain at the nape of his neck. He lay with his face on the floor and his arms folded under his chest, as if at the last minute he'd pushed forward to save himself as he fell. In fact, I'd come between him and the floor. Anyway, he was too still to be breathing. Was it possible that this avalanche of a man had been brought down by a single blow from the slender Giulia?

'I don't know, I can't take it in,' I said. 'I ought to go up to him, but I just can't do it.' Then, as if it was the right time for it, I said what I was really longing to do at that particular moment: 'I must rest.'

Giulia looked at me as if she hadn't understood, then exclaimed: 'I've killed him. My God, I've killed him.'

'No, sir,' I barked. And she was suddenly silent, scared. 'You didn't kill him. And even if you did, it wasn't your fault. He'd have slaughtered the two of us.'

She had killed him, though. In the end I got up and went cautiously across, as if he were some wild animal asleep. I even leant over him, all my joints cracking: he wasn't breathing and the wound behind his head was still bleeding. I got up again and turned to look at Giulia. She burst into tears and ran into my arms.

The scene that had taken place before was now repeated, only the other way round: it was I who took her to the chair, holding her up. But she sat there for only a moment. I think she'd found better shelter in my arms, because she flung herself into them again. I hugged her hard, carried away by her bewilderment, and discovered that all my ribs, at the very least, seemed broken.

I then discovered, yet again, that disasters never come singly.

The latest—the most striking and monstrous of them all—was now a corpse. But the very last, more menacing still, if possible, was at that moment banging at the door.

There was no doubt who was thumping on the door outside; we could both hear it perfectly well, above Giulia's sobs. I was no longer in a state to behave with dignity, and looked at her in terror. I thought, and it was only for a moment: why the hell hasn't Luisella done anything?

On an impulse, convinced that Tonino would break down not merely the door but the very walls of the house, I flew to the window, dragging Giulia after me, though she was oddly reluctant: she'd turned to look at the giant on the floor and seemed fascinated by the sight of him. She was sobbing and moaning at once, and couldn't manage to climb over the low windowsill, so I had to lift her too, a dead weight or nearly so.

Opposite us was the windowless wall of the house next door, on the left a fairly low wall, on the right, at the end, the courtyard that led back to the entrance hall and above, the sky of a new dark, threatening day. It had rained in the night and the ground was wet.

There wasn't much to look at, it was all there; unless we climbed into the tree and perched there among the birds. This, and a long narrow ladder I saw lying on the ground under the window we'd just climbed through, gave me an idea.

'Is there an inside staircase leading up to the roof?' I asked Giulia.

She looked surprised, then shook her head. After which everything happened very fast. I resigned myself to the idea of another siege—but at least out of doors and I hoped in sight of the entire village—and prayed that Luisella would turn up with someone in time. And in a few moments we were both up on the wet roof of the house, cold, sitting close to each other on the hip between the two steep sides.

With no help from Giulia, and with one of my shoes missing, I'd hastily pulled up the ladder, leant it against the wall, seen with relief that it reached the roof, dragged Giulia up to the top rung and pulled the ladder up behind us. It was now lying there beside me and a good length of it stuck straight out beyond the hip of the roof, threatening to slip down at any moment. In spite of our shouts and noise, the whole village was still deep in a Sunday morning torpor and knew nothing; like the birds, who kept on chirruping. The tiles were freezing cold.

Tonino must have got tired of knocking and from the alley, which was invisible because of the gutter, no sound reached us. Knowing my vulture, though, I was sure he'd never go away. Meantime Giulia, in that thin cotton T-shirt, had stopped sobbing and started shivering, so I took off my jacket, put it round her shoulders, and took over her shudders. Then I took her hand and laid it on the ladder.

'Hold tight,' I said. 'Don't let it slip down, if you do we'll find him up here with us. D'you realise who it is?' She nodded. 'The man the monster was expecting.'

Creeping forward on hands and knees across the wet roof, I managed, without falling, to reach a point from which I could see part of what was happening in the road. Nothing was happening. Tonino was waiting, but he'd moved away from the front door enough to let me see his legs and feet, if I leant out as far as I could. It had now become a tradition with the two of us. The dandy had changed, though: no grey suit, no parti-coloured shoes: he was all in black, suit and shoes. Then the legs vanished and I heard him knocking again, stubbornly. But impatiently too. I was a few yards above him and I heard him swearing to himself.

It was as if he knew about the great dead hulk inside the house which was keeping the door shut and sealed.

From below I could see the whole of the little alleyway. Two figures were entering it at that very moment, on my right. When, with thumping heart, I began to make them out and saw that they were Luisella and a man in uniform, what oughtn't to have happened happened.

Giulia, behind me, gave a shout. I turned and was only just in time to save myself: the ladder was slipping faster and faster down the sloping roof. It passed a few inches from my nose and fell into the road, just at my feet, bounced and then landed with a noise that, this time at least, must have wakened the whole village. Tonino at once leapt backwards, almost hitting the garden wall behind him. He raised his head, looked up, and our eyes met. I don't know what there was in mine; his were flashing with a furious hatred that stunned me, leaving me there surprised and motionless on all fours on the freezing tiles. Dressed entirely in black as he was, he must have hurried from his brother's funeral to rush up here, in time for the funeral of another outsize beast.

He gave me a final glare of hatred and hurled himself on the fallen ladder, vanishing under the gutter. I turned to Giulia.

Sitting on the hip of the roof, holding on to the row of

horizontal tiles with one hand, she had her other hand up at her mouth and was looking at me with wide open eyes. 'It slipped away from me,' she exclaimed. 'It wasn't my fault, it was too heavy. It slipped away.'

At that moment Luisella saw me from a distance and started calling desperately. The policeman for his part shouted: 'Stop! Stop there!' and began running.

He was calling to Tonino who, I now saw, had lifted the ladder, laid it on to the gutter, and already had his foot on the bottom rung. He hadn't quite got the knife between his teeth but he was certainly going in for the kill, so he didn't stop when the policeman shouted, he just kept on climbing.

Still on my hands and knees, I reached the top of the ladder when he was already half-way up it and the policeman a few yards away. I seized the two uprights of the ladder and, on my knees, tried to push it away from the roof and overturn it. But it was jammed against the opposite wall, and so too steeply inclined, and was carrying the weight of Tonino, who, filled with hatred and savagery, was already more than half-way up it. I stood up, grabbed one of the uprights with both hands and tugged. The ladder swung round onto the other upright and began slipping along the gutter until it fell, taking with it Tonino and the policeman, who'd followed him on to the bottom rungs and had grabbed one of his feet.

The Lauria family must have been a race of panthers. Tonino leapt from the ground as if shot up on a spring and, whether bruised or not, wounded or not, was on his feet in a moment in front of the policeman, whose reflexes were slower and more human, and who, above all, was the older of the two. The policeman had only just managed to get on his knees when Tonino flung himself upon him, ready to tear him apart. Shouting continuously, Luisella leapt on his back like a gazelle and clung there, banging him with feeble fists. But he took not the slightest notice and continued squeezing the neck of the kneeling policeman who with one hand was trying to free himself and with the other was fiddling with the holster of his pistol.

I was watching from above, quite powerless. Luisella shouted to me to do something and I tried frantically to loosen one of the tiles. It came away at the very moment in which Luisella had in desperation left Tonino and run to the door of the next house, which had opened at last. Without taking aim and with the risk of hitting the policeman as well, I hurled the tile. It fell about half a yard from the pair of them and broke into a thousand pieces. Meantime, a tall strong man in a woollen vest had come into the road from the house next door. He made ready to rush at the two but then stopped suddenly. I don't know when he'd pulled it out, but Tonino was now waving a knife.

The second tile came away more easily; I threw it and this time hit him on the shoulder just as he was aiming his blow, which was turned aside. The blade sank into the policeman's arm, just as he managed to get out the pistol, which fell from his hand. Tonino kicked it away towards the man in the vest, who was still watching the scene indecisively. Luisella shouted something to him and he leant over to pick it up, but hesitated a little longer, holding the weapon.

At the same time the black panther leapt backwards, pulling the blade from the arm it had sunk into and approaching the third tile, which hit him in the small of his back. The policeman, still on his knees, was collapsing breathlessly, his arm bleeding. Then Tonino turned and looked up at me and I was just in time to bend forward and avoid the knife, which hit the tiles behind me, bounced and slipped down into the gutter. He must have felt powerless then, because he fled. He had lightning reflexes; in the same movement with which he'd used his arm to throw the knife, he turned right round and ran off.

His black figure scarcely skimmed the large paving stones on the ground as he flew towards the entrance to the alleyway and finally vanished behind the angle of the roof, even before the man holding the pistol had overcome his obvious reluctance to act.

I rang Miletti from the hotel. The sighing had vanished and instead he was grunting. What did this mean?

'You woke me up, Iovine,' he said. It was two in the afternoon and Luisella was asleep as well. She'd flung herself down on the bed the moment she got into the room and passed out. 'I hope you've got important news, at least. Have you found Giulia?'

I told him where and how I'd found her and what had happened inside and outside the house. All I forgot to tell him was that I'd lost and recovered a shoe; about the rest, I omitted no detail. The first amazing question he asked me when I'd finished was: 'And where's Tonino now?'

'Nobody knows. He may have emigrated to Switzerland, which is just down the road here, or he may have gone back to Naples. He's travelling in a hired car, so it'll be hard to stop him on the motorway.'

'And the other one? That Pappa?' He knew the monster as well.

'They haven't taken him away yet, maybe they're waiting for a bulldozer. What did you say his name was?'

'Pappalardo. He's one of Casali's old trusties. He must have sent him ahead to give the other one time to change his suit.'

'But how come he knew of the old woman's existence, or her address?'

'Iovine, wake up,' said Miletti. 'Marullo. Haven't you got there yet? In the early days that ugly bastard used to send my money to that address, and Casali thought of the old woman and sent Pappa straight off to her.'

'But Giulia mightn't have gone there,' I said. 'In fact, it was just a chance that she did. If she'd stayed with her stepmother...'

'Well, she went there, stepmother or no stepmother. Where better to hide?'

Nothing happened in which the little cripple wasn't involved. I told Miletti this and asked him how and why it was so.

'He loathes me, as I've told you. And his complicity with

that woman set him definitely against me. So he went over to Casali and told him everything that might harm me. But don't make me talk too much, my lungs get tired and I've got to be careful. Tell me about Giulia. Where is she now?'

'With the police. They've kept her. We're waiting for the magistrate to come from Domodossola, but you'll see, he'll let her out on parole right away.'

'But why?' he asked, to my amazement. 'Didn't you take on responsibility?'

'Well really . . .'

'How could it possibly happen? A little girl killing a man like that!'

I still hadn't told him of Giulia's unexpected gesture. The fact was that she'd told the police that at the time it happened I was tied up in the other room and she'd freed me after dealing the monster the blow that killed him. And I'd said nothing. I'd even been thanked by the policeman who intervened with Luisella, for saving him from getting the knife in his heart, and praised for my silly idea of dragging Giulia up on to the roof. An idea that served only to increase Tonino's hatred and rage, by exposing me up there. If I hadn't been there he mightn't have attacked the policeman who tried to stop him, but might merely have run away when he saw him.

'Don Michele, it wasn't possible . . .' I stammered.

'Not possible? So I'm paying you to send my daughter to gaol, am I?'

'I don't understand, Don Michele,' I protested. 'Am I supposed to go to gaol myself? For what I haven't done?'

'Of course,' he said, indignant and angry now. 'I certainly didn't expect this. All right. All right. I'll get in touch with my lawyer straight away.'

'Your daughter made a statement first, telling the truth. I couldn't deny it; it would have complicated things for her as well.'

Miletti took no notice, but considered the matter again. 'Legitimate self-defence, anyway. They can't do anything. All right,' he conceded, not at all persuaded. 'That's how it had to be. If only Lentizzi were still around; it would be useful.'

I expected this no more than I'd expected what he said before. 'What could Lentizzi do in this case?' I asked. 'Why, what's happened?'

'Everything's going wrong for me,' he said. 'They've suspended him. It's just happened.' He must have turned that little room in the nursing home into an information bureau. 'So I'm losing people all round.' Another illusion? But he was now beginning to lose his grip.

Among other things, he didn't know what cards Assenza held. It wasn't the right moment to tell Miletti this, though; I put it off and thought of Lentizzi instead. And of Assenza, who clearly never missed a trick. But how had he got as far as Lentizzi?

'Everything's going wrong for me,' Miletti went on. 'In any case, stick close to her now.' And, still the sibyl with pneumonia, he added: 'Look after your own interests, this time at least.'

I left Luisella asleep in the hotel and went back to the police station. The policeman's wound wasn't serious, and I found him there with his arm bandaged. Giulia was there too in the bare little room, sitting on the bench in front of the sergeant's table. Old Carlinda was beside her, holding her hand.

She was old, but her face was fresher than Elena Miletti's; her cheeks were red and her white hair was drawn back into a bun. Her hands were the only thing that betrayed her age, they were wrinkled and blotched on the back and remarkably large; hands made to welcome a child, to give him shelter and comfort, as she was now comforting this other child, with her loving handclasp.

'Mr Iovine,' said the sergeant, in a friendly voice, still grateful to me. 'The magistrate will be here in a few minutes. When you've repeated your statement you can go, if you like. But I'm afraid you'll have to come back. If not here, to Domodossola.' I had stated, and signed, only part of the truth: I'd gone there to fetch Giulia on her father's behalf and had found myself in this trouble. Giulia and Luisella had confirmed this.

'And what about Miss Miletti?' I asked.

'The magistrate will decide.'

Giulia said nothing. She was gazing into space with the concentrated expression given only by resignation to suffering. Carlinda had laid an old pullover over her shoulders and she was no longer trembling as she had been the last time I saw her. I wondered why she'd wanted to exclude me from the least bit of responsibility for the killing.

'Giulia,' I said. I'd gone up to her and she raised her head, but this time her eyes weren't smiling. 'I didn't say anything before, I didn't contradict you because I didn't want to complicate things.' This was partly true. 'But . . .'

She indicated the sergeant with frightened eyes. I then turned to him, sitting there embarrassed and bandaged.

'Sergeant,' I said, 'might I talk to Miss Miletti alone? Just for a moment?'

He cleared his throat before answering. 'Well I don't know . . . Look, I'll go and get my cigarettes from in there.'

When the three of us were alone, I found that Carlinda's presence wasn't that of a stranger. The free hand lying in her lap might offer shelter and comfort to me as well. At that moment, anyway. She never said a word, she sat quite still, not even listening. She merely comforted us.

'Giulia, will you tell me why you did it?'

No answer.

'I talked to your father a while ago. He says I mustn't leave you alone. He'll send a lawyer. He's still in the nursing home himself, unfortunately.'

'I hope he stays there,' she replied unexpectedly. 'He never ought to get out again. He must never get out and harm anyone else.'

I couldn't understand her stubborn hatred. For Pino, all feeling had gone: for her father she'd fan the flames of hell. 'Giulia, you mustn't . . .'

'Talk like that? Don't make me laugh . . . Sasa.' She didn't use my nickname in a contemptuous tone, not at all, but her tone wasn't particularly familiar either. 'Let's drop my father. I'm really dropping him. For ever. You want to know why I did it. Because it didn't change anything for me. I killed him, and it would have complicated things for you. And I want you to go away at once. You must go to Elena. Give her this.' She spoke slowly, as if with an effort, and as she did so unstrapped the man's watch she was wearing on her wrist. 'It's Pino's. I'd bought it to give him when I found I was pregnant by him. Before he was to have run off with me. Now it belongs to Elena.'

I took the watch. 'I don't understand, Giulia.'

'You never will. Take it to Elena. As soon as possible.'

'But you can give it to her yourself, it's just a question of . . .'

'I haven't the courage, even to ring her up, after . . . after I left her as I did, and at that time. And tell her I won't have an abortion. That in spite of what I've been through just now, nothing's happened to the baby. Tell her I'll have it.' She looked round at her old nurse beside her and squeezed her hand more tightly. 'Carlinda will look after me and the baby.'

The other hand, the one which had been lying in Carlinda's lap and might have protected and comforted me, moved across to cover the back of Giulia's, which was so much smaller and frailer, and was thus completely covered.

24

We managed to set off for Milan only early on Monday morning. The magistrate had arrived from Domodossola at six in the evening. It was Sunday, and as far as they were concerned this explained everything. We were free only about ten o'clock, after I'd been to the hotel twice to wake Luisella; the first time, when the magistrate arrived, the second around eight, for some confirmatory questions. Luisella was longing to sleep. Missing a night was fatal to her. She'd spent the previous night in the street, the square and the police station, where the policeman hadn't dared to take any initiative without orders from the sergeant who was up on the Piana. It was Saturday evening when she turned up at the police station for the first time, and this explained everything too, as far as they were concerned.

Later, in the hotel, she curled up round my bruises and fractures and went suddenly to sleep for the third time. Holding her in my arms, I thought of Giulia and of what we had been through together. And of her eyes, which when we said goodbye a little earlier had lost their light. They were sending her to Domodossola next day, where I was to present myself half-way through the week. Then I fell asleep too.

On the journey, after the first hour of silence, I told Luisella that we would have to go to Elena Miletti's before leaving. She said nothing, she was now very sweet to me. But she wanted to see the watch, of course.

'I understand her,' she said, making me furious. But what the hell? I didn't understand a thing. Maybe she was right, all I understood was business. And what business.

'You don't understand Don Michele though, do you?' I said.

'No, I don't,' she said. Firmly. And we spoke no more of him.

When we went into via Macedonio Melloni, I saw at once that something was different about it. First of all it wasn't raining any longer, then the street seemed livelier and this, as we approached the house, gradually became less of an impression, more of a fact. As we passed the front door we saw a crowd surrounding an ambulance and some grey-green police cars, with the lights winking on their roofs. And a couple of black cars too.

I found a place to park much further on and we walked back. Outside the entrance there was a proper crowd, held in check by a couple of policemen. At that moment Assenza was coming out, with another man dressed in a dark suit, another policeman. He looked very busy and wasn't wearing sunglasses. He saw me at once.

'You've come at the right moment, Iovine,' he said, coming across to me. He wasn't smiling and there was no irony in his small eyes. 'Come along. Is the young lady with you? Come along, both of you.'

He took us in and went ahead of us through the street door. Behind him was a short staircase with a red runner down the middle. He stopped at the first step, with the other man still beside him, and turned to us.

'May I ask you something you asked me? Precisely, last Friday. How on earth do you come to be here? And in such a mess, too. But please don't answer with another question.'

'Well, I was just going to ask what's happened,' I said.

'I'll tell you later. Satisfy my curiosity first.'

I told him why I was there. Going back in time, I told him about the watch I was bringing Elena, about Giulia being held at Domodossola, about the wounded sergeant, the raging Tonino, the dead Pappalardo, and almost all the rest. Almost, but not quite all.

'So in the end you found Giulia and Tonino found you,' he said. 'And where is he now?'

I said I didn't know and he was silent for a moment, then he spoke suddenly. 'You're Signorina Luisella, aren't you?' he said. But perhaps the question was meant for me.

In any case, I replied: 'I'm sorry, I haven't . . .'

'Don't be ridiculous, Iovine, this isn't a party. You wanted to know what happened. Well, I won't tell you, I'll show you. Come. In fact, come along, both of you. You come too,' he said to Luisella.

We went up. The landing, when we opened the lift doors, was full of people. The neighbours were all there, and on the stairs as well. The door of the flat was open and obstructed by two uniformed policemen. Inside the flat, though, they were all in plain clothes, at least those I saw.

We went into the sitting-room-cum-dining-room, where there were other people, all very busy. Black marks were everywhere, an army of insects of all sizes that seemed to have attacked every corner of the room and every object in it.

Assenza stopped inside the doorway and, indicating the sofa, said to Luisella: 'Will you be so kind as to wait for us a minute? You can sit there, if you like.'

Then he turned to the dark, silent man who had followed us. 'Monaco, don't leave the young lady alone. Iovine, come with me.'

We went back into the passage that was partly the entrance hall, at the end of which was a door: the bedroom, obviously. We went in.

At once I realised why he'd left Luisella outside. It was made clear to me the moment I was inside the door by the condition, and not merely the physical condition, in which I found myself. I had in fact to lean against the doorpost, and if I hadn't been fasting for so many hours, I'd have thrown up on the spot, under the gaze of those solemn-looking gentlemen discussing things in the room, as they stood round the body of Elena Miletti.

She was lying on the floor between the bed and the window, her legs wide apart, as could be seen from the feet which poked out from under the sheet that covered her to the waist. The rest of the body must have been uncovered a little earlier for the magistrate to see it, but even he hadn't been able to stand it and, clearly shaken, was talking to the others with his back to it. Elena Miletti no longer had a face, only a horrible red mush in its place. A thousand blows couldn't have reduced it to that state, it must have taken ten thousand or more, and blows delivered with a force that suggested the most sadistic, inhuman madness. The temples were in no better state; the whole skull must have been smashed. The mass of hair was reduced to a stringy red, soaked, but not only with blood. Under her the carpet had changed colour, had become a single red stain.

Assenza took my arm. 'Come along,' he said.

We went back to the other room and I sat down beside Luisella. He sat in one of the armchairs, the one in which Elena Miletti had been sitting two days before. Around us the men moved as silently as shadows.

'Monaco, please fetch me a glass of water,' said Assenza to the darkly-dressed silent man, revealing an unexpected thoughtfulness.

The water was warm, obviously run straight from the tap. I drank half, then made ready to listen.

'Iovine,' Assenza said at once, 'I must tell you that basically I like you.' Very nice of him. But he hurried on to add: 'Why I like you I can't imagine. Maybe because through bravura, natural talent, you manage to slip away from me. I ought to catch you but you get away. In the full sense. In other words, I mean that I don't understand you.'

'What should you understand?' I asked. 'And catch me in what?' I wasn't in the ideal mood to follow him or to keep up with his imaginative oratory.

'It's out of proportion,' he exclaimed, as an inadequate answer. Then he went on: 'D'you realise that you're holding back information, and that's an indictable offence? There's no proportion between what you're risking and what you're gaining. If you're gaining anything.'

I didn't know what to object to this. Immediately I thought of the old sibyl and his promise, the last thread on which I was hanging, like a spider disturbed in his web.

'And there's no proportion between this crime and the interest you have in covering up whatever you're covering,' he went on. 'That's why I brought you up. That's why I made you see it with your own eyes.' He looked at Luisella, sitting beside me in silence, bewildered. 'A horrible sight,' he told her. 'It horrified even us, and we're used to such things.' Then he turned back to me. 'She was killed with a rolling-pin, imagine. After being knifed in several places, including the thighs. It happened yesterday afternoon, when the neighbours say they heard bumps and screams. God knows why they didn't come and see. It was discovered this morning by the porter's wife, who worked as her cleaner and had the key.'

He recovered his breath and went on, reporting it in detail. 'Bloodstains led her to the bedroom, where she made the horrible discovery. They started from there.' He pointed, and Luisella and I turned together to look towards the hall. Luisella was tense looking and now clearly uneasy. The stains were there, a great many of them and very noticeable, ringed round with chalk marks.

'It's obvious what happened,' he said. 'The murderer caught her by surprise out there, after some excuse to get her to open the door, and then, although she was already wounded, she ran into the bedroom. She must have been in time to shut herself in, because the door was forced open.' This I'd noticed mechanically: the door without a handle, the lock hanging on the screws around which it had twisted after being wrenched out of the wood. 'There she was caught and killed. Whoever did it was a mad criminal, a fury. He left his prints everywhere, fingerprints and wet shoe prints, even in the kitchen. God knows why he went and got the rolling-pin. He was alone.'

After which we stayed silent, all three of us. I was as shaken as Luisella, yet lucid enough to realise that Assenza was in fact the spider: he was spinning a web much more effectively than I'd managed to do with my poor little efforts. He never ceased to surprise me.

'Have you heard about Lentizzi?' he suddenly came out with.

'Is he dead too?' I asked. Everyone seemed to be dropping down dead around us.

'No, he's just been suspended from duty. A very serious charge, as you can imagine. Not transferred, suspended. Didn't your friend Miletti tell you? You keep in constant touch on the phone.' So he knew this too.

'Well, yes, he did tell me.'

'Lying there on his bed of pain, the grand old man manages to keep in touch with everything. But don't think it's any merit of mine.'

'What is?' I asked.

'Getting to the bottom of things with my—well, let's call him my colleague,' he said. 'The fact is, I was sent the evidence. Documented, too, with plenty of photocopies. What was he— employed half-time by the old boy? He even put his signature on things, the idiot, which the old man kept carefully, in case his friend saw the error of his ways and reformed. D'you know something? I've taken the guard off his room, at the nursing home. And d'you know why?'

'Taken it from Don Miletti?' I said. All this chat was getting me confused. 'Why?'

'Nastiness,' said Assenza. 'I'm nasty too, did you know?' As I said, he liked talking in this sort of way. 'He won't talk. Right, I won't guard him. That'll teach him. When his friends catch up with him. D'you know Improta, for instance?'

'I've often heard him mentioned and I've seen him sometimes. He's the old man's factotum, he gets all the heavy jobs. I think so, anyway. I've never liked him, with those crazy eyes of his.'

'Right. Let's get back to what you're not telling me.'

'At this point, Inspector,' I said, 'I think you know a lot more than I do. What else d'you want to know? D'you see the state I'm in? Well, I'm even worse inside. You've been given documents and photocopies, you've had things whispered into both your ears, what else d'you want? You've got all the winning cards.' And I saw Luisella looking at me with surprise, even more bewildered than before.

'Signorina, take no notice of him,' said Assenza. 'He's a good actor. It's one of the things I like about you, Iovine. You've asked me what I want to know. Well, let's pull in our ears.' The expressions he used. 'You're not officially involved in the business of the contract,' he went on, 'but the whole thing's blown sky high. What's more, you've seen that poor soul in there. Don't you see that you shouldn't be shielding anyone any more? Not anyone, d'you understand?'

'What d'you want to know?' I said. Who could deny what he was saying?

'I'm not asking what you agreed with Casali that would hurt Miletti or with Miletti to hurt Casali. I don't want to know a thing, in any case I know it all. I also know why you were following the old man's daughter and why Tonino was following you. I don't even want to know anything about the car accident, either, that's between you and your conscience. Formally, you're in the clear at the moment and that's fair enough. There's just one thing I want to know. Just the one—it's small but important.' He left the two adjectives to seep right down inside me.

'What did Signora Miletti tell you?' he asked at last.

Seeing me still bewildered, he explained: 'You beat me in getting here. I was delayed in Naples—you can imagine why—and got here only this morning. In time to make this other discovery, like you. I wanted to talk to the lady, though, whereas you're the one who actually did. And you mustn't deny it. You got here on Saturday morning, you saw Signora Miletti and you spoke to her. What did she say to you? That's all I want to know.' Then he added, implacably: 'For the moment.'

A fly in his web, I thought. And I now thought, too, that I

didn't give a damn for Miletti's private affairs and that we might just as well hang his dirty linen out in the sun to dry. 'Well, everything,' I replied.

'Try and remember. I imagine the poor soul confided in you. It can happen. Sometimes, when a person's had a shock, he pours it all out and confides in the dustman.' Just to show he liked me, this. 'So I imagine she told you the life history of Pino Gargiulo, which I know myself by now. But she must have said something else. A sentence, that may have seemed quite insignificant. Try and remember.'

I remembered perfectly well the apparently insignificant sentence, as I remembered the woman's agonised face as she said it, and had no difficulty in telling him:

'She said she was certain, but had no proof.'

'I see. Did she say anything else?'

'That she meant to go to the police and tell them everything.' And before he could answer I warned him: 'But of course she didn't tell me what, although now I think I understand, more or less.'

Luisella was lying against the back of the sofa. She no longer seemed tense, merely impatient. Assenza, grown suddenly hasty, got up with a grunt. Perhaps because the magistrate had at that moment come out of the bedroom with his retinue and was going to the front door. At which, as if at a signal, two figures in white overalls went towards the bedroom, pushing through the crowd out there: they were trundling a wheeled trolley.

'Well, Iovine, I don't think there's anything else,' said Assenza. 'I suggest you take the young lady away.'

As before, he met us at the door again. 'Are you going back to Naples? Try and avoid Casali.' Once again he'd taken on his mysteriously allusive manner.

We didn't take the lift, there were already some plain-clothes policemen waiting and the red button was alight. We walked down, for the first flights between two lines of people—tenants from the building, leaning on the banisters and standing against the walls, silent and curious. They were waiting for the gentle lady on the third floor, whom they had probably never even greeted when she was alive, to be brought past them, dead.

When we were in the street the people crowding round the front door made way for us, also looking curious. We walked to the car without looking back. Luisella's eyes were glistening.

I put my arm round her shoulder and drew her to me. 'Come, Luisella, you never even met her,' I said.

'I know, but it's terrible all the same. I don't know how I stood it up there, while that man talked and talked. The description he gave was . . . I can't think of the word. Yes, I can—it was evil.'

We went back to the hotel to get our cases and return the car. By taxi, we got to the airport just in time for the last two seats on the afternoon flight to Naples, and so we missed having lunch. Apart from a roll on the motorway that morning, I hadn't eaten since midday on Saturday. Endless cups of coffee had kept me, and continued to keep me, on my feet. Apart from I don't know what else. Certainly not hope.

25

In Naples it had been raining too, we found. But the sky was clearing up: in a few hours the sunset would be perfect. Quite clear, the clouds blown away by the wind. The cloudiness would be in myself.

Luisella was surprised, of course, when I changed and prepared to go out as soon as we got home. To her, the bright sky was merely a good omen, a sign that our idyll would be taken up again at the lost point where it was interrupted, and everything that had happened in between was part of an unrepeatable bad dream. Like the hurricane that had swept through the flat, which was still upside down.

'Have you forgotten the Twin?' was the first thing she said.

'No, but I'm not afraid of him any more. And if he is back, this is the first place he'll come and look for me.'

'And you're leaving me here alone?'

'I'll soon be back,' I said.

'You'll find me dead,' said Luisella.

She came to the door with me. 'Barricade yourself in,' I said. 'I'll tell the porter to let no one up.' As if that would do, in an emergency.

'I bet you won't even notice when you find me laid out cold,' she almost shouted, leaning over the banisters on the staircase.

I took the Alfetta out of the garage and immediately compared it with the one I'd hired. No doubt about it, beauty's in the eye of the beholder, even when it comes to engines. This reminded me of that carefree thinker Assenza. I almost wanted to see him again.

Miletti, on the other hand, I had no wish to see. I merely had to, and this time entirely on my own account. Luckily there was no difficulty in doing so: outside the door of his room a nun told me that his temperature had gone up and that I mustn't tire him. After which she let me in. The passage was empty.

Because of the clumsy position of his shoulder in plaster, he was three-quarters over on his side, facing the window. Perhaps that was the only thing wrong: there oughtn't to be anything else. He was looking out, his eyes reduced to two cavities, and when I came in he turned. He must have recognised my footsteps.

'Come in, Iovine, sit down. Have you shut the door?'

I'd shut it. I sat down on the chair by the white table against the wall, at the foot of the bed. From there I could see his face between the bars of the bedhead.

'Giulia? Did the lawyer get to her? Did you hand her over to him?' He must have lost track of time. If the lawyer had left for Domodossola at once he couldn't have got there before that morning. And I was already back in Naples.

'Your daughter was held and taken to Domodossola,' I said dryly. 'There was no point in my staying there. So I came here.'

He turned his head slowly and almost raised it, moving it from the pillows into which it had sunk. Immediately afterwards he gave a grunt, but I didn't hear what he said. I was thinking of what I had to tell him.

'Elena is dead. They killed her yesterday afternoon.'

He gave another gurgle that this time hid no word. Perhaps it was a grunt of satisfaction.

'You're pleased, aren't you? Are you glad now?'

His head dropped on to the pillows and his eyes closed. 'Yes. It's like being freed from a burden.'

'Because that woman, as you call her, represented your shame—is that why? A kind of trick, the only one in your life, which you'd been the victim of for fifteen years, is that why?'

He nodded, moving his head slightly on the pillows. The folds in his chin had increased in number.

'Whereas the tricks you've gone in for, they don't count, do they? They don't cry for vengeance.' What was happening to me? I was talking like Assenza.

'What are you saying, Iovine?' And I realised he'd lost every winning card, not just a few. I saw his face between the bars: pale, ill, the face of a man who was finished. 'I ask you about Giulia and you tell me about that woman. Yes sir, I'm free of a burden. I had it here.' And he raised his hand, theatrically, to his stomach.

'Giulia won't be back,' I said. 'They'll admit that she has every possible and imaginable excuse and she'll soon be free. But she won't be back. She's decided to have Pino's child.'

It was as if I'd fired a shotgun into his face. He took the hand from his stomach up to his face and covered it, and his head seemed to sink even further into the pillows.

I had three things to say to him and I'd already said two of them. I waited for him to recover, before saying the third. I'd seen his reaction to those two pieces of news; now I wanted to look him in the face while I told him the third. So I waited. But he interrupted my train of thought.

'What I can't understand,' he said, 'is why both of them told you everything.' He too. Was it only Assenza who understood the unexciting reason for inexplicable things? 'Instead of being ashamed.'

'They must have found something human in me,' I boasted. 'In you they saw only an animal.'

'Don't you dare talk to me like that, Iovine, or else . . .' He shook all over, his head flicked up a second and fell back again. Then he began shaking his hand, as if groping for something, but without closing his fist.

'Or else, Don Michele?'

He fell back and didn't answer. Instead he looked at me from behind the bars.

'I came to tell you one last thing, Don Michele. I want those fifty thousand francs right away.'

'You want. You can want the moon for all I care. How dare you?'

'Apart from the fact that you owe them to me, after all I've done and gone through for you and your interests . . .'

'You were supposed to bring Giulia back to me safe and sound, that was our agreement. Whereas you got her into gaol. You haven't even stayed up there with her.' After each sentence he drew breath.

'. . . apart from that, as I was saying, you know perfectly well that I can now force you to pay your debts, as you called your promises.'

'What d'you mean?' he said.

'A friend of mine tells me he doesn't mind the word blackmail. I've discovered that I don't mind it either.'

'You've always been a blackmailer of every sort, Iovine. What's happened, are you suddenly turning honest? All at once? And would your friend be Casali, by any chance?'

A moment earlier he'd seemed to be having a stroke, completely collapsed. Now he suddenly recovered his usual clear-sightedness.

'Casali's no friend of mine. He just wanted to get in on the act and asked me to give him a hand. I didn't, and he turned Tonino on to me. Or vice versa. But it doesn't matter. You're going to pay me now, though, Don Michele, and on the nail. Fifty thousand, that's flat.'

'I'm asking you again: what for?' He was still staring at me through the bars, panting.

'Don Michele, are you trying to gain time? Are you waiting for the office in Lugano to shut for the day? In summer we're an hour ahead of them; that's one thing at least we're ahead in. So there's still half an hour, and if you want to spare your breath you can get a move on. But if you haven't made that call to Benetti within half an hour I'll open the door and you won't see me again. You'll see someone else. You wanted to set me up for life. Generous of you. But all I want is this one hand-out. It's the tip you give anyone who does you a service, especially when it wasn't owed to you.'

He said no more and even closed his eyes again. Then he became agitated, all grunts and gurgles, but in the end, without even turning, he waved his fingers frantically to indicate the telephone.

I got up quietly, lifted the receiver and asked for the number in Lugano. They said there was a delay and I waited, we waited, Miletti turning his back on me deliberately. When the phone rang I answered. They put me through to Benetti and I stayed for a long time with the receiver at my ear counting the unanswered rings it gave.

'They shut at four up there,' the old man gurgled ironically. 'That's five o'clock here. An hour after the exchange office has shut. We'll have to put it off till tomorrow.'

Nothing was going right for me either. When I went out, the passage was still empty.

From via Caravaggio I turned into via Manzoni and went right along it to the end, as far as Posillipo. There, the gulf with the dead volcano in it opened up before me and, high up, the stage was already set: the empty sky behind the peak, ready to absorb the first variations in the light. Then, from that speedy, sparse flow of traffic I plunged into the heavy, almost standstill traffic of Mergellina.

Casali had his office in via Elena and the coincidence certainly wasn't deliberate; just as surely, he wasn't expecting me now. I was taking a risk, but not a big one. For the moment, in fact, Tonino wouldn't poke his nose out from where he was holed up. But it was just a matter of hours; his precautions wouldn't last longer.

Casali was sitting behind his enormous desk, and gave the impression of sitting on a pot. The cuirass of fat on his capacious belly made several tyres that ran right round him. He saw me come in, with surprise.

'This time you can't say you were thinking of me, Don Nicola,' I said.

'Come in, come in,' he cried. 'You're quite right, I wasn't thinking of you just now.'

Unlike the office in via Marina, this one was completely modern, according to the idea that creature might have had of the modern. Everything made of steel, to stand up to his weight wherever he moved and leant on it, obviously. I sat down in front of him, on the other side of that showy desk.

'Well,' I said, 'a nice mess you've made for me. Benetti hadn't heard a squeak about those ten thousand francs. Did you really think I wouldn't telephone him to check?'

'Checking's something that's always foreseen,' said Casali. 'Or do you think me so ingenuous? Let's say it was an indirect warning.'

'The direct warning was brought by Tonino, I suppose? By him and that Pappalardo. What orders had that beast, come to think of it?'

'You're making a great fuss, aren't you?' said Casali. 'But I'll tell you just the same. To find Giulia and the papers, as you can imagine.'

'And once they were found? Why was he expecting Tonino? Couldn't he get the papers himself? He hadn't even looked for them. What was Giulia, a hostage to put pressure on Miletti? All those papers were used for was to get an idiot like me running round in circles. Why don't you come clean?'

'Iovine, if I'm to confess the truth I'd better do it to you,' he said, all understanding, with the air of a nasty, repentant child. 'It was another accident.'

'Why do accidents always happen to you? What on earth is this crew around you? A gang of incompetent oafs. If I were in your shoes, I'd change a bit. Get a change of air, for a start, because Assenza's after you, and then some order into things here.'

'What the hell are you on about now? Are you sitting in judgement on me? Things have always been all right the way they are. Why change them?'

'Because times have changed, that's why,' I managed to say. 'In any case, you'll soon find out why. In the meantime, d'you see what's happened? Nobody's won. You said it was both or nobody. Well, it's over and there's nobody.'

He looked at me above a smile that wasn't just a crack made by stretching his lips but a real gap opening up in his great cheeks. 'You're losing your way in this chat,' he said. 'Why have you come?'

'To satisfy my curiosity, first of all.'

'Go on.' He was still smiling and helpful.

'Why did Marullo always confide—let's call it that—in you? I don't think it was for money. He sent Pino to you as well, and you welcomed him. Why did he hate old Miletti so much?'

'You can ask him,' said Casali.

'As if he'd tell me. He's walled up inside that hump of his like a shellfish and if he let anything out to you it was to get his revenge. What for? Don Nicola, if you tell me this I'll mind my own business in future.'

'What do you mean?'

'I mean Assenza,' I said. 'He's after you, I tell you, and all he wants is witnesses to link you with Tonino, and the bomb, and those who died in via Orazio. Apart from Pappalardo.'

He thought this over seriously, without smiling; then he said: 'Well, it's not really such a secret, it'll come out sooner or later. All right. You met Elena Miletti? You saw her?'

'Alive and dead,' I said.

He didn't bat an eyelash; he already knew.

'Didn't you notice anything about her? About her face?'

I shook my head. He looked at me still, then absently flicked through the papers in front of him.

'Elena was Marullo's daughter.' He waited for that to sink in, while I thought of the two faces of Elena Miletti that I'd seen. 'She ran away from home with a man called Gargiulo,' he went on, 'moved to Milan, and when, after his death, she got in touch with her father again, she'd settled up there. She met Miletti by chance, a long time later, ten years later, the one and only time she went to see her father in the office. Talk about bad luck.'

No, nothing in Elena's face had reminded me of Marullo. 'But she was tall,' I exclaimed in the end, ingenuously.

'Mother Nature is unpredictable,' declared Casali the fatalist. 'There may have been a giant in the family.'

'And Miletti? Did he know?'

'What questions you ask. Of course he knew.' And he'd continued to take it out on Marullo, I thought. Once again I saw the hunchback bending over the desk he was chained to, with that everlastingly frowning, disgusted expression.

'Don Nicola, you know so many things. Tell me one more.'

'The last one,' he said, unexpectedly agreeable.

'How was it possible for Marullo's child to keep her own child hidden for so long?' What was I doing, playing on words? Or was I still muddled about this network of children? 'Why, when she didn't leave her husband, did she leave her child in a way? It's not credible. In fact it's not human.'

'It *is* human, her reason for doing it,' said Casali. That mountain of nastiness looked at me with an inspired, angelic air. 'She did it to save her father from gaol. When her lover, that bloke Gargiulo, died, her father asked Miletti for a loan and signed some promissory notes. Not much, less than a million. Gargiulo was in hospital for more than a month, in the intensive care unit, and when he died she hadn't a bean. Her father helped her and then went on for years renewing his promissory notes, which now ran into millions. Then he had the idea of forging Miletti's signature on a big cheque, but of course it went wrong and the cheque ended up in the old man's hands and he hung on to it. It took a shit like Miletti'—you'd think he was the Angel Gabriel, himself—'to nibble away at his father-in-law for all those years. What could the daughter do? Go and confess all, and so turn him against her father? She supported the child with its nurse and later on in Milan.'

'But when the shit, forgive the expression, came to hear of Pino's existence, why didn't he avenge himself on his father-in-law right away?'

'Obviously he thought up a slower, nastier revenge. Marullo's been on starvation wages for years. Even shits have their generous side, as you see.'

The mouth of truth. For once in its life, that oven or sewer had become the mouth of truth. He was now suspicious, and never took his eyes off me. 'Satisfied?' he said.

'From now on I'll mind my own business, I've said so and I'll stick to it,' I replied. 'For total satisfaction, though, I need those ten thousand francs.'

The great hole cracked open again in his face. 'And why, this time?' he said.

'I don't mind the word blackmail either,' I said. 'Assenza's still after you.'

'Iovine, you slay me, you really do,' he said at once. 'Assenza may be after me, but I'll whisk him off like a fly. I talked to you before not because of this ridiculous threat of yours, but to satisfy your curiosity. You asked me so many things but you haven't said a word about Tonino. Well, I'll tell you. They arrested him in Milan late this morning. The idiot got himself caught at the station. What the hell did he have to use his knife for, and on a copper at that? In any case, this doesn't bother me in the least. Your friend Assenza, whom you seem to be starting to like, hasn't a shred of proof against me, and you can't go talking to Tonino. D'you want any more? In these last few days I've got rid of Miletti as a partner and completely changed COOFA, even its name. He knows nothing about it, but he's in such a mess that even when he does he won't notice. And here's the last straw: we've got the contract. Not two contracts but one, better concocted and thought out. And two billion bigger.'

'And what about my evidence?'

'Well, you know what you can do with that. But I forgot to tell you that from tomorrow Assenza's being transferred to other duties. He was already at Castellammare di Stabia as a punishment, and now he'll go to the interior of Sicily. Our friend Lentizzi's coming back to his old job. For the moment. Later, something better may be coming along for him. And all it took was a little trip to Rome, while you were swanning around between Naples and the Alps. A day return in the early afternoon.'

26

I almost ran up all three floors of the old building in via Marina, and when I got upstairs I was coughing and out of breath. The door was open, wide open in fact, but the three dreary rooms were empty. I went round them twice, as if Marullo might be hiding under a chair or the wicker-work sofa. That ridiculous signal on the last door was lit up in red. Or perhaps it was the blood in my eyes that made me see it that way.

Empty-handed, that's how I found myself. My two efforts

today had been a total failure, completing my first hurried plunge into sincerity. What was happening to me? I no longer recognised myself. I'd have another try with Miletti tomorrow: but as consolation, this was pretty feeble.

Suddenly I remembered the old man, and it cleared up everything: I realised where I'd find Marullo. I dashed down the stairs and ran to the car, which I'd left in a hurry at the front door with its wheels on the pavement. All this took a few seconds; reaching via Caravaggio seemed to take a century.

It was late now, at least for a nursing home, but the porter at the counter said nothing when I dashed past. On the third floor the passage was still empty and the door of Miletti's room closed.

I opened it, burst in and stopped suddenly, relieved. There they were, quite quietly: Marullo sitting on the chair at the foot of the bed and Miletti sitting up in bed, raised high on the pillows, still three-quarters turned on one side. He wasn't looking at the window any longer but at Marullo, who was looking back at him, his great head twisted with that kind of stiff-necked air. And they were saying nothing.

I shut the door, went over to the bed and gradually, one detail at a time, I took in the scene. Miletti was panting hard and from his open mouth, in waves, came a continuous gurgle, louder than usual, almost a rattle. And he had one, two, three ... I counted up to five dark red stains, on the shoulder that wasn't in plaster, on that side of his chest, and on the opposite side, on his free arm. But there were more, many more. And they stood out against all that whiteness and were spreading as I watched.

In the hand which Marullo held open on his knees, in that uncomfortable position of his, was the weapon that had produced all these stains: a cheap knife, not even very long, with a sawtoothed blade, curved at the end and with a yellow plastic handle. He held it there, as if to keep showing it to the old man in the bed, after he'd cleaned the blade on the piece of sheet there beside him, making further stains. Behind him, on the table against the wall, the television was flashing noisily.

I went over to it and switched it off; then I went round the bed and to Marullo, took the knife from his hand and laid it on the bedside table, as if I'd come in to tidy up. The hunchback's fixed stare was the last terrifying detail I noticed.

The old man in the bed was saying something. I went closer to him and had to lean over to hear. 'I want to go to confession. Call a priest,' he managed to say, his expression lost in those opaque eyes of his.

'Yes, yes, all right. But don't move, you'll lose blood,' I answered. That precious, carefully hoarded lifeblood he'd talked about.

Behind me, unexpectedly, I heard Marullo's dark voice. 'Take no notice. He's going to die like a rat, without absolution. In any case, hell's waiting for him.'

I turned: with his head twisted, Marullo continued staring at Miletti. 'He had your daughter killed, didn't he?' I asked him.

'He killed her himself, with his own hands, for fifteen years,' he replied. 'He got someone else to give the final blow, but he killed her with his own hands.'

'I want to go to confession,' the old man behind him rattled once again.

I leant over him. 'You can confess, Don Michele,' I said. 'We're here on purpose to hear you.'

'The priest,' he repeated, as if he were still in a state to give orders. 'The priest.' Moving his eyes, turning them away then staring straight into mine, in a way that reminded me of Giulia, must have meant an agony of concentration for him. But they were opaque, not limpid like hers, which were blue like his yet so different.

'Did you have Elena killed?' I said. 'Answer. Confess.'

'Improta,' he whispered. The stains were spreading. 'The priest.'

Two almost equal, indistinguishable pants. I turned to Marullo again, who was now shaking his head. 'What's he saying?' I asked.

'Improta. He's named a man who's possibly more evil than himself. With the excuse that he's raving mad.'

This was the missing detail: the name of the actual executioner. I then remembered having seen him in the old man's office the very day on which it all began, thick-set, dark, with madness flashing in his light eyes. A dark shadow, often mentioned but always invisible in the days that followed. That Wednesday, obviously, he had turned up to report.

The old man in the bed became excited again. He leant right out on one side, as if he wanted to vomit. We took no notice, neither Marullo nor I: perhaps God had marked us both. Him with his hump, me with what?

I took his arm. 'Come along, Marullo.'

'I must stay to the end,' he said. 'It's a sight I've paid dearly for.' He turned his head with that continuous movement of his and looked at me. 'You haven't done anything and you can go. I'm staying.'

Before I opened the door I turned to look at two final things: Marullo's big head, which had remained half-turned, as if the mechanism had once again been blocked, and the telephone on the bedside table, on which I wouldn't be ringing Benetti the following day. Then I turned the door handle.

Assenza was out there, sitting in the little enclave opposite the door of Miletti's room, with two short stretches of passage on either side, still as empty as ever. He was smoking and in his other hand still held a packet of Nazionali, which I'd never seen him bring out before.

'We got here too late again this time, Iovine,' he said, without smiling, without irony, as in Milan that same morning. But his small eyes now hid anger. He must have been full of it: it must have been piled up inside him, enough to make the foot of his crossed leg tremble. So we'd said goodbye to the phlegmatic thinker and the mathematician; he even smoked now, as well.

'Did you see?' I asked, and took the armchair beside him.

'I opened the door and looked in. You were busy and didn't

notice, neither you nor Marullo. And Miletti was busy dying. I must admit that in its way justice is triumphing among us . . .'

'And you didn't do anything?'

'I'm now authorised to wash my hands of it,' he said, no longer chatty. 'And anyway, I came just out of curiosity, to get it confirmed for myself, let's say. I got here too late to stop Marullo. Like you. I'm sorry about him.'

'It was Miletti.'

'We realised that in Milan, when we saw the poor woman killed in that way.'

'He mentioned Improta. He must have sent him up to Faito too.'

'An old acquaintance of the police. A mad criminal I should have arrested long ago.' And he repeated bitterly: 'Should have. You can do anything, with good will, but with Miletti around, even that was impossible. They're holding Catello and his wife again instead.' And he fell silent.

I lit a cigarette too, a Gala, and waited for him to get over it. I thought of that wretched pair but asked nothing about them; at that point, details weren't important.

It was he who broke the silence, with one of his unexpected remarks. 'How do you feel?' he asked.

But he wasn't wandering off the point this time. I understood him and replied: 'Done in. How about you?'

'The same.' This time I was moved. Where would I find another Assenza? 'You know, Miletti didn't send Improta to Faito. In a way it was Tina who got him there. I'll explain: Miletti knew his wife was unfaithful and had set that killer on her track. She went up to Faito and Improta followed her. But he didn't act at once, he asked the old man for instructions first.'

'How do you know?'

'The idiot rang the office and Marullo heard. Marullo saw and heard everything. And he talked to me for a long time.'

'Was he disturbed by Giulia turning up?'

'Exactly.' The professional was getting the upper hand. 'He

saw her and rang the old man, who gave him orders to hang around. When the girl left, the madman struck. This time he found the right moment. But the way things went, it was as if Miletti himself had struck the blow. Marullo was right.' He'd been in time to hear that.

'So you heard from Marullo, indirectly, of Giulia's comings and goings at Faito?'

'Yes, from the first, when she went up on Tuesday afternoon, thanks to Improta's phone call which Marullo told me about. Her second trip we knew about from the Bellellas, and from the suitcase and the bag she'd forgotten.'

'There was a third one, too,' I said and told him what Giulia had told me in the hotel at Formia.

'So everything works out. As for Elena, I didn't ask you before but I'll ask you now: when you spoke to Miletti on the phone did you repeat what the poor woman had said to you? That is, that she was going to the police? Don't feel guilty about it, though.' Fatherly now.

'Yes. But, looking back on it, what could that have produced?' I hadn't realised that I could have felt guilty about it; I realised now, and my empty stomach heaved.

'When Elena called him that Saturday evening, Marullo told her about Improta's phone call, that is, that the man who'd sent her son's murderer into action was her ex-husband.'

'So when she spoke to me on the Saturday morning, Elena still didn't know about the phone call.'

'What she said to you, Iovine, was more than enough to alarm the old man, who already hated her.'

'And Marullo didn't say anything to his daughter until Saturday?'

'He kept putting it off. He confessed to me that he'd had neither the courage nor the strength to do it. So he put it off. You've seen him, haven't you? Shut in like a sea-urchin.' That word reminded me suddenly of Luisella. The time had flown by, would I still find her at home? Clutching a kitchen knife too, perhaps? Oh, what the hell.

'You know, Iovine,' said Assenza, 'you aren't the fool I took you for, after all. Irresponsible, yes, but not stupid. You knew less than I did, you didn't have Marullo's outbursts to go on, yet this morning in Milan you understood everything straight away. Only you've got to change your life. Not the way you're going but your whole life, and then things will go a bit better for you.' Decidedly fatherly. 'Just take a look at yourself: and you'll damage yourself even more, if you carry on. Take my advice and change your life. And hang on to that Luisella of yours.' It was a farewell rather than a piece of advice.

But he didn't get up; I did. I was now in a hurry, clutching the telephone money in my pocket. Yet I had to ask him something. 'Why did you advise me to avoid Casali?' I said.

'I thought you'd try and recover those francs and I didn't know Tonino was still in Milan, where they arrested him later. In other words, I was worried about your safety.'

'Marullo?'

'Yes, I heard that from him as well. Casali'd told him about your gentleman's agreement.' So no-one had managed to keep a single secret. 'Did you try?'

I nodded, and he understood, from looking at my face. He held out his hand and repeated: 'Change your life.'

I shook it, looking back into his small eyes. Then, almost clearing his throat, he said: 'They've transferred me. I heard today and I'm leaving tomorrow morning.' So his discomfort in the little armchair wasn't just a result of having his belly squashed between its two arms. 'You know, Iovine, this is a country where killing's forbidden, yet everyone kills, just the same.'

Downstairs in the entrance hall, opposite the porter's counter with the switchboard still grumbling into the silence, there was a public telephone.

I dialled the number and when she replied said: 'Luisella?'

As promptly as she had lifted the receiver she answered: 'I'm not here. I'm dead.'